I0628325

WIGGINS:

SON OF SHERLOCK

BY

DOROTHY ELLEN PALMER

© Copyright 2021 Dorothy Ellen Palmer

The right of Dorothy Ellen Palmer to be identified as the author of this work has been asserted by her in accordance with the Copyright, Designs and Patents Act 1998.

All rights reserved. No reproduction, copy or transmission of this publication may be made without express prior written permission. No paragraph of this publication may be reproduced, copied or transmitted except with express prior written permission or in accordance with the provisions of the Copyright Act 1956 (as amended). Any person who commits any unauthorised act in relation to this publication may be liable to criminal prosecution and civil claims for damage.

All characters appearing in this work are fictitious or used fictitiously.

Except for certain historical personages, any resemblance to real persons, living or dead, is purely coincidental. The opinions expressed herein are those of the authors and not of Orange Pip Books

Paperback ISBN 978-1-78705-723-4

ePub ISBN 978-1-78705-724-1

PDF ISBN 978-1-78705-725-8

Published in the UK by Orange Pip Books

335 Princess Park Manor, Royal Drive, London, N11 3GX
www.orangepipbooks.com

Cover design by Brian Belanger

To all my decades of Drama students who taught me to see
and observe The Great Improvisor,
and to the generations of little girls – my nine-year-old,
limping, redheaded self, included –

who longed to slip their hand into his and go off
adventuring

with Sherlock Holmes.

"There's the scarlet thread of murder running through the colourless skein of life,

and our duty is to unravel it, and isolate it, and expose every inch of it."

- *A Study in Scarlet*, Sir Arthur Conan Doyle

Chapter One: Our Red-Handed League

It was the coldest morning of my young life. It was the winter of my fifteenth year.

Inspired and abetted by the wily London snowstorm that so fittingly shrouded the debut of 1891, the great detective who was my father summoned me to breakfast with New Year's first sun, where – before so much as a single bite of crumpet – he decreed my death at dawn.

"How are you? You have been lying in a Whitechapel gutter, I perceive."

His first words were not a question, but an affirmation of instructions. I nodded and wished him, "a most deductive New Year," a phrasing I had crafted with considerable cogitation hoping to please him.

Instead, he snorted, "Exposure can be deadly, Wiggins. Disrobe immediately!"

Breakfast nudity – now that was an odd request, even for my father. While we often dined in costume, all previous performances before an attentive audience of toast points had included pants. But that morning, ignoring both the irony of his request and the dismay it caused me, he vaulted from his chair to capture my beloved cap.

When an oblivious elbow dashed his morning pipe to the floor, glowing ash from reclaimed plugs and dotties singed the bearskin rug. Insensible to the notion that even guttersnipes are entitled to a privacy of their persons, he began my interrogation, whilst stripping the beggar-boy's coat from my back.

"None observed your arrival, Wiggins? Neither your person, nor your footprints?"

I nodded.

"You journeyed to Baker Street circuitously, walking backwards in the snow?'

I nodded again.

"Having adhered to my methods, you can swear you were not followed?"

I could.

"You have put it about that you were unwell, suffering from cough and fever?"

I had.

"You have coughed convincingly in public places? I do not wish to know if you spit."

I grinned. When I puffed my cheeks and mimed a well-aimed stream, he neatly pulled his boots beyond my improvised trajectory. An expert hand pretended his own quick handkerchief, whipped from breast pocket to wipe imaginary spittle from his toe. A sideways flick sent ersatz spittle back at my face. I ducked. When he applauded, I bowed. He then raised a stopping hand.

"Unlike this improvised tom-foolery, Wiggins, the play I debut this New Year's morn is formidable and far-reaching. As its curtain rises with the sun, I must know with certainty that you have dressed the stage to the best of your amateur abilities."

I watched the invisible handkerchief be returned, inch by inch, to his breast pocket. It was, as always, effortlessly perfect, exemplifying the theory and practice of his heralded monograph, *The Science of Improvisation and the Detection of Belief*:

"Everything, real or improvised, has a history. Like their human creators, improvisations have provenance. They neither materialize in the ether, nor return to it. Improvised objects must be seen by all to have a genesis, a physical birth, an identifiable on-going use and belonging, and a final resting place."

Once the improvised hankie rested, Father's nimble hands reached for my throat.

"My next question is of urgent import, Wiggins. Answer it exactly."

I struggled, but could not prevent the unbuttoning of my collar.

"You were seen to fall asleep for three nights as instructed, in the appointed bend of your designated gutter, wearing the exact costume you are currently, if inefficiently, re-providing me?"

Beneath the threadbare shirt being tugged over my face, I emitted an affirmative grunt.

"Good! You shall die directly. Alone in a gutter, in rags. A cast off in cast offs. But, console yourself," he added reaching for my left pant leg, "Your death ensures my resurrection."

If I did not appear delighted, he did not appear to notice.

"In Act Two, the second demise will be mine." Freeing my pants from my person, he began whipping them overhead, narrowly missing the green gasogene. "It's a cracking plot, my boy! An international stage. A climax thrilling! In operatic finale, the vital moral of the story will be secured."

He lowered his whip, lowered himself to his red leather chair, and began rolling my clothes into a ball. Sighting an old medical bag, he yanked it from its shelf. Contents dumped in a tinkling of glass, thankfully adding no vial of anything no-longer medicinal, but still flammable, to spots of bearskin still smoldering. In typical disregard for property not his own, he began feeding my only apparel to the bag's chomping mouth. I kicked my beloved cap under the settee, a bare half beat ahead of the detective-turned-rag picker whirling back into my face.

"A certain scribbling physician will mourn me in his little magazine as he and the Empire grieve my loss. I dislike deceiving our good Dr. Watson, but must do so to ensure his safekeeping. You recall two years ago, in *The Adventure of the Dying Detective,* when I had to convince him I had a deadly virus? In that case and this, Watson's grief must be credible and he could never credibly pretend it." Holmes rolled his eyes, "I remind you of his face in any game of Whist."

I returned his smile. The good doctor's tell-tale flying eyebrows broadcast his every card.

"Watson's current consort – number two or twenty, I can never tally the man's amative accoutrements – will no doubt console him. Our longsuffering landlady is likewise safe. No one suspects her importance to me. At my insistence, Watson has portrayed her in his stories as merely a fussy flibbertigibbet. When I am gone, I imagine the fictitious Mrs. Hudson will withdraw into a hermitic self-consolation via the creation and consumption of sticky pudding. An addiction, I must add, of which she is much too fond for her corset's liking."

I smiled again as required. Equally on cue, Holmes pushed for the punchline.

"As we say in the theatre," he rounded his shoulders and inflated his belly, instantly transforming his tall, svelte self into a portly silhouette, "Adipose... ruins the pose."

Flipping a fleet smile in my direction, he added, "I shall relish this pose, then recompose."

If you find this Sherlock excessive, Perplexed Reader, you have yet to meet the bodacious bedlam of the rest of my irregular family. If this Holmes is not the cerebral sleuth you expected, that is Watson's creation. That good doctor shrunk all my father's excesses to fit Victorian propriety. My

Sherlock is of a more theatrical bent, if not a fully-smoked theatre ham.

Father closed Watson's case. He raised a tensed leg to straddle his chair, narrowed his gaze to an aspect somehow both innerved and entirely still. As always, he commanded the room.

"When Moriarty comes for you, my dear boy – and make no mistake, he cannot not suffer me to live on in any capacity and so come for you he most certainly shall – unlike Mrs. Hudson, you can find no solace in the soporific over-ingestion of comestibles. Unlike Watson, you cannot find your missing manhood in an inkpot." A well-buffed finger executed one smart tap to his nose. "So, my young apprentice, deduce the obvious: what must you do to protect yourself?"

Fisting his best gloves aloft like dark wings of a bird of prey, his talon-grey eyes targeted mine. But I kept silent. As my dear mother had often explained, all Holmes' questions were reductively rhetorical; any answer by anyone else was incorrect by default of not being his. In the theatre of deduction – in truth, before any audience of any size either of my parents ever garnered – the first line, the best line, the punch line, and the last word must always be theirs.

"What is plainer than a child as plain as you, hidden in plain sight?"

I had no time to take offence at this slur of a riddle given how he solved it.

"A dead child." A lean black finger stabbed the air. "Already buried. Flat in his grave!"

6

When my eyebrows flew, Father gave one sharp-bursting bark like a sleek, exultant hound.

"Hah! No one shall come looking for you, Wiggins, if they believe you dead. See it plain. I have made career and reputation from the simple precept that most people cannot see things for looking at them. Fewer still have the deductive capacity to outwit danger, to escape it true and in time. But you and I, my young friend, in a triangulation of triumph, shall do all three."

I had no memory of him ever touching me in kindness.

It confounded me beyond uttering when he set his hand, albeit a gloved one, on mine.

"That any of our friends – that you especially, Wiggins – are now in danger simply by virtue of proximity to me, well, it is indefensibly intolerable."

As I clutched my chest in my thinnest smallclothes, the last of which I was grateful he had not removed, his gaze warmed. His eyes crinkled. These were soft changes, so rare the world seldom saw them. But the merest morsel of affection is a dangerous meal to a father-starved child.

The odd gentle word kept me in his thrall as surely as the razor of the Ripper at my throat. It gave me hope when I must take none. I must not let the beast who defiled my mother anywhere near my heart. Then, of course, with a snap of insulated fingers, he spoiled it. Holding out an imperious black hand, he demanded my cap. I fetched it from under the settee and dropped it into his bag.

"I go post haste to your gutter to display a dissembling decoy. Frozen in your place, comporting your garb, he is a stiffly simulated Street Arab. He is —"

Here Holmes paused with eyes downcast in a practiced abashment, a coy telegraphing of insincere apology sent whenever he knew his next line to be both unseemly and unstoppable. "He is... an indigent urchin icicle."

The great detective restrained his self-congratulation poorly. He smirked.

Knowing he expected it, I snickered back. He bowed and exited the room.

I take the moment of his absence, Empathetic Reader, to assure you that I quickly regained my cap and to ask you this: please be slow to judge him. On this frosty first morn of 1891, I had not told Holmes I was his child.

It must also be said that had he deduced my paternity, it would not have altered his tone, nor temerity. Quibble it homicide or filicide, he had computed my death by the mathematics of his method. Ergo, killing me was not a drug-induced seven percent solution; it was the only solution. To call it the loss of a sacrificial pawn, would suggest there was loss. Safe in his warmest coat and the certainty of his convictions, there was none. At least not for him.

I must here contradict the esteemed Mr. Darwin, who asserts that all evolved creatures have conjoined heads and hearts. While I agree that Holmes branched as far from the simian as only the singular member of his species can, as the self-evolved Homo Detectus Cerebellum, Father's skull housed a raging intellect so hot that it furnaced all but hard fact. Logic and the science of deduction consumed his every effort, including, sadly, those a child needed most: encouragement, patience, and the occasional approving smile.

I told myself that he needed a torching eye in his profession. I conceded that despite his fame, he remained a private, introverted man. But I could never forgive him for burning my mother out of his heart.

History labels Holmes an unfeeling machine of a man. But Watson is less to blame for this misrepresentation than I am. At fourteen, I was too young to understand that my father kept his feelings cunningly warm, his own soft-glowing plugs and dotties, tucked under the cold cinders he showed the world.

That incandescence you will see anon, Dear Juror, assuming your own heart is not charred irrevocably against him in the future time and place wherein you hold this book. Watson got as much wrong as he got right, but I grant him this: he did his best to tell their story.

I never tried.

Until now, a lifetime later, when it is all but too late.

Like Watson's service revolver, truth is my family's weapon of last resort. Our willingness to withhold the truth is the cold, confounding, calumny of this story, but not its heart. For my father especially, improvised deception was but a carapace; a shell game planned and perfected, necessary falsehoods fabricated and finessed. This is the unmasked truth: beneath his maquillage of icy masculinity lay a soft-beating heart. One courageous enough to be broken more than once and still risk love again. Holmes had such a heart, as did my beloved Danny.

There, I have said his name. Forgive me if I cannot do so again for some time.

Knife in hand, my father returned. He carried a keen, collapsible blade with a unique turquoise handle – a gift from Utah in the case Watson called *A Study in Scarlet*. Knowing I would pay handsomely for it, many a Baker Street Irregular had more than once attempted to pinch this prize from Holmes' pocket. Not even the lightest fingered ever succeeded. I didn't want to own it, or to pawn it; I wanted to chuck it in the Thames.

For me, the terror of Jack the Ripper did not end with the death of Mary Kelly on November 8, 1888. In dark dreams that began with my mother's illness, night after screaming night, I met the Ripper's razor blade. Saw death flashing turquoise in my father's lean hand. Unable to run, I never escaped its thrust. That morning, in menace calculated and casual, Holmes repeatedly snapped his blade, enjoyed it glinting and retracting as he spoke.

"Consider the irony of your urchin icicle, Wiggins. This impecunious boy gives you a princely gift. Because he dies for you, you shall be reborn. So, rejoice, Wiggins! Dead, you are the smokescreen of my best of tobacco. Dead, you are the reddest of my scarlet herrings. Another boy takes the death you would have had without me: starved in a gutter, shrouded in snow."

"How'd y'get a body? Where's he at? Tell me it hain't an Irregular? What's 'is name?"

Father frowned and pocketed his knife. I assumed such questions had not bothered him and thus could not possibly be worthy of anyone's consideration.

"I do not know his name. He was dead of influenza before I made his acquaintance. I do know he was not one of your merry band of Irregular miscreants. He was a runaway Home Boy, one unwilling to be sent to the colonies, now sadly disqualified for any new life. I got him from a doctor at St. Bart's. A colleague alerted to my need for a dead redheaded boy. Given the necessity of maintaining his rigidity, your deceased doppelganger is laid out on the woodpile. I note the urgency to fetch him before Mrs. Hudson goes in search of kindling to fire up her teapot."

Father stepped to my side and lifted his hat to hold my eyes.

"Your decoy messiah could not be saved, Wiggins, but he saves others. That is all the heroism we may ever hope for. You and I, by conspiring to expire, we shall save other lives."

I must make my complicity clear. When my father cast a dead boy in my role, I could have protested. I did not. I could have refused any part in his macabre play. Again, I did not.

11

As all Irregulars knew, Home Children were not always homeless, or even orphans. Many were simply poor, wrested from destitute parents by the uniquely Victorian blend of arrogance, avarice and pity. To save the public purse, claiming it was for the little beggars' own good, church and state shipped children to the colonies like cattle.

It felt dead wrong to benefit from a dead boy's fear. I could have investigated his provenance and sent anonymous recompense to his family. Bare minimum, I should have marched out to the woodpile to thank a frozen face. Instead, I gave myself an excuse and took it. I told myself my angel mother would wrap loving arms around a small boy new to heaven. To honor her, I must be the boy Father would have me become.

"Where'll I be goin' then, guv, now that I'm a goner?"

Father's face split into a prizefighter's grin.

"A pun, Wiggins! You may be dead as a doornail, but there's a rusty hope for you yet! I assume our joint exile to the colonies is at least perfunctorily preferable to full corporeal demise?"

In the long hindsight from which I pen my words, it has oft occurred to me that the very words Holmes used to address me said he knew I was no gutter rat. But I must not sentimentalize the data. He spoke that way to all and sundry. His Shakespearean vocabulary raised his status. It erected walls. If someone couldn't scale them, he had no use for their company.

"You, my puerile punster, shall go straight from your last breakfast to entombment –" he waited, enjoying my obvious alarm, "at the Diogenes Club, to benefit from Mycroft's tutelage."

He hefted Watson's case and aimed for the vestibule, then leapt back into the study and, ignoring my sputtering protestations, ran quick exploratory gloves over my capless skull.

"Mycroft and I have a small wager as to how much your little Irregular brain can absorb without cracking." Here he shrugged. "I shall endeavor to prove the phrenologists wrong. If they are not, I shall write the definitive monograph on your genetic and cranial limitations."

Upon his exit, I replanted my cap on said cranium, imagining internment with the warty, mono-syllabic Mycroft to be the worst of all possible fates.

I was wrong. That arrived when Father's footsteps returned.

I had just enough time to thrust my cap beneath me when his smiling face rounded the doorway and he protractedly cleared his throat. I should have been warned by this tactic. I knew it for one he used without shame on Watson and Mrs. Hudson – a prelude to tossing a last bit of bombast before evacuating the premises to spare himself the explosion.

"Central to your studies, Wiggins, will be the peoples, flora and fauna of the fledgling Dominion of Canada – a new nation born in 1867, now poised to celebrate its first quarter century. In five months – four in the unlikely event you prove smarter than your skull suggests – you will be a reborn spring lamb gamboling in the charming Canadian hamlet of Mayfair, Ontario."

When I tried to protest, he stared at the ceiling until I stopped.

"Mayfair's founders, the Mcleans, are stalwart Scottish farm folk from the hardscrabble Argyle parish of Kilcalmonell, recommended by Sir Henry Baskerville himself. You'll recall the tale of the giant hound, last year? Sending Watson on an extended constitutional in Grimpen Moor, I raised Sir Henry from colonial farmer to baronet when I solved the murder of his uncle using only a pair of boots. Such fine footwear – Sir Henry's, not Watson's – made by one Meyers, Toronto. We must look them up upon arrival. Speaking of boots and backwards in the snow..."

His eyes lost focus, fluttered, then closed. Whether induced by injection or epiphany, this departure signaled his best plans in their hatching. When his eyes reopened, he grasped my chin, rotated my jaw, and evaluated my teeth and tongue, all with a practiced performer's eye.

"Acceptable flexibility. I trust you can ape a Scots-Canadian accent by spring?"

He leapt from the landing taking the spotlight with him. As always, in a grandstanding exit he ran down his seventeen steps matching each footfall to a shouted seventeen-beat last line: "We can blame a witless foreign mother for your sad lack of Gaelic."

That rankled. In one of the many things he must never know, I had Mother's facility with languages and was proud of it. Her father was a Highland Scot, fluent in English and Gaelic, her mother spoke German and Polish. Like mother, I knew all four tongues. Given her profession as an opera singer, we also spoke a working French and Italian. One of my aunties, who married a seafaring Scot – one admittedly more pirate than sailor – had also impressed upon me the value of a language that in an emergency only your chosen clan understood. In short, I had words in seven languages for the brute abandoning me all but buck-naked on Baker Street.

A lack of Gaelic was the least of my problems.

But I must also admit to this: a teenage tingle. Father and I would be explorers! Brave as *les coureurs de bois*, we would track wily fur traders, face vicious mountain lions, and meet fleets of feathered Indians like those in *The Last of the Mohicans*! Shake your head, Modern Reader, at how I elevated lore over data. I anticipated a wilderness romance the likes of which only a child confined to a life of London smog could see. In equal geographic error, I imagined Mayfair, Canada, to be but a stone's throw from somewhere I did want to go: my birthplace in Egg Harbor City, New Jersey.

Poised for his final exit, Father called me to the landing, then fired his best puckish smile.

"One trivial finality, Wiggins, a small step for your protection. You shall arrive in Mayfair unexpected, appearing on the McLean doorstep as the child of a long-lost black sheep, one who fifteen years ago fled farm and country for the continent. The family knows of your birth, but none has ever met you. Unfortunately, lacking the convenience of any long-lost male progeny," he stepped outside and pulled the door to frame his face, "You must present yourself as a girl."

I wailed the unintelligible and lunged after him. But this was his script. I had no lines.

"Fret not, Wiggins. You need become Miss Euphemia Hortensia Mclean for only a short hiatus." He smiled into the crack. "A year at best. Or possibly two."

He winked. With one quick pull, his door banged shut.

Of course, exactly as he staged it, by the time I limped down his bloody seventeen steps, I stood alone in my long johns and he was long gone. I could have chased after him, but I am no John L. Sullivan, the champion of bare-knuckle boxing that Holmes so admired, and for whom my insufficient attire was named. I hate the cold and Holmes knew it. It elevates my pain and worsens my limp. In the cold, my tiny feet turn a few more degrees inward, exacerbating their abnormality.

When I realized Father had not taken my boots, it curdled my heart.

Of course not. No one but my lovely mother could bring themselves to touch my feet.

In full redheaded temper, I damned Holmes to hell for all of Baker Street to hear. Hurling every street slur the

Irregulars ever taught me, eviscerating the third commandment, I blasphemed the Heavenly Father for giving me a parent who would exile me to a snowy land of backwoods and beavers. I swore into the face of a most alarmed pedestrian – a costermonger with a cart of spotty oranges – that under no circumstances would I become his conspiratorial Canadian icicle.

I slammed the door. Perfectly-timed three beats later, it cracked back open.

"You may keep the cap, Wiggins. I have, of course, made a copy."

Insulted by his retreating back, how I longed for definitive data! Left shivering on that icy threshold, dreading the pain of remounting his bloody seventeen steps, I could not untangle deduction from deceit. Had Holmes improvised Miss Euphemia Hortensia Mclean as punishment? To mock me? To cripple this little cripple with the most execrable name in history?

Or was it an invitation to a kind cross-dressing? Had he used his methods to expose my secret desire: that I craved the swish of skirts to cover my feet?

I had no logical answers to these most vital questions.

Did he know I was his child?

Did he know me for a girl?

Chapter Two: This Boy's Last Bow

It is January 1, 1967. It is the winter of my ninety-first year.

Please bear with me, Indulgent Reader. Before we return to that shivering child abandoned on a Baker Street stoop, I ask you to please first pause a moment to appreciate the distance from which this grateful old crone pens her tale. As you carry the image of the irregular urchin me in your head, please also see me as I am today: an anachronistic academic, antique pen in hand.

To celebrate the first day of Canada's Centennial year, this ancient wreck of a Wiggins has been freshly diapered and wheeled out to the living room. The gleaming metal tray that fronts my wheelchair has been wiped clean of mashed carrots. It holds my fountain pen, my crystal inkwell, and a pile of pink paper. I insisted on pink, and I am not yet entirely doddering, so the offspring took me seriously. We all know this is my last chance at a full confession.

Here in the London, Ontario, seniors' home that is my final home, it's Sunday night. Jostling in front of my week-old Christmas present, a brand new colour TV, are my own Irregular, red-headed army: children, grandchildren, and great-grandchildren. We're all anticipating *Walt Disney's Wonderful World of Color*, followed by their generation's P.T. Barnum – a wizened, bellowing imp named Ed Sullivan. Tonight, my *TV Guide* says Ed will bring us a really big show: jugglers, a black ballet troupe, the singing Castro Brothers, and a young comedienne named Joan Rivers. Mother would have loved a funny woman adventuring. Watson would have chuckled whether he got her jokes or not. Behind the newspaper shielding his face, Father would have laughed 'til he cried.

But I have left all masquerading roles behind.

Today, I enjoy my family openly, as myself, and see the long ago days of Victorian London in a light less refracted by a longing for home. This New Year's debut is thankfully not a dead boy. It's a folk singer with the euphonious name of Gordon Lightfoot, singing *The Canadian Railroad Trilogy,* commissioned by The Canadian Broadcasting Corporation, and released to welcome our Centennial. It charms me, as does the gift from my youngest great-grandchild – a gold centennial lapel pin. Symbolizing the ubiquitous flora of my chosen homeland, the Maple leaf, it has eleven equilateral triangles: one for each province, one for the north. In every triangle, I see the three sides of this tale: Fiction, fact, and uncertainty. Why has it taken a lifetime to share them with you?

I feared getting it wrong; I dreaded getting it right. And I struggled to be fair.

It's hard to review a show when you are a lead actor in it. I shrank from spending years in reflection only to look up from the last jot of blood and ink and be no more enlightened than the day I first took pen in hand. In further truth, I liked keeping my loved ones to myself. Once you give them to an audience, once they all take their last bow, the show is irrevocably over.

But enough excuses. Bastioned by a full wall of thumbtacked photos – my progeny's Centennial Projects of embroidered tea towels, time capsules, birdhouses, lumpy pottery and tree plantings – I can face what Holmes would have called, "my profoundly puerile performance of puffery and pride." I ask your forgiveness at my poor attempts at levity, like this one. A joke, however feeble, gives both improviser and audience time to breathe. It reminds me I shared moments of silly joy with both my parents and gives me heart to continue.

As Wiggins, I failed to honour either my mother, or my father. I plead a conundrum of impossibility: to honour one was to dishonor the other. While it could be argued that my parents never let me be a child, that both used me to adult ends before I had a fully sentient self, I neither plead this defense, nor seek its pity. I knew what I was doing. As the real Phineas Taylor Barnum – whose own good heart you shall meet later in these pages – once put it, I played my father for a sucker, a chump and a fool.

As always, this little pawn obeyed the real chess master: The Woman. It was she who birthed me, she who raised me and she who loved me beyond reason.

This is my earliest memory: standing in my mother's closet, surrounded by the lushest of forests, garments of every shade of green, from spring mint to deepest jade. I reach out for the caress of silk, for the stiff rustle of taffeta, and warm stroke of velvet. As actress and opera singer, my mother's closet was a place of wonder for a child.

The name you know me by, the only name I shall share with you for now, came from her closet. Quite the baby peacock, I loved getting layered with as many costumes, jewels, and wigs, as my small body could bear. Then we would perch on the chaise lounge in front of her practice mirror, and watch ourselves taking imaginary tea. Whenever she invited me to this game, "Let's play Wigs and Crumpets!" I was delighted. But with the pronunciation of the word *crumpet* being yet beyond me, I'd yell, "Wig ands! Wig ands."

Of course, christened with one ruffle of my hair, I became, "My dear little Wiggins."

Thus was a wily street urchin born. But Wiggins did not remain our private game.

He became The Woman's secret weapon. In her own operatic plan, Mother raised me to one purpose: to ruin the man who called himself Sherlock Holmes. But she would never give me the backstory. She refused to say when, or where, or how, she met my father. Most confoundingly, she would not tell me why she would not tell me. She said only this, "All will be revealed in the fullness of time. For now, you must live for only one thing: to make him pay."

Why did I obey her? It is both simple and simply too complicated to explain. My complicity grew from the most bonding of loyalties – a lonely child's need.

Mother kept me close. Never abandoned me.

Except to row twice a week on the Thames, we seldom left the house. Lest you think our isolation confining, it was not. Her imaginative company provided all I could wish for. As parent, teacher, nurse, and playmate, I never felt crippled in her company.

I did worry why she kept me from public company. Because it was a question I could not ask aloud, with incomplete data, my deduction assumed the worst. I decided that if my mother had a fault, it was vanity. That a plain girl was no asset to a beautiful mother, and a disabled daughter no fit companion for a famous celebrity who rowed her own boat like the strongest of men.

But I must not suggest that any one in my family ever treated me like an invalid.

Just as Mother taught me to read and to sew, she attempted to teach me to shoot and to ride. She hid her disappointment that my uncertain balance ruined my aim, and that feet bouncing in stirrups made me cry. She could not hide her regret, however, at my total lack of musical talent. My attempts on the violin never progressed past the wailing of dying cats. For reasons obvious, I couldn't play any instrument which required standing for long periods of time. I played a little piano, but not with any promise, and not happily when a piece required me to stomp the pedal. I told myself it didn't matter. I told myself, like her, I could sing.

Thankfully, my family never stopped teaching me all the skills I most needed to learn.

I occasionally wished I could have attended school with other children, but I never once wished I had any other kind of lessons, or any other school mistresses. At my mother's hands, I learned how to fill our conservatory with her favourite wild lilies: *Hemerocallis Fulva*. At the hands of my aging aunties, I learned how to maim and murder men. On a voyage to Japan, in hiding from maritime police, they learned the ancient martial art of jujitsu. Always progressive, my aunties were some of the first in England to combine jujitsu with French kickboxing, cane fighting and boxing, to become practitioners of the new martial art of bartitsu.

For an hour each day in the garden, every resident of Pictavia practiced unfailingly.

I had some skill at cane fighting, but couldn't kick anything without falling to the ground screaming. If I needed to sit to practice, no one stopped me. But I must never miss practice, my aunties insisted, because a family that fights together stays alive.

When Holmes took up the craft, they scoffed at how the prudish Watson sanitized "bartitsu" to "baritsu," all to avoid putting Holmes in hand-to-hand combat with anything that sounded too titillatingly like mammaries.

How we laughed! At the boys of Baker Street.

At the glory of life.

Each morning, my mother lovingly brushed my ever-tangled hair. Every night, in the greatest gift a parent can give, she read to me. Long after I passed the age where I could read to myself, she read to me. Such a cornucopia of voices!

Recitations from Shakespeare to the worst penny dreadfuls, from Tennyson to Tacitus, from *Tales of Tippling Tinkers* to *Beowulf.* I loved *Little Women* and *Rose in Bloom.* She loved the villains: Long John Silver of *Treasure Island*, and Fagin in *Oliver Twist.* If she was training herself to be underhanded, I did not see it at the time.

To train both of us in their methods, and because Mother did not want me thinking Watson had invented the genre, we read every detective novel ever published. Any success I have had as a professor of Victorian Detective Literature began at my mother's knee. We read Dupin and Lecoq. We studied *The Woman in White* by Wilkie Collins; *The Nottinghill Mystery*, by Charles Felix, and Mary Elizabeth Bradon's *The Trail of the Serpent.* Our favourite was *The Leavenworth Case* by "the mother of detective fiction," Anna Katharine Green. She wrote thirty-two novels and thirty short stories, the first a full decade before a certain scribbling Scottish doctor.

From winsome to wicked, from rafter-splitting rage to sweet sotto voce, Mother read every part in role. Whispering, cackling, enticing, and singing – always singing – each night, she tucked me into bed with song. She loved all kinds of music: arias, hymns, scandalous music hall ditties, and especially folksongs.

Our favourite was my lullaby, *The Skye Boat Song.* She sang it to remind me how another true Catholic, Bonnie Prince Charlie, disguised as a woman, had outwitted British soldiers and escaped in a rowboat to the isle of Skye. When she sang, "Speed, bonnie boat, like a bird on the wing," I felt as beloved as "the lad that's born to be King," and longed to sail "over the sea to Skye," and on to dreamland. Instead, with each goodnight kiss, Mother made me repeat the litany that bound me in hate to the man who made me a bastard.

"So, dearest child, does the Heavenly Father put us on Earth for a reason?"

"Yes, Mother. His eye is even on the sparrow."

"And tell me, what does He expect of my little sparrow?"

"I must improvise the role of a beggar boy. I must insinuate myself into my father's sin-filled life until damning evidence can be found. Then I must ruin the man who has rejected the Holy Mother, dishonoured my own mother, and refused to honour the bastard that is me."

"Chirped well, my little songbird. Let us pray to Mary, Mother of us all."

In the last days of 1890, she grew rapidly frail. Her prayers grew more explicit: "Precious Lord, bless her Majesty the Queen and Mary the Queen of Heaven. Help me smite the vile heathen serpent Sherlock. Make strong my child's arm to slice his tiny, disease-ridden organ from its host, so that in eternally exquisite suffering, he shall never spawn again. Amen."

Was my own dear mother insane? By the day of her death, uncontrovertibly so. I heard my aunties whispering, "Syphilitic and unrepentantly murderous."

I hoped Mother had contracted it from the King of Bohemia, and from not my father. Whatever its source, from my first taste of mother's milk, I imbibed a steady diet of its venom. However toxic, it was my only sustenance. My only alternative was homeless hunger – to forage the streets with Danny and the Irregulars.

Today, that makes me smile. To my 1967 ear, they sound like a rock band on Ed Sullivan, like Eric Burden and the Animals, or Herman and his Hermits.

In Victoria's London, we banded for survival. A child who bit the hand that fed him went hungry. A child who ran away risked running into worse. Fleeing cruelty or perversity, manipulation or malfeasance, hands bruising, bloody, or thrust under nightclothes, it mattered naught; all homeless children had equal opportunity to be shipped to the colonies or starve.

So, I stayed put.

But I trust, Sympathetic Reader, you feel my double predicament. All families have their one bleaty sheep, an odd or eccentric ram or ewe. But both my parents were as potty as a pair of potted March Hares.

Perhaps the brilliant are always barking mad.

I can say with certainty that Holmes was frequently mad before breakfast. Perhaps, prior to egg and crumpet, his brain naturally secreted the chemicals that addle hatters. There may be sound precautionary wisdom in the dietary injunctions of Mr. Sylvester Graham and Dr. John Harvey Kellogg, both warning that both men named Holmes ingested too much red meat at Simpson's supper club. These doctors would have endorsed my fondness for crumpets, but not likely my belief they should attend every meal. Had Graham's crackers and Kellogg's flakes calmed my father, he would have labeled them poison.

My parents thrived on chemical excess. The heightened, altered states of righteousness and revenge, sleep-deprivation and cocaine all made life large and worth living. In equal truth, reflection is unnecessary to a man who is always right the first time and introspection is only useful to a woman interested in changing her mind.

I often asked myself what an innocent child could ever conceivably have done to deserve this most cruel dual punishment. My shame-filled answer as a child, the one I could never speak aloud and am sharing with you only now a lifetime later, came directly from Bible and pulpit.

I was not born innocent. Born deformed and illegitimate, I paid the bastard price. My conception is a crime we both must steel ourselves to hear.

Today, I know both my parents paid for their sins. But the child left alone on that cold Baker Street doorstep, believed that only Mother and I did. I paid as her guided missile, fired into hostile streets to wound my father. Mother paid with her life. In her dying days, it took both my aunties to remind her she was not the sinner, but the sinned against.

But in the largest truth, I must also add this: the childhood my parents staged for me, *The Wonderful World of Wiggins*, now that truly was a really big show. At their most erudite and charming, both my parents out-shone the night sky. When they left me, they sucked all light from the sun. Please note the fresh darkness of my loss.

On that first day of 1891, the great contralto Irene Adler had been dead but seven days.

She was thirty-two years old.

Having planned her exit, she entered Heaven on the morning of her Savior's birth. On Christmas morning, Tante Gisela delivered her note on the mantel to Messrs. Bennett and Shaw, Funereal Directors. The bewhiskered Mr. Shaw arrived immediately and left as quickly with my mother in his hearse. She had pre-selected her final costume: her favorite emerald gown with black piping and pink rosettes. She left instructions for no flowers but wild lilies, no publicity but a notice in the *Times*. She specified an immediate, private burial in St. Ambrose, our parish church.

At her closed-coffin funeral, my famous mother had only mourners five: myself, my Danny, my two great-aunts, and our good friend Godfrey. My aunties stood tall, identical auburn Amazons brandishing matching amber rosaries. I held the right hand of the woman who ran our household, Tante Gisela Adler, and griped the left of her twin sister, Tante Grizelda. I have always loved her name and how she most absolutely did not embody its meaning of "endless patience."

You will get to know my sweet Tante Gisela anon, but you already know her sister. My impatient Tante Grizelda is the woman you know as Mrs. Hudson.

I know this is not the way you heard our story, Startled Reader. I'm sure you're wondering why Watson never shared the truth about my dear red-headed league?

A man cannot tell you what he does not know.

For the full roles played by my family, you will have to wait. For now, we must all take this as our working truth: on that sad Christmas morning, I knew exactly for whom the bells tolled.

They rang for Irene Adler, a woman born to staunchly Catholic parents: a German mother, Gerda Adler, and a Scottish Highlander father, Alexander Mclean. They rang for their only child, one christened with a euphonious hybrid name: Catriona Magdalena Psalmonia Adler Mclean. Named Catriona and Magdalena after her Scots and German grandmothers, Psalmonia was an Adler encumbrance. In a family that loved to sing, too many innocent babes needing a saint's middle name by Catholic tradition got burdened with the moniker of St. Psalmonius, sainted for his wondrous singing of psalms and for turning snakes into donkeys.

A feat that no doubt inspired my mother when planning justice for my father.

In her teens, Catriona took an Anglicized nickname: Irene. Ever mercurial, she embraced it in all its pronunciations: as the American "I-reen," the more European "I-ray-nay," and "I-ree-nee," which she shortened to "Reenie." After the break with her father – something I did not understand and always got hushed for asking about – she took her mother's maiden name: Adler.

But, in one of the many instances when I failed to see the facts before my eyes, on that New Year's morning when Holmes mentioned the Mcleans of Mayfair, as implausible as it sounds, I thought it mere coincidence. It was such a common name: in Gaelic as MacGhille Eoin, as MacLaine or MacClean in English. Many Irregulars had Scottish names. In an exploding diaspora of kilts landing all over the planet, three generations of Scots had been driven from their crofts in the Highland Clearings, many into the streets of London.

Father's Mcleans lived in the backwoods of Canada and I knew Mother's people came from Egg Harbor, New Jersey. Her grandmother Adler was a concert pianist, her grandfather, a respected doctor. In youthful snobbery, it never occurred to me that hardscrabble colonial farmers could be any kin to my sophisticated, professional, city-dwelling European-American family.

Do you hear that, as I do? To my shame, pride contends. Pride sneers. Despite my lack of ability to observe the obvious, I actually believed I could out-perform the greatest improvisor of the day, and outwit the greatest brain of the century.

I told myself it was never Holmes' game afoot; it was always mine. Mine and Danny's.

Here, I must say his name to give him fair credit. Whilst running the meanest streets of London, all the while appearing to faun at Father's beck and call, we artfully dodged our Fagin. Whenever he yelled, "Bring me data! I cannot make bricks without clay," we snickered. Keeping the richest clay to ourselves, hoarding the very cornerstones of truth, we practiced all kinds of tomfoolery behind his back.

And gloried in it.

Each evening, after a queen's repast in Pictavia – our wholly-owned Georgian hideaway in High Kensington Street, mere blocks from Holmes' shabby rented hovel – Danny, my aunties and I gathered in the library to toast the end of Sherlock Holmes. We raised our glasses to the fine array of my mother's portraits.

My favourite was a small study, a *memento mori* of a girl with streaming russet hair running through a field of wild orange lilies, her face tilted up to the sun.

Tante Gisela loved it, too. Finding kindness even in sorrow, she said it reminded her of her niece's happiest moments, sharing her love of lilies with her lovely daughter. Tante Grizelda and Danny preferred another, more scandalous frame. To spare him career-ending ridicule, I won't name its famous portraitist known for a realistic rendering of human anatomy. He squinted at us for days, deftly producing a fine likeness of Mr. Wiggins and Master Wiggins, both in identical stalking caps, all without noticing a foursome of perky breasts and a dual lack of Adam's apples.

But enough of my old tongue's wagging.

This penitent little puppet must pen an apologizing pile of pink paper knowing it is a poor Pinocchio that impersonates a living soul. I write that sentence of which Father would be proud, knowing my musings here also violate his most sacred rule – one Watson actually quoted correctly in *A Scandal in Bohemia*: "It is a capital offence to theorize before one has the data. Insensibly one begins to twist facts to suit theories instead of theories to suit facts."

But in his brilliance, in his impenetrable arrogance, Father failed to advise how the rest of us miserably inadequate pawns should make peace with life when the one unalterable fact of our story remained: we were never given all the data. People who claimed to love us kept vital facts from us. We had to make our bricks out of insufficient clay.

In summary, Well-Warned Reader, please remember that every word you read here comes from *The Wizened Wheelchair World of Wiggins*. Please hear my long view of history in every word. I long for you to carry in your head the same conflicting joy and grief that I do.

I offer you these tidbits of my life knowing them insufficient fare. Mashed carrots keep us alive, but always leave us hungry.

Chapter Three: My Adventuring Red-Headed League

I slammed the door on Baker Street and went in search of my beloved cap.

Wearing it kept Mother close. She knew what they called her after her scandalous liaison with the King of Bohemia, but shrugged it off, "When we had to leave Warsaw in 1879, I was all of twenty-two years old. I said to myself, so be it. If I'm an adventuress, I shall have adventures. How perfect! What shall I wear? I shall make myself an adventuring cap!"

She fashioned a dashing deerstalker, accessorizing a masculine hounds-tooth tweed with a feminine hint: a blood-red silk ribbon, a scarlet bow to hold the earflaps up. She wore it in our dress-up games and whenever she went out in her "walking clothes" dressed as a man. She made me my own in 1887 when I turned eleven. I still hear her laughter the first time she pulled it over my unruly curls to complete my transformation into Wiggins.

"Behold, a new adventuress is born!"

Unfortunately, my wayward Medusa locks more than spoiled the effect.

In my best gift of heredity, I had hair like my mother's – luxuriant, shiny, smooth curls alive in bouncy spirals. An auburn that glowed like chrysanthemums in the sun, warmed to a deep chestnut at twilight.

Famous for her talent, but memorable for unmasking her glorious head of hair, at curtain call Mother always doffed her wig. It began as an accident. Relived to survive her Warsaw debut, she bowed so low her wig fell off. When catching it and holding it high elicited a standing ovation, it became her trademark. Audiences loved the revealing tumble of waist-length curls, loved it best when it was a man's wig she doffed. Mother had never cut her hair and loathed the idea of chopping mine, but I risked being unmasked because Wiggins could not wear his cap nonstop.

When my curls fell from my face to the floor, she held her tears. At the sight of mine, she responded with an act of instant solidarity. With one strike of the scissors, she slashed her own braid back to a manly bob.

"A dual improvement, don't you think, my dear? Less work. More fun."

I often think of the generosity of that gesture. It made her as brave as my literary heroine, Josephine March. In *Little Women,* Jo cut and sold her hair, her "one beauty", to send her mother to nurse her gravely ill father, to save his life and bring him home.

For the next four years, I slept with my cap under my pillow. On Boxing Day of 1890, I laid my mother's cap in her coffin.

On New Year's morning at Baker Street, I pulled Watson's settee as close to the fire as I dared and kept shivering. Only one thought warmed me: I had some operatic plans of my own. You shall remember, Retaining Reader, how on that January morning I had grunted at Father's gutter inquiry? Technically, I answered true, but I relished the dissemblance I proffered.

Yes, I had been "lying" in a Whitechapel gutter, as in, not telling the truth about it.

Anyone who spends a long December night in a filthy ditch when they have their own hearty supper and warm featherbed awaiting them is a danger-courting dunce. I imagine it never occurred to Homes that I might actually succumb to snow, or rats, or rozzers, the Home Children patrol, or beasts known to hunt children in the depravity of ditches. Had I died, would he have shrugged it off and joined Mrs. Hudson in the sweet consolation of sticky pudding?

I forced my mind to a better matter: my first case! It little mattered I had my foolish self as a client, or that I had so far found but one obvious clue. I had vowed to best both Holmes and Watson, to both solve and pen the deed. In nose-thumbing plagiarism, I entitled my detecting debut, *A Study in Scarlet Ribbons*. To date, I had deduced nothing more than the title. I had what Holmes would have called "a three pipe problem."

On Christmas night, I found Mother's final gift to me. Given its staging, I know she expected me to find it. Wrapped in a purple velvet shawl, hand-beaded with wild orange lilies, her bundle of letters presented a lumpy replacement for her pillow on the first lonely night when a grieving child climbed into her bed, hoping against all logic to find her there. While Irene Adler's desk was a disaster, with old play bills and crumpled sheets of libretti bursting from each drawer, these letters were pristine. Each worn page was carefully re-creased, restored to its original envelope, and reset in chronological order. I recognized the blood-red ribbon that bound them immediately. A fresher length of it held my cap's earflaps up. I recognized her hand, a more immature and exuberant script, but still so welcome, so hers.

Right on cue, on my first night alone, I heard my mother's voice.

July 1st, 1872

To My Dearest DAMM,

On this wondrously glowing new summer day, I shall begin writing you the letters that I vow to write until the day I become your wife. There is something so delicious in using only your initials. Like a secret language, DAMM is a word that rings of you and the forbidden.

How perfect! That is exactly how our new love feels!

Mutti says I'm being an utter goose and whoever the poor fool is, I'll scare him off for sure, because fourteen is still a baby and far too young to claim you're in love at all, let alone that you're certain as the sun you know the boy you're going to marry and love forever. But she smiled when she said it. That kept me from pointing out that I am almost as old as she was when she met Da. And theirs was a true love story right from the start, so I know ours will be too!

She can't be entirely against it, because she handed me this ream of pretty pink paper she had been saving as a present for Tante Gisela. She told me to write all the lovey-dovey out of my system and to stop traipsing around the house, singing my love-sick lungs out. When I said I'd been told I sounded just like Jenny Lind, I would have also told her it was your dear self who said so, except Da darkened the doorway and grunted, "More like, Jemima, the Lindstrom's cow."

But that evening, he set aside his whittling and pulled out his violin.

He smiled when Mother moved to the piano and I joined in. Our three-part harmony would have turned Jemima's milk to cream! For all his silences, Da is indeed the most artful man in all of Caradoc County. Who else can both sing and play with such feeling? Who else can whittle such tiny, exquisite figurines?

Mother says that his little shepherd boys, once they're cunningly painted, look just like the china children that lived on her mother's grand piano. Tonight, when I stopped singing and watched them perform, I felt myself newly older; a woman grown!

If my parents often seem sad, they still sing beautifully together. We will, too, because the words you said today have told me you love me. During your first lesson on Da's violin, you said, "I vow to play only true music, born of uniting the heart, the head, the body and the soul!"

If I could tell my parents your beautiful words, they would know we have been blessed with a love as strong as theirs. But when she kissed me goodnight, Mutti wasn't smiling. She made me say an extra Hail Mary, "Da must never see what you're writing." When she hugged me, her cheek was cold and her whisper colder. "He'll cut off your hair and throw it in the fire."

Could you imagine what Da would do, my darling, if he knew it wasn't just some Mayfair boy – that it was you? You, you, you, my amazing, inspiring, miraculous, beloved cousin!

At least Da approves of your lessons. For now, that is enough. We will keep our true music secret.

Kissing my pillow and knowing someday soon it will be you I kiss,

Catriona Magdalena Psalmonia Adler Mclean,

and your Reenie

While I had no willpower whatsoever when it came to devouring novels and crumpets, after committing this letter to memory, I had decided to ration the rest. I vowed to read them sparingly, in reviving tonic, when I needed my mother most. Swaddled in a bear rug, I decided not to dwell on my parents' absence, but instead to use Father's methods to solve my case. I began my self-interrogation with what I assumed would be his first question, "Why would a woman have her own letters?"

The first was penned in 1867, when my mother was fourteen – my exact age. But none of the letters had stamps. They were either hand-delivered, or never sent. For reasons unknowable, someone had inked out every jot on the front of every envelope. Since the redactions took different lengths and shapes, I deduced that both recipient and sender had lived in more than one place over time. That left only one clue. In her salutation, Mother used the man's initials: DAMM.

Why did she not use his name?

Why, and from whom, had she hidden it?

Where were these letters' mates – the replies DAMM sent in return? Or were there none?

When I shared this letter with him, cuddled up in our own warm fire, Danny had suggested that Mother had written this man for years, but never received a reply. I needed him to be wrong. What kind of cad takes a woman's love, but neither rejects nor returns it honourably? I feared myself already tied to such a man, and didn't want to know my mother had loved another one.

Remember that man's caution about speculating before we have all the data? It absolutely applies to the reading of beribboned letters, but I speculated non-stop.

Perhaps DAMM never saw them? Perhaps, as miscarried as the letters of another Romeo and Juliet, someone intercepted them? Then, at some too-late date, cruelly returned them to my mother? Perhaps this explained the break with my grandfather? I longed to believe these letters would unlace a star-crossed love and a wronged, but honorable man. In the secret spot where we keep our heart's desire, I hoped he was the true husband of Irene Adler's heart.

In my secret heart, telling no one, not even Danny, I hoped I'd found my real father.

Those voices in our heads? It is so good of them to say what we most want to hear.

Perhaps bereaved bastard children are entitled to go barking mad. I shredded every pillow in Pictavia. I quite logically gutted the feather beds and upholstery. After prying up some floorboards, I bowed to Tante Grizelda's ultimatum I must not lift another or she would make me eat it. Tante Gisela calmly explained that my mother had left her letters hiding in plain sight. If there had been more to find, I would have done so already.

I reluctantly deduced that if the DAMM replies existed, they were not hidden in our home.

On that cold morning in Father's home, his bearskin would warm my shoulders or feet, but not both. I pushed a bear's teeth past my face and vowed to be my own Toby the Basset Hound. I would track my father until I found him.

I imagined a witty, musical lad from New Jersey, a boy with a shy, respectful smile; now a perfectly sane man with a perfectly normal name. Fighting sleep, I recited Mother's letter to an audience of andirons. Seeing Holmes' face with each blow, I struck the fickle fireplace coals with the poker whenever they faded and needed to be struck.

I wound bear paws tight around my chest.

Dead claws clicked. The fire faded.

Rudely awakened by Father knocking like a woodpecker on the brim of my cap, I jerked it from his reach. He had no right to touch it. For once, he seemed equally ill at ease.

"I was gone for an hour. For another seven minutes, Wiggins, I have been watching you sleep, embraced by a bear. I would not wake you from your ursine dreams were it not necessary."

I sat up, cold and groggy. If I did not appear delighted, again, he did not appear to notice.

"After depositing your doppelganger decoy, I paid one of your Irregular little birds to fly to Baker Street to report your al fresco demise. He arrives at our door in three minutes. In the interests of verisimilitude, to lower the curtain on Act One, I shall accompany him to identify your remains, then inter you at my own expense. Please assist me with the pecuniary exactitudes."

For a sleepy moment, I imagined he had learned my wealth exceeded his own and was asking me to lend him the money to bury me.

"Bein' sorry, guv," I faltered. "I hain't followin' you."

"Your name, Wiggins. Your full Christian name, for your tombstone, what is it?"

I panicked. How was it possible, that in all of Mother's scrupulously staged preparations, we never once expected this question? My bruised heart leapt next to outrage: how was it possible that we were right, that for all the years of our acquaintance, my father had never once asked my first name, content to summon me by a single moniker like a mutt, or a ship's monkey?

I knew I was pausing too long. Unable to improvise a Willy or a Sam, my eye fell on the table beside the settee, landing on one of Watson's magazines.

"Strand," I muttered.

"Strand?" my father raised one dark eyebrow. If he glanced table wise, I did not see him do so. "Your Christian name is Strand? You are properly called Strand Wiggins?"

"Mam was a great enthusiast, sir."

Two black brows arched higher. "Really, Wiggins, your mother could read?"

I quickly rectified that error.

"No, Sir. Mam was enthusiastical for th'pictures, for th'stories what got read to her in pubs." Then in for a drowsy penny, in for a sleep-addled pound I added, "I'm 'avin' Ambrose for a middle name, Sir, like all good Catholics, bein' after a saint."

His voice caught. "And your age, your date of birth?"

This was at least a question Mother had anticipated. Now a runty fourteen, I was born June 23, 1876, but Holmes must not know it. He must get a date that made me too young to be his child.

"I'm twelve, being born May Day, 1878."

A disappointed shadow crossed his face.

One he hid quickly.

"How festive, Wiggins. Remind me to erect a Maypole in your honor." Lifting his pocket watch, he added, "I shall return to Mrs. Hudson's excellent egg and crumpet. Tell her to have it ready in," he snapped his watch shut holding my eyes, "Exactly seventy-six minutes."

He raced the stairs, craning his long neck round the door jamb one last time to tie upon it a wooly cravat snatched from the coat tree. If it was Mrs. Hudson's and patterned with outlandish lavender lilies, he did not notice and I did not correct him.

"Be productive in my absence, Wiggins. You say you're broaching thirteen? Then, as I become your guardian this day," here he paused to plan yet another perfectly matched seventeen beat-seventeen stair exit, " I'd say it is long past time to ponder the question of girls and laps."

Then, doing what he did best, he made his exit.

Chapter Four: The Cross-Dressing Conundrum of Thor and Loki

At my second abandonment in a year but hours old, I gripped the sides of the settee the way I now grip the arms of my wheelchair when my most athletic grandchild pushes it – as if I expect to be tossed from it straight on my head. All these decades later, it is still hard to stomach his arrogance. With zero consultation, "the world's first consulting detective" threw me into a grave, then into a new life. The idea that mudlarks might have their own tides, might want their own clothes and some small, salvaged belongings to bring with them, that never occurred to him.

In fairness, Holmes had little attachment to his own possessions. In his Act Two, when he feigned his own death, he left all he owned behind, except his violin and his photo of "The Woman." It is equally fair to note he planned his demise sporting a full purse. He could replenish life with instant ease, purchase a new Churchwarden pipe, artisan blends of shag tobacco and a new Persian slipper, perhaps even a pair. He could – and did – buy any number of silk dressing gowns, be they blue, purple, or mouse-coloured. It is easy to reinvent yourself when you are rich.

Shivering on his settee made it icy clear to me that my life would be refurbished, if at all, at the caprice of his noblesse oblige. Mother may have costumed me in rags, but she would never have left me unclad for all of a winter's morning. Father's concern for his actors ended once they left his stage. But I had loved ones I would not abandon as lightly as he had me. I would reassure them that the boy about to be found dead in a gutter was not yours truly.

As I leapt from the settee, ursine claws sliced my bare leg. The droplets of blood on my exposed baby toe served as a keen reminder that I was not clad for any outing, let alone a London snowstorm. Despite his claim to a precision of plans, I could spy no attire of my size at hand. If this lack of costuming was designed to ensure that I followed his stage blocking and "stayed put," then I would happily go off script.

I crept down the stairs in search of Tante Grizelda's mending bag, habitually hung on the back of her kitchen chair in both her houses. As my frozen feet limped down colder stairs, however, I realized this – I could not be sure whether either of my parents told the truth.

Were Mother's letters authentically from her youth? That froze me mid-step.

Her every pink page may be fraudulent, written in a final mad desperation in the last days of sanity-stealing illness. I hoped her letters true, but could not prove them, or her, to be so.

My reservations had begun with her second letter, read for the first time last night. Danny and I had slipped away from a small celebration of my mother's life, away from my aunties, the Marx family, and Godfrey. After our private celebration, we read the second letter together. In truth, I read it aloud a full three times to an increasingly frowning listener.

"As much as I loved your mother, you must see it? She's not telling herself the truth."

Danny's direct honesty was one of the things I appreciated most, even when it hurt me. In pointed example, I had not realized how my entire family had humored me about my belief that I could sing as well as my lovely mother until one year at Christmas carols, when Danny exploded.

"You sound like a burping bullfrog. It's bloody god awful. Please stop."

This time, so close to my mother's death, I wasn't ready to hear his truth. I did what all my family does when uncertain: I retreated into silence. I asked Danny and my aunties to please let me read the letters in my own time, with no further questions. I promised to come to them when I was ready. They reluctantly agreed. By my own hand, I slammed the door to their counsel. When I later blamed others for keeping the truth from me, I should have remembered I had done likewise.

August 1, 1872

My dearest, most deliciously distant DAMM,

How excellently you feign your disinterest! I am certain no one suspects a thing. But I do not have your skill at keeping the secret of our singing love! I fear it shall burst from me like the best of Mozart. Thankfully, delightfully, you let me know in all the endless codes and double meanings between us, that your love for me is boundless and true.

Today, I let your "brother" carry my books from Caradoc Academy.

I confess I did so in hopes that keeping your hands free meant you would reach for mine. I don't know why Home Boy bothers to converse with me at all, but I actually agreed with him when he said we were so lucky to have a school where both boys and girls can prepare for university. I was surprised he knew my desire. But surely, he must see he will never be allowed to graduate.

He will always be the servant boy who takes off his only pair of shoes to muck dung in his bare feet. Your family is kind to have taken him in. Uncle John and Aunt Ada show further Christian charity when they lend him out to Da. I do what chores I can, but it breaks Mutti's heart to see me dressed as a boy. I don't mind. Pants are more comfortable than crinolines.

I do mind how Home Boy thinks me weak. When I was chopping firewood, he tried to take my axe. To put him in his place, I asked him if he even knew where he came from. "London," he said with silly pride as if it were an address. I asked where in London, knowing he could not know, being so young when he came here. "All of it, he replied. Every street of it is home."

How absurd.

One of the best things about you, dear cousin, is your sense of propriety. Today, you insisted Home Boy walk between us to ensure no breath of scandal. When we stopped at the ravine, you jumped up to swat a honeybee buzzing near

47

my feet. When Home Boy stayed your hand, you did not hit him for his insolence. He said, "Let the creature be. It cannot sting. It lives only to make life a little sweeter and should not die for it." You squashed the intruder dead with your foot, saying, "It is buzzing around Miss Catriona. That is good reason for it to die."

I sent you a smile that said you make my life so sweet that should I ever feel the sting of separation, I would die. I saw the sly, warning smile you gave Home Boy. How clearly that look told him I am yours and yours alone. If you weren't going to run your father's farm someday, you could grace the stage like Edwin Booth. I'd willingly be your Sarah Bernhard.

But she sleeps in a coffin. I suggest a warm feather bed would be much nicer for us.

Now and always, buzzing to be yours,

Reenie

Donning cast-offs in a cold kitchen, I decided that was the shabby punishment Holmes had intended. Replacing rags with more rags, another staging to keep me in my place. Another test, much like the one he had set when we met, when he observed me closely to see if I flinched from his tale of *The Giant Rat of Southampton*. When I somehow managed to hide my fear, he shrugged. "I will teach you, Wiggins, but do not, for one fraction of a second, ever believe you can hope to know all I do. It is inconceivable."

Clearly the most welcoming job offer in the history of sleuthing apprenticeships.

Upon his return from my burial, Father chided his now dead apprentice for my laziness. Please pause, Tickled Reader, to enjoy the delicious impossibility of that sentence.

As for what he had expected me to have done in his absence, I freely admit that I lacked the ability to read his mind. As Watson correctly noted, in Holmes' attic brain, he kept only what he considered useful. That morning, Holmes retrieved a useful topic Watson would never have admitted his friend and flat-mate knew intimately: the art of cross-dressing.

In another scandal the class-conscious Watson omitted, we often breakfasted with Mrs. Hudson in her kitchen. I sat down anticipating the solace of hot crumpets, hoping they would make the breakfast lecture bearable. As I waited, I decided I must be the only child in human history to have two cross-dressing parents. It opened career doors for my mother and doors of data for my father. But a mind such as Holmes' could easily have devised equally impenetrable masculine disguises to ferret out the same information. Clearly, there was more afoot here than necessity.

I assure you, Robbed Reader, my father flaunted feminine attire on far more entertaining occasions than Watson ever shared.

To my future profound regret, I underestimated the danger of exposure. Since the world found Mother's cross-dress charming, I naively assumed they would view a man's likewise. I should have known better. I could only deduce that Father computed that risk acceptable, believing himself too good an improvisor to get caught.

As a child who cried alone each night in an absent mother's closet, I also knew this – wearing another's clothes kept them with you. When you reanimated their clothing, you reanimated them. The textures, scents, colours and sounds of their life returned. As you stood in their second skins, you were both yourself and them. You were incongruously congruent, singularly and jointly, vibrantly alive. And because it was forbidden, it could also be exciting. Arousing. Titillating.

Because, of course, a modern alienist would also see sex in it. When you were a heterosexual Victorian man temporarily costumed in woman's clothing, you became a man entering the forbidden female form. Conversely, through men's clothing, my mother reclaimed the power a man had stolen, when, without her consult or consent he removed her clothing and entered her unwilling body. For my parents, cross-dressing offered a conundrum: it provided both a shield against and a reminder of rape.

I understood this, because running the streets as Wiggins offered me a similar escape.

Wiggins was not real. He was my game afoot. In release and respite, not only could I be a clumsy boy, one who fell, got up and laughed, I could join a small Irregular army of invalids.

So many street children were disabled.

Missing fingers, arms and legs, all taken by factories that chopped children up then spit them out. Limping on feet that had been crunched under carriages and horses' hooves. Lifting purses with broken arms that never received medical attention and never properly reset. Born with lazy eyes, living with rickets, driven to madness and hunched to skeletons by coughs and illness and smoke and soot and starvation. As just another broken boy in streets full of them, no one stared at yet another limping boy. For the first time, in cross-dress as a poor boy, I found myself in good company and right at home.

Suffice it to say, my addiction to over-analysis may be tainting the data.

Perhaps, for my parents, the truth was simpler. They both bored so easily. Perhaps nothing tantalized them more than a perfumed or pantalooned passage to a secret second life. In costume, they took that escape, enjoyed its adventures, all while wearing a second protective identity. Cross-dress gave them proximity while ensuring emotional distance. However their stand-ins were treated, their true selves never got touched. That clearly appealed to my intimacy-adverse parents.

But not to me. I longed to be touched.

My Tante Grizelda, who in real life had zero use for propriety, brought my wandering teenage mind back into focus by playing a proper Mrs. Hudson.

"My dear Mr. Holmes, you must cease and desist. It is far too early of a New Year's morning for such lewd discussion. I will hear not another word of cross-dress at my breakfast table, thank you very much."

A senior flibbertigibbet indeed.

What she really wanted, of course, was her boarder to go upstairs and leave us alone.

Father insisted no more time could be lost in the matter of my education and if the topic was *too outré* for his *dear landlady*, she could not possibly object to a little good literature? Snapping up the first crumpet of 1891, he scolded me for not figuring out for myself that by his instruction to, "ponder girls and laps" he meant me to begin with *The Collected Works of Shakespeare* sitting in plain sight by the settee, as bookmarked by *The Strand*. Before so much as my first bite, he waved me off with an eggy fork, sending me back upstairs to fetch it.

I found his curriculum scribbled in the preface: *As You Like It, Merchant of Venice,* and *Twelfth Night.* I understood *Taming of the Shrew* and *The Merry Wives of Winsor*, where men masqueraded as women, but questioned *Two Gentlemen of Verona* and *Cymbeline* where women passed as men. I carried it downstairs, annoyed to have to feign ignorance. Mother and I had committed much of Shakespeare to memory. She taught me how to embody a character in mind, body, and soul. I refused to share those heavenly memories with my heathen father. I should have been smiting his diseased organ, not playing the monkey to his Elizabethan organ grinder.

When I returned to the kitchen, scowling, cold as my crumpet, Holmes made it worse.

"I have added King Odin's sons, the mighty Thor and the cunning Loki, to our list. These sons of the God of War dressed as bride and bridesmaid to retrieve Thor's hammer, Mjölnir. That should be sufficient consolation, Wiggins, to your own less-athletic aspirations of manhood."

He did not need to know I knew a lying Loki hungered for Odin's throne.

Father next quite logically jumped from Mjölnir to *Huckleberry Finn*, and began to read in a grating falsetto, choosing the moment where Huck, dressed as Sarah Williams, got exposed by the widow Douglass. Poor Huck closed his legs to trap a thimble the widow has thrown, as opposed to opening his legs to catch it in his skirts as the widow insisted a girl would have done. When Holmes read to me assuming me illiterate, I longed to make him stop by throwing my own thimble or perhaps a fork or two. Instead, Tante Grizelda and I suffered the frothy projections of minimally masticated egg and crumpet.

Mid-scene and mid-mouthful, Father pitched Huck clear across the kitchen with lethal aim into the fire. "Enough, you posturing poseur! I call you out!"

Have I mentioned that Holmes frequently pitched things into fires? Often things that had no place in fires, that constituted a danger to all and sundry near said fires.

Mrs. Hudson, more fed up than frightened, played her flibbertigibbety part to perfection. She screamed, then rushed to the rolling coals and flying cinders, shoving all things incendiary back where they flaming belonged.

I froze, certain he meant me. Certain that, like Huck, this imposter had been unmasked.

"Heed me, Wiggins! It is a mistake to see men and women in the maths of Moriarty, in binary opposition. No, in both skirts and trousers, once predators gain their prey, they secure it. In short, all traps snap shut." His eyes narrowed. He steepled an accusatory spire of fingers under his nose. "If I had the tendencies of a modern alienist, I might conjecture unkind thoughts about the sexual dishonesty of Mr. Mark Twain." His hands broke apart; one flew dismissively past his face. "But in deference to his reputation, our good landlady's suddenly Puritan sensibilities, and your youthful ignorance, Wiggins, I shall not utter my suspicions aloud at this time. Not one word."

Mrs. Hudson snorted. "Bravo, Mr. Holmes! As you fully intended, you have successfully disparaged all of us, by mentioning none of us aloud at this time."

How Father laughed! Watson so correctly described it in *A Scandal in Bohemia*, Holmes collapsed with tears scoring his cheeks and a snorting inability to take his next breath.

My face laughed along, but not my heart. That mocking man had just put a dead boy in my grave.

In pricked teenage pride, I longed for Twain to be right and Father wrong. Just once. About anything. I longed to ask why Home Children were being sent to America if it was already full of homeless Huck Finns. Would we all end up polling down the river alone?

After breakfast, when Holmes dispatched me, costumed yet again in castoffs, to the Diogenes back door, I finally understood my bit part in his great plan: he believed my only role was to play a grateful, broken beggar to my betters. I trudged along, mentally throwing things at my father, but did not restrict myself to thimbles. Or forks. I tossed books, boots and rocks – some small and some not big enough – all to see if his legs would open or clamp shut.

You realize, of course, Insightful Reader, that I was both fuming and frightened.

Seeking solace, on that first night at the Diogenes, I opened my mother's third letter.

August 15, 1872

My dearest DAMM,

Some people search their whole lives for a partner to take their second oar, but we found each other just across a ravine, your father's barn in sight of mine. Your proposal today was as romantic as that in Little Women, where Laurie says, "I would always like to row in the same boat as you, Amy." I record your clever words here, for the future delight of our grandchildren.

Today was one of those oven hot days, too hot for dragonflies to buzz or frogs to sing. We met at the ravine, but it was too hot for even me to row. I hiked my skirts to wade in the cool water and you lay on the bank to laze in the sun and watch me. When I slipped, it was Home Boy who shot out a hand to save me. We caught your frown. Then you smiled.

"Home Boy, ask Miss Catriona what she sees as the best quality in a husband."

Home Boy said nothing. You repeated your request louder, so I answered.

"I want a husband who values me. A man who trusts me and trusts our love."

"Home Boy," you continued. "Tell Miss Catriona what you want in a wife."

I confess I giggled. The notion he could ever marry is so utterly impossible.

Home Boy looked up to answer, not at you, but at me.

"My wife must value truth above all things. In its seeking and sharing, we must be peers."

When you laughed, Dear Cuz, you did not have to roll on you back and howl like a giant hound. Yes, it is a ludicrous notion that Home Boy could ever think he'll find a peer. The Fergusons have a Home Girl from some dirty town in Wales, but she's quite daft, and if you have to grant anything about Home Boy, he is intelligent. Now that you are studying away, he has stood first at Caradoc Academy and still does all your family chores. I fear he never sleeps.

After your clever declaration of love through Home Boy, why did you say nothing more?

I shall deal directly with what I'm sure based your hesitation: the anticipated opposition of my parents. Let me begin here: I am a woman of fourteen. When our grandfather, the first Duncan Mclean, married our grandmother, Mattie Mc Kniven, he was twenty-three and she sixteen. I count seven years between them, and only five between us. Our fathers fell out when Da became a Catholic, but unlike Montagues and Capulets, there need be no uncivil blood between us.

So I spoke to our uncle, Father Mc Kniven. He assured me there was no law of God or country against cousins marrying. My father converted to marry my mother, so that is clearly something a Mclean does. For the love of his life, surely another Mclean can do so again?

In truth, while I am thrilled by the clever way you proposed through Home Boy, I shall also insist on being be asked directly. Shakespeare often had lovers speak through stand-ins and suffice it to say, that seldom went well! Let us not to the marriage of true cousins admit impediment!

Your soon to be kissing cousin,

Reenie

After a sleepless night at the Diogenes, alarmed by my young mother's increasing self-deception, I arrived at this deduction: the true cross-dressing conundrum of Thor and Loki wasn't that they might someday get caught. It was that they might never get caught. That they would be forced to forever play out their days in an inauthentic role. This new insight embodied my current dilemma – perhaps the cross-dress my father offered me reflected a Moriarity binary that was in fact the opposite of kindness? Perhaps it was simply cruel? Perhaps he preferred to see me as a pretending boy, because he did not want to have to look at a deformed girl?

Hope said, "He plays along because he loves to play with you."

Doubt warned, "Do not sentimentalize the data. The facts are inconclusive."

Hate pricked, "What good is a parent who sees their child's pain, but does nothing?"

Chapter Five: Born of the Bodacious Bedlam of Bootlegging

That morning, after a bowl of cold prunes that never deserve the title of breakfast, Mycroft gave this cheery greeting to a child who had just lost his mother, "You are dead. Ergo, you cannot be seen in the streets. For the next four months, you are forbidden to set foot outside the club."

Late that night, I opened Mother's fourth letter, desperate to keep something of home alive.

December 12, 1872

My dearest most devoted to his studies DAMM,

Oh my gracious heavens! I have such a surprise for you! Thanks to luck and Our Lady my father didn't catch us! To be fair, I must also thank the quick-thinking Home Boy.

While I far prefer rowing to skating, the ravine is beautiful in winter, isn't it? A kiss of pure white fairy dust with every icicle hand-painted by pixies.

It is our place and I could scarcely be blamed for wanting to visit it, even if Da had forbidden it. He could give no reason, so I saw no reason to obey him. You have been so busy with your studies you have no time left for me. When I mentioned one lunchtime to Home Boy that I wanted to visit it, he frowned. Then smiled a half smile. "Let me consider it, Reenie. There must be a method. One that is safe for all concerned."

What a caravan of silly snow camels we made!

When Home Boy first suggested I walk behind him in his footsteps, I was insulted. I am not his little dog. I didn't think it would work, but he convinced me to try. We practiced in the school yard behind the barn, where no one could see us. To my surprise, after more than a little laughter at our drunken-looking selves, it took only a small adjustment in his gait for me to match him. I wanted to go straight to the ravine, but he said there was more to learn of his methods.

The next day we again practiced behind the barn, but this time we went backwards!

It is more than clever is it not? I saw the brilliance of his plan immediately. Together, side by side, we walk home as usual, taking two sets of footprints to my door. Then when he turns around and heads across the field for home, I follow in his footsteps to the ravine. After our visit, I trace those steps backwards to my front door. Utter genius!

Today, we had arrived successfully, decamped on our usual log. I, of course, was insisting that now that we knew his method worked, he must ask you to join us. It was growing dark when we heard Da and another man approaching. It was with a speed I could barely comprehend that Home Boy pulled me backwards up the slope, proving that we could indeed run backwards together in our own footprints. When we collapsed in laughter afterwards, I'm sure God smiled.

So our plan is afoot! We will wait every day, my dearest. Please come at once! If it is inconvenient, our love is at stake, so come all the same.

Your impatient and cunning kissing cousin,

Reenie

With this letter, I gave up all interest in DAMM being my father and began simply to treasure the happiness in my mother's young voice. I am reduced to an old Wiggin's tears all these near-eighty years later at the fragile joy it still brings.

Her snowy adventure of fairy dust and pixies recalls my joyous first adventure with Danny, and I know I must bring myself to speak of him now. But first, I must be clear: our romance could not have blossomed without without my aunties, who repeatedly saved both our lives. My aunts in all their wisdoms and tales of daring-do deserve their own book, but for now, Patient Reader, it will suffice to trace the strands of their backstory to my love story.

Born in 1840, my great-aunts were eighteen years older than their niece. Since Mother was eighteen when I was born, that made them only thirty-six years older than yours truly. In 1891, when to fourteen-year-old me they seemed egregiously ancient, they were not yet fifty. As the babies of their family, as the thick-as-thieves twin daughters of Laurenz and Magdalena Adler, they were always free spirits.

All three daughters – Gerda, Grizelda and Gisela – were born in one of the oldest "twin towns" of Europe, the

German-Polish city of Gorlitz-Zgorzelec, on the Oder-Neisse River. In 1854, the Adlers came to Egg Harbor City, New Jersey, a haven for Germans being persecuted by Know Nothings, rabid "patriots" intent on ridding America of Germans and Irish Catholics.

Embracing their new freedom, they became Abolitionists. Concert pianist Magdalena saw it as integral to her Catholic faith. Dr. Laurenz Adler considered anti-slavery an extension of his Hippocratic Oath. None of the family cared one whit for what Watson considered the true jewels of the British Empire: manners, decorum and propriety.

My aunties shrugged at the English fetish for good breeding, saying that while they were thankful pedigree applied to dogs and horses, it had no role in human worth. Had they lived in the 1960s, they'd have donned bra-less tie-dyed tank tops and stormed the patriarchy with placards waiving. In their generation's version of radical love, as family lore tells the tale, Gerda, my grandmother, met my grandfather, Alexander Mclean, at an anti-slavery rally.

After their wedding, having no sons to send to the Civil War, the Adlers sent their school-teacher twin daughters to be the Florence Nightingales of the Union Army. Across five long Aprils, from 1860-1865, my nursing aunties saw unspeakable horrors. It gave them the take-no-prisoners nerves of steel later required to sign up as pirates.

Tante Gisela lost her young man at Gettysburg. She never married. When the war ended, both aunts headed back to Egg Harbor City, to the teaching of other women's children. Five years later, at the un-marriageable age of thirty, Grizelda eloped with a sea captain and proud Scottish nationalist – one Hamish Hudson. As an athletic girl who loved the water and spent every possible moment on the Jersey shore, she jumped at the chance to marry a man with a really big boat.

As first mate and cook, Tante Grizelda ran the ship's galley. I'm sure tough tattooed sailors accustomed to hard tack and wormy biscuits welcomed her crumpets. Tante Gisela ran the rigging of sails and sailors, keeping both better mended than brigands left to their own bilgy devices. Captain Hudson ran the whiskey running. The profits on the finest of Scotch Whiskey from his own distillery in his West Highland hometown, the port of Oban, were booty indeed.

Suffice it to say this Scot saw bootlegging as his personal revenge for Culloden.

Having read many letters between the twins and my mother, I know my Tante Grizelda sailed as Captain Hudson's first mate in the truest sense of the word. In the seediest ports, she wielded both a coquette's wiles and a cocked pistol. In 1879, when Captain Hudson met his untimely death at the hands of another irate pirate – or possibly a pirating New Jersey financier, the data is unclear – Mrs. Hudson wisely decided to relocate herself and her ill-gotten gains to London.

Knowing American authorities described her as "the German wife," she and her twin arrived with her dearly departed husband's Scottish accent blooming like heather in the highlands. Claiming they'd just come over the hills from Skye, they bought a home in High Kensington. When things went sour in Warsaw, they invited their niece to join them.

Enjoying their rebirth as Scottish selkies, and to honor the Picts who lived north of Hadrian's Wall, free clans never subdued by invading armies, my aunties christened their grand white house Pictavia. Mother hung her legitimately Scottish Mclean family crest over the fireplace: *Virtue Mine Honour*. Tante Gisela added a cross-stitched motto in scarlet embroidery floss in Polish: *Witaj w domu! Tu, tam wojownicy.* Welcome Home! Here, there be warriors.

My Pictavian warriors fought on every conceivable front of the war for women.

They read newspapers. They read lewd and scandalous novels and discussed them aloud – *Leaves of Grass*, by Walt Whitman and *Madam Bovary*, by Flaubert. They read Mr. Darwin and Mr. Marx. They befriended the Marx family, who often joined us for dinner in what Karl liked to call "The Salon Pictavia." Eleanor "Tussy" Marx, being the exact same age as my mother, was one of her bosom friends. Together, we attended all manner of unsuitable public events, including those demanding, "Votes for Women!"

Unlike Emmeline Pankhurst, my aunties never chained themselves to Buckingham Palace. As life-long abolitionists, they loathed all manner of chains and unnecessary violence.

Unless provoked, my Tante Gisela wouldn't swat a bee. I cannot vouch likewise for the Pictish Warrior named Tante Grizelda.

Many a family legend affirms she protected smuggled booty by any means necessary. My sweet Tante Gisela never had the same killer instinct, but I am forever grateful to report the one exception – on one fine spring day in Hyde Park, my bee-saving auntie broke a man's neck.

I was almost six years old. It was the spring of 1882.

We were on our way to the London Zoo to say good-bye to my beloved friend, Jumbo the Elephant. Despite a letter-writing campaign to Queen Victoria from 100,000 children, yours truly included, Jumbo had been sold to P.T. Barnum to headline his circus. That forced relocation against my friend's will gave me nightmares. I woke screaming at the sight of my beloved Jumbo frightened and alone, far from the warmth of home, entombed in cold American snow.

I felt two incompatible things: that Jumbo had abandoned me and that I had failed him.

Our brougham had taken a Park Lane shortcut, but in Hyde Park, we stopped dead. When I protested the delay, Tante Gisela explained that Speaker's Corner was typically full of working men spouting ideas that would never work without a revolution.

Our driver, Godfrey Norton, awaited the crowd, when a marvelously mustachioed man thrust hairy hands through the open window and grabbed me. He would have pulled me clean away, were it not for one small pink boot that landed like a guillotine, neatly severing the cervical vertebrae where skull meets spine.

To this day, I still marvel at the skill with which my quiet auntie felled her foe.

When an officer arrived, one with a new uniform and ruddy cheeks, he found a dead man dangling in our window. He also found a hysterical little old lady, one who trembled so badly she kept spilling her smelling salts. She said the crowd had jostled the cab and in the kerfuffle the thief hit his head on the window frame. The young rozzer did ascertain that there was no further injury to the body. He had no other explanation for the contusion on the dead man's skull, as there were no weapons in the carriage, and clearly, no person in said carriage capable of wielding them.

When I tried to assist by correcting my frazzled aunt that the intruder had not been a thief, but a kidnapper, Tante Gisela reached beneath my petticoats and gave me a nasty pinch. When I howled, more in outrage than pain, she burst into tears and thrust me into the copper's face.

"The poor baby needs a new nappy. Oh, I am too weak to change her. Will you?"

Moments later, how we laughed at the face of the panicked young rozzer who was far more frightened by a diaper than he was of a dead body. Too frightened, fortunately, to ask our names or addresses before sending my improvising auntie on her merry murdering way.

When I think of how close I came to losing my life – I mean truly losing my life and being forced to live another one – I marvel at the linked coincidences necessary to produce that moment: German-Polish great-grandparents who emigrated to America, a great civil war, a great-aunt with a twin sister who met a smuggler, pirates in hiding in a remote village in Japan, and the Pictavian practice of a hybrid martial art. All this, and a man who came to London to buy an elephant.

Now that, Well Entertained Reader, has all the makings of a really big show.

In my cynical old age, in these diminished days of mashed carrots, I do not believe in miracles, but it is the Age of Aquarius. These coincidences hypothesize a hidden, mystical connection of all things, a humming beneath the surface, a binding of one to the other. With good reason, I will always believe in the serendipitous salvation of pink boots.

But, sadly, the saving of my life is inextricably tied to a moment a half hour later, when I failed to save the sad-eyed elephant I loved.

I still hear my Jumbo, trumpeting his distress.

When our brougham pulled away, I could not help him. I could only wave good-bye. When I put my hand out the very window that nearly took my life, then and only then, I began to cry.

To this day, I am grateful to Tante Gisela. She didn't pat me on the head and tell me it would be all right. She didn't tell me to stop. She nodded.

"Losing someone we love is hard. And it's never fair. You go right ahead and cry all you want. That's what human tears are for."

As my mother's fifth letter confirmed, crying was something she knew more than a little about. She was what Dr. John Harvey Kellogg would have called "A Dangerously Modern Girl," no stranger to tears caused by the swampy moral landscape of gossip.

Pretty women seldom are. They're the ones who have to kiss the most frogs.

April 28, 1874

My dear DAMM,

This is not the first time I have asked you to stop using Home Boy to hurt me. I am sixteen and you are a man finished his studies and ready to wed. As a young woman who has spent years loyally believing herself your woman, I am crying and confused.

Some women would be flattered by the recurring gossip that two men have repeatedly come to blows over her, but I am not one of them. I do not care who threw the first punch. I most particularly do not care who bested the other. Given his crutches, the bruises on his face, and his obvious pain both standing and sitting, I'm surprised he had the courage to come to school. Since you are older and bigger, I can only assume you were the victor.

But again I say, I do not care. I care only that you know and believe what I have told you already: that nothing that spindly urchin says or does, today or tomorrow, now or ever, is of any merit to me. He is barely a man. He is shy and bookish. He would rather read than run, rather write than ride, rather stick his nose in some book or newspaper, than flirt with any woman, including me. What kind of man is that? He is not half the man you are.

That leads to my confusion. Why did you need to beat him so badly, yet again?

Yes, there were times when I have enjoyed his company, but only as a poor and temporary replacement for you. To be jealous is to think I would stoop to prefer a boy over a man of breeding. To be jealous is to call me stupid and cruel, to think I would indulge in an unkind dalliance with a penniless boy, when I love a fine man set to inherit one of the wealthiest farms in Caradoc County.

If my parents will have trouble accepting you, there is no possible way they would ever give their only daughter to an illegitimate servant boy, one sent here from the dirtiest slums of London. Home Boy is not on my level. He will never be my peer.

But none of that is the point. I am. We are.

Do you not see that another altercation with Home Boy is a blow to me and my judgment? Please have more faith in me! Please leave him now and forever alone. As the bard said so well, "Love is an ever fixed mark that looks on tempests and is unmoved." While I admit to being shaken, I cannot, and will not, ever be moved. I am immovably, devotedly yours, and only yours,

    Reenie

    I hoped Home Boy would soon fight back and give DAMM a damn good licking. The image of an abandoned orphan being beaten repeatedly bloody right under the noses of adults sworn to look after him did not help me rest easy. Home Boy's pain felt too close to home. He could have been any of the Irregulars.

    He could have been my Danny.

    How did we meet? Suffice it to say, that thanks again to my Pictavian warriors, Danny came into my life five years after waving good-bye to Jumbo.

    It was the hottest moment of my young life.

    It was the best day of my life when we met in the course of a crime gone dreadfully wrong.

Chapter Six: The Misadventure of the Solitary Thief

It was my first robbery. On August 1, 1887, I was all of eleven and had just been given my cap. I'd been running the streets as Wiggins for days; of course I was ready.

My family provided every creature comfort. Unfortunately, those all belonged to my mother, or the pirate's widow, my Tante Grizelda. When I became Wiggins, I deduced that I needed things that were mine, or could be sold as mine. In perfect logic, I decided to become a thief.

When I assessed my qualifications, a tiny frame, a forgettable oval face, and the nerve to slip through crowds, hedgerows, and back doors, I decided it didn't matter if I couldn't run well. I would be better than fast; I would be sneaky. I needed to help feed my large Irregular family every day, not just when my father tossed us a few pence.

After watching Sally's Second-Hand Emporium and Pawnshop for all of one afternoon, I concluded sufficient surveillance had been conducted. At nightfall, I scaled the ivy and entered an open second-story window, intending to steal a few inconsequential baubles that could be sold by a child without raising too many questions.

Before you ask, Indignant Reader, no, none of my family knew anything about my sudden turn to crime. Mother, in particular, would have been livid. She had just released her Wiggins into the street. Should I ever be caught, it would ruin all her plans. Which is why I didn't tell her.

As Wiggins, I'd made my first human friend, a flower girl named Tansy. She had a rattling cough that worried me. I needed medicine from a real doctor, not a quack. I felt no guilt about stealing from Sally's because Mr. Sally was a truly vile species of scum straight out of Dickens. The Irregulars knew him well. If we were wary of those charged to help us, if we feared being pressed into a Home Child ship, we knew this perverted pawnbroker fenced both stolen merchandise and stolen children. Tales of who he sold them to, and what they used them for, were worse than nightmares.

They were true.

My blood still freezes at how close I came to being sold to child rapists.

I had stealthily grabbed a few items, a sparkly ring, a pretty tortoise shell comb, and a golden bracelet. I had one foot on the windowsill poised to flee by the same means as I arrived, when a dirty hand reached up from the ivy below and clamped my ankle.

No one touches my feet. It hurt. I did what any expert burglar would do – I screamed.

My captor released my ankle and re-clamped his free hand over my mouth. To my surprise, it was neither Mr. Sally nor his watchman; it was not even a man. It was a boy, one several shades dirtier and inches shorter than I was.

I quickly realized that clad in black, with soot-blackened hands and face, he must be a far more experienced burglar than yours truly. At the sound of angry shouting on the stairs, he pried the baubles from my hand and launched himself back down the ivy.

When I hesitated, he hissed, "C'mon, I haint getting' nabbed cossa you."

And yanked me backwards out the window.

My head shaved the frame, scraping my cap to the floor. My hand shot out to save it, but grasped only air. When I tried to go back for it, the boy shoved me down the ivy, a beat before the reach of two hairy, adult male hands trying to drag me back through the window.

This was too much déjà vu for me. I froze.

Had not my liberator half-carried me down the ivy, I might have been hanged as a thief, or sold for worse. I caught one glimpse of the enraged Sally, sallying forth in a soiled night shirt that failed to cover his hairy bottom. When someone did what any sensible pedestrian would do and screamed, he reconsidered his nocturnal omission of clothing and went back inside.

Belatedly remembering Holmes' methods, I quickly assayed who had the bigger feet. The boy did. I pushed him ahead of me and followed, ensuring that my indicting tiny, turned-in feet got masked by his larger imprints. In the safely of several blocks away, we threw ourselves down behind a wagon and began to giggle.

When he asked why I had moved to run behind him, I replied, "It's muddy. Walkin' in your footprints, it looks like it's only one 'a us."

I saw the first flash of respect in his eyes. He saluted me with a tug on his cap. When that triggered the realization of my own lost cap, then, and only then, I began to cry.

"Hey, wotcha doin' that for? I didn't 'urt ya, did I?

"No, it's my cap. I've lost it. It's gone."

"Well, get churself anuver one."

"I don't want another one. It's got to be that one."

My Whitechapel accent left me. High on adrenalin in the first adventure of my life that included both danger and camaraderie, I told him everything. Well, almost everything.

If I neglected to mention I was a girl, I did tell him I wasn't really a burglar, a fact I imagine he had surmised for himself. I told him about Tansy's cough and why I needed money. I told him I lived in High Kensington, that my mother – a world famous opera singer – dressed me up as a beggar boy and sent me into the streets to get close enough to my father to ruin him. He was a detective on Baker Street. Maybe he'd heard of him, the equally famous Sherlock Holmes?

I can still see Danny's face. Black curls, green eyes. Utterly focused, absorbing every word. Then exploding into a smile of a thousand stars. He draped himself over the wheel of the wagon and howled until he cried. It annoyed me no end. He laughed just like my father.

"You haint much for thieving, but y'can talk yer way outta any prison they try t'stick you in. That's a good one, mate. That's summa the best made-up patter I ever 'eard."

Furious at being disbelieved and laughed at like a child, I told him to follow me if he dared. When we reached Pictavia, too angry to remember my training, I stomped up to the front door. As I reached to open it, Danny slapped my hand away.

"Enuf's enuf. Yer brave to do it, but ye hain't getting us caught twice."

I imagine the ensuing argument grew a trifle energetic. Tante Gisela opened the door and before Danny could run said, "Good evening, Master Wiggins. And who might this be?"

I turned to a boy with his mouth hanging open.

"His name is—" Then, of course, I realized I hadn't a clue.

"Daniel P. Barnum at your service, my lady," said my companion, suddenly become much better spoken and a little charmer, lifting his cap and beaming at my aunt. "My father being the great Phineas T., also Barnum. He sired me on the trip to London wherein he first set eyes on my lovely mother and on the famous Jumbo at the London Zoo."

If I had been old enough to faint, I would willingly have done so. Tante Gisela shook Danny's hand, trying unsuccessfully not to smile.

"Well then, Daniel P., also Barnum, welcome to Pictavia. It's the home of Master Wiggins and quite possibly the second greatest show on earth. Perhaps you best both come in."

Tante Grizelda, who escaped from Baker Street whenever she could, had fired up the teapot with Godfrey. I ran upstairs for Mother. Together, all six of us spent the first of many a happy hour in the warmth of our kitchen. Danny ate two full plates of lamb stew and enough crumpets with honey to clean out a beehive. All went well, until it didn't.

"So, Danny, do you know where Mr. Barnum and Jumbo are performing now?"

Danny paused to swallow his last sweet bite.

"You hain't heard? Jumbo got smashed by a train in Canada. He's dead, mate."

Heed the lesson, Reflecting Reader.

Like blood, the truth will out.

My mother and my aunts had chosen not to tell me that Jumbo had died in 1885 – a scant three years after I waved him good-bye at the London zoo. The details were grisly. While boarding a train in St. Thomas, Ontario, Jumbo had been hit full on by another train, cracking his skull. I little heard my mother trying to console me with the story of Jumbo's heroism, that he was alleged to have died saving a tiny toy elephant called Tom Thumb.

It mattered not one whit. Jumbo was still dead.

My entire family had still lied.

As parent and grand-parent, I now appreciate the desire to protect a child from bad news, but that night I was still enough of a child to resent being treated like one. When Jumbo died, I was nine years old. It was completely illogical

76

for my family to claim I was then too young to hear of an elephant's death, but at eleven I could be sent alone into the carriage of a stranger who would shut the door and terrify me with the story of a giant man-eating rat from Southampton.

For the first time, I doubted and resented my mother.

What else had she chosen not to tell me, telling herself it was for my own good?

Unable to be openly angry at her, I glared at Danny.

"P.T. Barnum came to England and bought Jumbo from the zoo five years ago in 1882. You must be a liar, Mr. Calls Himself Barnum, because you are obviously not only five years old."

Danny surprised us all. Reaching into his pockets for a pencil, he quickly illustrated his story with a neat timeline, complete with dates and events entirely legible and spelled correctly.

"My father, the great P.T., also Barnum, first visited London on his European Tour with Tom Thumb in 1844, when they met Queen Victoria and the three-year-old Prince of Wales."

My Tante Gisela, the historian and newspaper addict in the family, nodded.

"My father returned to England after the death of his first wife in 1873. That was when he met Jumbo at the London Zoo. On that visit, he also met the governess of Sir William Flowers, one Amelia Worthington. Too recently single for it to be seemly, and because at sixty-five, my father was thirty years her senior, they married in secret. My father promised to return for her. But she died in childbirth, seven months later in 1875."

I caught lightning-quick glances between my mother and aunties, but could not read what they telegraphed.

My mother said only, "My condolences, Mr. Barnum. Please continue."

Danny explained that he had only recently learned that Barnum was his father. His grandmother, who did the best she could until she grew a tad too fond of her gin pot, confessed it only on her deathbed in 1886. In deeper deceit, she had falsely written Barnum claiming both mother and child had died. For the last year, Danny had been living rough, finding boltholes, how and where he could.

Mother saw straight to the vital moral of his story.

"Today, at twelve, you are a child alone."

Danny nodded.

"But not tonight, and I thank you and Master Wiggins for it."

When Mother turned her gaze on me, demanding to know why I had been out long past my curfew, Danny instantly covered for me in an improvised patter of his own.

"That was my fault, Ma'am. Tansy, one of my friends and me, we met Master Wiggins outside the chemist's shop in Baker Street. Tansy needed medicine for her cough. But she got worse, too weak to stand in line, and Master Wiggins kindly volunteered to take her home. I was somewhat detained, the line being long, and after we looked after Tansy, who is doing much better, thank you, I thought it best to walk Master Wiggins home."

If Mother knew that for a whopping load of elephant dung, her smile hid it well.

Hoping to divert her, I picked up some bits of paper accidentally pulled from Danny's pockets. They were all notes on Jumbo! They detailed how, in a single day, Jumbo could eat two hundred pounds of hay, several bushels of potatoes, and a dozen loaves of bread. His trainer, Matthew Scott, reported that Jumbo also enjoyed the occasional cask of beer.

I could not let a boy who so loved Jumbo lie for me. I opened my mouth, thanked him for saving me, and then told my family the truth about my short-lived career as a thief.

It was the longest I ever saw my mother and my aunties sitting perfectly still. It was absolutely the longest they ever went without uttering a single word.

That silence hurt more than my feet.

It frightened me more than any bungled burglary.

Mother asked only one question, "Why did you feel the need to steal?"

I replied that it really was for medicine for my new friend, Tansy, but Danny, who had been on the streets longer proved much better at explaining things. After hearing how children like Tansy and Little Pip had banded together for friendship and survival, but still went hungry and had no medical care, my mother looked at my pleading face, then at my aunties who nodded. She made the offer sound casual. As if Danny would be doing us a favour.

"We could use an enterprising young man such as yourself, Mr. Barnum, for a variety of jobs both inside and out. We are in particular need of someone to help young Master Wiggins make his way in the outside world with which you are more familiar. Would you be interested?"

The first time they saw him smile was the second for me, and they were equally moved. Delight, gratitude and an intelligent vitality, all beamed like the sun. Should anyone ever ask, Sweet Reader, if it is possible to fall in love at the first sight of a smile – you know my answer.

Mother offered him a room off the kitchen and a wage I thought small, but that Danny later told me was twice the going rate. He declined only the offer to retire for the evening, saying there was something he must do first.

Next morning, when all sensible Londoners sat down fully clothed to eat their crumpets hot, Danny reappeared. Noting my transformation to a girl, he took one step back, then two forward.

"That's good, then," he said. And set my cap on the kitchen table.

Beside it, each wrapped in brown paper, we discovered two further gifts.

The first box, from my aunties, held all the medicine a score of coughing children would need for the winter ahead.

The second, from my mother, held a mason jar heavy with coin. The card read, "Please use this money at your discretion to keep your irregular army strong and healthy. Then you can march through any London street you choose to conquer. P.S. This agreement is null and void if either of you ever practice any further thievery of any kind."

Danny grinned. "I'm sure all us Irregulars say thank you, Ma'am."

And thus, with that third smile, my second Irregular family was born.

Watson introduced us in his very first tale, *A Study in Scarlet*. Set in July of 1881 when he and Father met and took up residence, it appeared in *Beeton's Christmas Annual* in 1887 – the year I met Danny. In the Irregulars first appearance, when Father summoned us to his new flat in Baker Street, he had clearly sought our help before. He calls Wiggins his first lieutenant and *spokesman of the Street Arabs.* Calling us, *the Baker Street division of the detective police force,* he added, "There's more work to be got out of one of those little beggars than out of a dozen of the force."

He was, of course, oblivious to the fact we shared his low opinion of rozzers, given the harm and death they brought us. He did note that all we lacked was organization, but did nothing to help us organize. Tussy Marx and my Pictavian warriors helped fund and organize us for years, an activity occurring right under their noses that neither Holmes, nor Watson, ever noticed.

The irony must be stated clearly.

They saw, but they did not observe.

Accordingly, Fair Reader, please do not ever attribute the name of the most beloved set of child characters in English literature to either Holmes or Watson. That credit belongs, like so much in this story, to my aunties, my beloved Danny and a kind benefactor named Catriona Magdalena Psalmodia Adler Mclean, a woman who always insisted on rowing her own boat.

June 23, 1875

Dearest devoted Duncan,

Now that my family knows the truth, my darling, I shall use your Christian name. No matter what happens next, I will say this first. Tonight was such a lovely summer evening at our ravine!

Drifting down the creek, pulling against the current to row us back, only to drift back under the summer stars again. When Da caught us, I honestly don't know what he was most angry about – that I was with you, or that I was the one doing the rowing.

It was unkind of him to refer to you as a lazy lump of lard. I tried to tell him I liked to row. I tried to explain rowing gave me the strength to better do chores and play the violin, but Da was having none of it. He kept yelling that no "lazy pansy-pants boy" was going to make his daughter row the boat. That he'd "tell Uncle John the truth," that he had "a no-good, nancy boy wastrel for a son." That you "better leave my daughter alone, if you know what's good for you."

I was a tad disappointed, dearest Duncan, that you did not oppose him. I suppose I should commend you for holding your temper. The last thing I want is more fisticuffs. A father thrashing a nephew would lastingly bruise you both.

And all because a girl rows a boat! Lord what fools these manly men be! If I can chop firewood in an icy winter, if I can stand in the sun pitching hay all day long, I can row a little boat. Da is entirely hypocritical to put me to work like a man, but expect me to be a dainty, helpless little girl.

Suffice it to say it's a darn good thing he didn't find us an hour earlier when we were both swimming under the stars as free as God made us.

What would Da have done to find us so unmasked, my darling? I'm sure he would have forced us to get married on the spot. My, oh, my, that wouldn't have been anyone's plan, would it?

Your mermaid, unclothed and unafraid, but unfortunately still a maid,

Reenie

Despite her scandalous exposure here, this remains one of my favourite letters, and not just for the lovely coincidence that it is written on my birthday exactly one year before my birth. I admired the spirit of this youthful adventuress. I wished I could be more like her, but knew I had little of her athletic bravery.

It was likewise becoming clear to me that Duncan Mclean was worse than a coward. Who could respect a boy who refused to stand up to my grandfather and defend my mother? A boy who bullied and beat not just a smaller boy, but a forsaken Home Boy, on a regular basis?

I liked this Duncan chap less with every letter.

I did my best to give Home Boy no further thought. Whatever had befallen him, I could do nothing about it. But I know my worry for him stayed silently with me.

Even with the comfort of Mother's letters, during my long months of entombment in Mycroft's secret bedroom at the Diogenes, I often awoke screaming. But it wasn't a rat, or the Ripper, or a turquoise-handled knife in my father's hand that horrified me.

It was me.

The sight of my body abandoned, flat on my back in a snowy Whitechapel gutter. Wearing nothing but my boots, I couldn't scream and I most certainly couldn't run.

I could only watch as, spade by spade, this crippled girl got buried on top of a cold, dead boy.

In a grave with a lying stone, one engraved with neither of our names.

Chapter Seven: *A Scandal in Bohemia*: First Abridged, Then Corrected

As my pile of pink paper grows, my most literary great-grandchild dutifully comes twice a week to feed white paper into her typewriter and turn my scribblings into clean typed copy. As I review these manuscript pages, after all my years teaching books, I think I finally begin to comprehend the difference between being a reader and a writer.

As a writer, as you weigh and place each brick in the story you build, you are simultaneously evaluating how the story is being told. In creative symbiosis, you discover how your story can be constructed and how you will be changed by its construction. With every brick, you are also constantly assessing its potential impact when it gets flung into the lap of its audience.

My father had his own critique of the bricks flung by one John H. Watson. Before you trust even one word of Watson as storyteller, Judicious Reader, please first consider the infamous list that stuck in my father's craw for decades. The list Watson embarrassed himself beyond measure by publishing in *A Study in Scarlet* as *Sherlock Holmes – His Limitations:*

1. Knowledge of Literature – nil.
2. Knowledge of Philosophy – nil.
3. Knowledge of Astronomy – nil.

4. Knowledge of Politics – Feeble.
5. Knowledge of Botany – Variable. Well up in belladonna, opium and poisons generally. Knows nothing of practical gardening.
6. Knowledge of Geology – Practical, but limited. Tells at a glance different soils from each other. After walks, has shown me splashes upon his trousers, and told me by their colour and consistence in what part of London he had received them.
7. Knowledge of Chemistry – Profound.
8. Knowledge of Anatomy – Accurate, but unsystematic.
9. Knowledge of Sensational Literature – Immense. He appears to know every detail of every horror perpetrated in the century.
10. Plays the violin well.
11. Is an expert singlestick player, boxer and swordsman.
12. Has a good practical knowledge of British law.

This list should correctly be read as topics my father saw no point in ever discussing with anyone named Watson. As proof, please see Watson's own words. In many of his stories, from memory, Father quotes Latin, Shakespeare, Goethe, the Scriptures, and even a letter in French from Flaubert to George Sand. Watson complains about annoying sounds from Father's violin because he does not recognize the sound of scales and exercises. As for "art in the blood", Holmes was no more related to Vernet than yours truly, but he had taught himself to paint. He had painted a small study I quite admired, of a joyful redheaded girl running through a field of lilies.

Please keep this one undeniable fact ever in mind.

I knew what Watson did not.

From my eavesdropping auntie, from firsthand experience with Danny and the Irregulars, I knew every detail of Father's cases first. As a receiving scrivener, Watson knew only what Holmes chose to tell him. It is Watson's voice you hear, but Holmes was always the Great Oz behind the ghostwriting curtain. Watson was but the straw man into whom Holmes stuffed selected fodder.

Watson then skimmed off the grains of truth he liked, sieved them through Victorian morality, and baked it up sweet enough for the public to swallow whole. In a fare more than fair, in academic expertise, I hereby offer my own list – *A Baker's Dozen of John H. Watson's Authorial Shortcomings*:

1. *Watson often did not know the truth, or knew only part of it.*

2. *Credulous to a fault, he believed every word Holmes ever told him.*

3. *Watson never realized he did not know the full truth and always wrote as if he did.*

4. *Sometimes Holmes purposefully told him things that were untrue, or half true.*

5. *Sometimes Watson knew the truth and chose not to tell it, or not all of it.*

6. *In the interests of friend, class and Empire, he often soft-pedalled it.*

7. *He wrote for a prim Victorian readership who demanded happy moral endings for all.*

8. *His reputation and fame depended on pleasing his audience.*

9. *As a failed physician, his family's livelihood depended on pleasing his audience.*

10. *Watson had created a literary persona for himself as a good man, and believed it.*

11. *He could not tell the full truth about Holmes without also condemning himself.*

12. *It would hurt his pride and self-respect to ever admit there were times he and Holmes failed.*

13. *He would never admit any truth that condemned his beloved England.*

Father cared for his Boswell, I do not dispute that. But he was equally fond of the practical joke. Father loved to egg Watson on, to say outrageous things simply to see what Watson would believe and publish. In short, in matters intellectual, Holmes considered Watson as but another Toby the Basset Hound: useful, companionable, indulged and oft-petted, but never an equal. He found Watson's writing too wordy, too sentimental and lamentably old-fashioned.

"I am a detective, not a Luddite," Holmes once snapped at his flat-mate. "Although it is often my opinion,

Watson, that your prose could be improved by the application of a hatchet."

I'm sure if he knew I was finally exposing my truths, Holmes would insist that I first take a hatchet to all of Watson's tales. In compromise, I will correct just two of Watson's erroneous works. Because you need to know his version to appreciate the truth, I will first faithfully abridge Watson's version, using only his own words to do so. I thusly hope to preserve something for which my scholarship has long given him credit: his rapid-fire dialogue which disdained long-winded fashionable Victorian tag endings such as:

"'Pass the sugar,' Vincent said languorously while stroking his vermillion waistcoat with a pale but polished hand and dreaming coquettishly of a brood mare named Innisfree.'"

Accordingly, Resigned Reader, I hope you enjoy at least some of the following – *A Scandal in Bohemia, by John H. Watson, as Abridged by an Ancient Wiggins.*

To Sherlock Holmes, she is always the woman. She eclipses and predominates the whole of her sex. Not that he felt any emotion akin to love for Irene Adler. All emotions were abhorrent to his cold, precise, but admirably balanced mind. Love would have been a distraction, grit in a sensitive instrument, a crack in a high-power lenses. And yet there was but one woman to him, and that was the late Irene Adler, of dubious and questionable memory.

One night – it was on the twentieth of March 1888 – I was seized with a keen desire to see Holmes again. After some observations as to how my person reflected marital bliss, he threw over a sheet of thick, pink-tinted note-paper. Undated, without signature or address, it stated that a masked visitor would call at eight o'clock. At a brougham's arrival, I stood to go, but Holmes insisted, "I am lost without my Boswell."

His masked visitor was six-foot-six in height, with the chest and limbs of a Hercules. His dress was a richness akin to bad taste. This Count von Kramm bound us to secrecy for two years, stating that "at the end of that time, the matter will be of no importance," but now "it may have an influence upon European history."

When he admitted "the title by which I have just called myself is not my own," Holmes drily observed, "I was aware of that." At which our visitor tore the mask from his face, revealing himself the King of Bohemia, and explained.

"Some five years ago, during a lengthy visit to Warsaw, I made the acquaintance of the well-known adventuress, Irene Adler."

I quickly found the index and handed it to Holmes.

"Born in New Jersey in 1858 – hum! La Scala, hum! Prima donna Imperial Opera of Warsaw – yes! Living in London – quite so! Your Majesty became entangled with this young person, wrote her some compromising letters and is now desirous of getting those letters back."

"Precisely so. But how—"

"There was no secret marriage, no legal papers or certificates?"

"None."

"If this young person should produce her letters for blackmailing or other purposes, how is she to prove their authenticity? The writing could be forged and your photograph bought."

"We were both in the photograph."

"Oh, dear! That is very bad! You have compromised yourself. It must be recovered."

"She will not sell."

"Stolen then."

"Five attempts have been made. Twice burglars in my pay ransacked her house. Once we diverted her luggage. Twice she has been waylaid. There has been no result."

Holmes laughed. "And what does she propose to do with the photograph?"

"To ruin me. I am about to be married to the second daughter of the King of Scandinavia. Adler has said she will send it on the day the betrothal is publicly proclaimed. That is Monday."

"Oh, then we have three days yet," said Holmes with a yawn. "As to money?"

"There are three hundred pounds in gold and seven hundred in notes."

"Good night, your Majesty. And Watson, please call at three o'clock tomorrow."

I arrived at three precisely. Mrs. Turner informed me Holmes had left that morning. At four, the door opened and a drunken-looking groom, ill-kempt and side-whiskered, with an inflamed face and disreputable clothes, walked into the room. I had to look three times before I was certain. Holmes laughed heartily for some minutes, until he was obliged to lie back, limp and helpless, in the chair. He then recounted his day spent as a groom, chatting up horsy men.

"I received as much information as I could desire about Miss Irene Adler, the daintiest thing under a bonnet on this planet. She has one male visitor, dark, handsome, dashing: Mr. Godfrey Norton of the Inner Temple. Was she his client, friend, or mistress? I was still balancing it in my mind, when a handsome man emerged from Briony Lodge and shouted at his driver, 'Drive like the devil to the Church of St Monica. Half a guinea if you do it in twenty minutes!'

"At the church, Godfrey Norton spied me and whispered, 'Come, man, only three minutes or it won't be legal.' I was half-dragged to the altar and found myself assisting in the secure tying up of Irene Adler, spinster, to Godfrey Norton, bachelor. They were married in an instant. The bride gave me a sovereign, and I mean to wear it on my watch-chain in memory of the occasion."

"This is a very unexpected turn of affairs," said I. "And what next, then?"

"She told him that she would go on her usual drive from five to seven o'clock and they drove off in different directions. I went off to make my own arrangements."

"Which are?"

"Some cold beef and a glass of beer," he answered by ringing the bell. "By the way, Doctor, I shall want your cooperation. You don't mind breaking the law?"

"Not in the least."

"Nor running a chance of arrest?"

"Not in a good cause."

"When Mrs. Turner has brought in the tray, I will make it clear to you. Now," he said, turning hungrily on the simple fare, "We must meet the lady when she returns from her drive. There will be some small unpleasantness. It will end in my being conveyed inside. A window will open. When I raise my hand – so – you will throw this into the room and raise the cry of fire."

He took a cigar-shaped roll from his pocket. "It is an ordinary plumber's rocket, fitted with a cap at either end to make it self-lighting. Your task is confined to throwing it. You may then walk to the end of the street and I will rejoin you in ten minutes."

He then reappeared in the character of an amiable and simple-minded Nonconformist clergyman. It was not merely that Holmes changed his costume. His expression, his manner, his very soul seemed to vary with every fresh part he assumed. The stage lost a fine actor when he became a specialist in crime. It was already dusk as we paced in front of Briony Lodge.

"But it has twice been burgled! Where will you look?"

"I will not look. I will get her to show me."

As the landau pulled up, several bystanders rushed up to open the door in hope of a copper. A fierce quarrel broke out. Holmes dashed into the crowd to protect the lady, but gave a cry and dropped to the ground, with blood running freely down his face. Irene Adler stood on the steps with her superb figure outlined against the lights of the hall, looking into back the street.

"Is the poor gentleman much hurt?" she asked. "Bring him into the sitting room."

I never felt more heartily ashamed of myself in my life when I saw the beautiful creature against whom I was conspiring, or the grace and kindliness with which she waited upon the injured man. And yet it would be the blackest treachery to Holmes to draw back now from the part which he had entrusted to me, and so, I hardened my heart.

I saw Holmes motion like a man in need of air, and a maid threw open the window. When he made the sign, I tossed my rocket with a cry of "Fire!" then made my way to the corner.

"You did very nicely, Doctor," Holmes remarked upon arrival.

"You have the photograph?"

"She showed me where it is, as I said she would."

"I am still in the dark."

"The matter was perfectly simple," he laughed. "You saw, of course, that everyone in the street was an accomplice. They were all engaged for the evening. I had a little moist red paint in the palm of my hand, clapped it to my face and became a piteous spectacle. It is an old trick."

"I guessed as much."

"When a woman thinks her house is on fire, her instinct is to rush to the thing she values most. I have more than once taken advantage of it. The photograph is in a recess behind a sliding panel just above the right bell pull. I caught a glimpse of it as she drew it out, then replaced it."

"And now?" I asked.

"We shall call with the King tomorrow at eight in the morning. She will not yet be up. We will be shown into the sitting room where his Majesty shall regain his image with his own hands."

We had reached Baker Street. He was searching for his key when someone passing said, "Goodnight, Mister Sherlock Holmes."

The greeting appeared to come from a slim youth in an ulster who had hurried by.

"I've heard that voice before," said Holmes. "I wonder who the deuce it was."

In the morning when the King arrived, we left once more for Briony Lodge.

"Irene Adler is married," remarked Holmes. "Yesterday. To an English lawyer."

"But she could not love him," the King protested.

"I am in hopes she does. If the lady loves her husband, she does not love your Majesty. If she does not love you, there is no reason why she should interfere with your plans."

"Well! I wish she had been of my own station. What a queen she would have made!"

The door of Briony Lodge was open and an elderly woman stood on the steps. She watched with a sardonic eye.

"Mr. Sherlock Holmes, I believe? My mistress said you were likely to call. She left this morning with her husband by the 5:15 train from Charring Cross for the continent."

"What?" Sherlock Holmes staggered back, white with chagrin and surprise.

He pushed past the servant into the drawing room, tore back a sliding shutter, and, plunging in his hand, pulled out a photograph and a letter. The photograph was of Irene Adler in evening dress. The letter was superscribed to "Sherlock Holmes, Esq., to be left until called for."

MY DEAR MR. SHERLOCK HOLMES,

You really did it very well. You took me in completely. Until after the alarm of fire, I had not a suspicion. But then, you made me reveal what you wanted to know. I found it hard to think evil of such a dear, kind old clergyman. But, you know, I have been trained as an actress myself. Male costume is nothing new to me. I often take advantage of the freedom which it gives. I ran upstairs, got into my walking clothes as I call them, and came down just as you departed.

Well, I followed you to your door. Then I, rather imprudently, wished you goodnight, and started for the Temple to see my husband. We both thought the best resource was flight, so you will find the nest empty when you call tomorrow. As to the photograph, your client may rest in peace. I love and am loved by a better man than he. The King may do what he will without hindrance from one he had cruelly wronged. I keep it only to safeguard myself and to preserve a weapon which will always secure me from any steps he might take in the future. I leave a photograph which he might care to possess, and I remain, dear Mr. Sherlock Holmes,

Very truly yours,

IRENE NORTON, nee ADLER

"Oh, what a woman!" cried the King. "Is it not a pity that she was not on my level?"

"From what I have seen of the lady, she seems indeed to be on a very different level to your Majesty," said Holmes coldly. "I am sorry not to be able to conclude this business."

"To the contrary," cried the King, "The photo is now as safe as if it were in the fire. Pray tell me how I can reward you." He slipped an emerald snake ring from his finger.

"Your Majesty has something which I should value more highly. This photograph."

The King stared at him in amazement. "Certainly, if you wish it."

Holmes turned away without observing the hand the King had stretched out to him. And that is how the best plans of Sherlock Holmes were beaten by a woman's wit. He used to make merry over the cleverness of women, but I have not heard him do it of late.

And when he speaks of Irene Adler, or refers to her photograph, it is always under the honorable title of The Woman.

I apologize, Long-Suffering Reader, for subjecting you to Watson's verbosity in even half its original length. Let me begin by correcting his most egregious error – *A Scandal in Bohemia* is not the only time Irene Adler appears; it was the only time Watson saw her. In many of Father's cases, she plated multiple roles, both male and female. In equal fact, supporting spying roles were also frequently played by my aunties and, on rare occasions, bit parts by yours truly.

The King may have offered Holmes a snake ring, but the true story of scandal, as authored by my mother, was entirely her own brilliant sting.

One that exposed prideful men as bumbling boys, and bilked them as they deserved.

Knowing the King would kill her once he secured their photograph, Mother made an operatic plan to save herself. First, she rented Briony Lodge and established a sham routine. When The King of Bohemia donned a mask to hire Holmes, she donned a servant's forgettable face. She secured a note in Tante Grizelda's hand saying that Mrs. Hudson was off visiting her sister for the day. Since the chortling twins spent it sharing tea and crumpets in Pictavia's kitchen, that was actually true.

Costumed in Mrs. Hudson's clothes, Mother aged three decades to become Mrs. Hudson's old friend, Mrs. Turner. It took a fine actress indeed to appear at Baker Street as a second senior flibbertigibbet in the morning, reappear that afternoon at Briony Lodge as a blushing bride, then resume her aged land-lady stand-in role in time to make Holmes' supper.

When Mrs. Turner, now also Irene Adler-Norton, supped with her real family, we rejoiced at how Holmes had fallen hook, line, and signature for her sham marriage to our handsome man of all work, Godfrey Norton. Apparently, even to a self-proclaimed preternaturally observant detective, any man in pinstripe looks like a Temple Bar lawyer and any old aunt in a cleric's gown doesn't look a thing like your landlady's twin sister.

Tante Gisela had been rather nervous about Holmes catching her out as she performed her cameo role marrying her niece to Godfrey, so the ensemble ensured it "was all done in an instant." In carefully rehearsed blocking, Father got rushed to the altar, prompted through the ceremony, and then Mother stepped in front of Mrs. Hudson's look-alike to hand him a sovereign.

It was a simple matter later that evening for Mother to stand in the hall with Holmes' cold beef and a glass of beer supper, eavesdropping on his plan to steal from her. It made her livid to hear a plan that would turn Holmes into a common burglar. Mrs. Hudson pronounced it worse: "pyromaniacly puerile and propulsively petulant."

In further impulsive boyishness, when he assumed the role of a "simple-minded Non-Conformist clergyman" the next day, Father failed to do his research and used the wrong prop. He ran to Mother's aid clutching a Catholic cross, complete with crucifix.

Of course, Mother knew exactly what she was doing when she invited her knight errant inside. An equally-obliging maid who made a quick-limping entrance to open a window would have been recognizable had Holmes bothered to look at her. After Watson tossed his little rocket, Mother let all go bang, then changed into her walking clothes and followed Holmes home.

When the three boys arrived at Briony Lodge the next morning at 8:00 a.m., exactly why they believed my mother would still be abed like a lady of leisure, remains a mystery. When they met yet another elderly servant "with a sardonic eye" – yes, Deductive Reader, it was my mother yet again.

She wanted to give herself the gift of seeing Holmes' face when she told him he had been bested by a woman. In stage blocking at its best, she awaited them on the porch. She spoke first, never gave him a chance to ask her name. When Holmes "pushed past her", she simply stepped off the porch and vanished – not for the Continent, but home to Pictavia.

For the record, the unmasked King of Bohemia was a thug and a bully who ordered ransacking illegalities and open assaults against a woman whose only crime was having her picture taken with a man she loved. He threatened her knowing she was ill. Knowing he had made her ill.

As I later overheard Mother telling my aunties, fully aware of his syphilis, in debauched frolics in London, King Siggy had made several women ill. Now, before his betrothal to a princess – the unlucky Clotilde Lothman von Saxe-Meningen – he was hunting them down to ensure they never talked. Mother knew until he believed her no threat to him, he would be a deadly threat to us.

As to why Holmes did not admit to already knowing Irene Adler, I cannot say. I think it likely Watson never knew. Even in the trusting, gullible Watson, it would have raised too many questions as to how, and where, and when, my parents made acquaintance. But Father certainly knew. Watson accidentally leaves several clues that prove Father knew more than he let on.

For example, please re-read Holmes' reactions to Irene Adler's biography in the index. Hear his comments as affirmation of data he already knew. Ask yourself how, if he did not know her, he could not possibly have known there were "letters extant" between "the king and this young person"? How else did could he possibly have known she possessed them and kept them?

At the time, I hypothesized the romantic and implausible: if my parents had an unspoken alliance. Perhaps, somehow anticipating each other's ideas, they made dovetailing plans. It made it possible to think Mother had decided she could count on Father's decency and that his chivalry, while not as commanding as Watson's, clearly drew the line at permitting the murder of innocent women. Consider that Holmes let her outwit him and escape, taking critical evidence with her.

In all of Watson's tales, does anyone else ever accomplish that feat?

While I enjoyed the idea of my parents as unspoken conspirators, I believed that the most likely explanation of Holmes' behavior stemmed from his obvious dislike of the king. Even after admitting he has failed his client, Holmes made no effort to return his princely thousand pound fee.

Please tally, Calculating Reader, the enormity of that sum. By 1967 standards, I estimate that to be about 7,000 British Pounds, or the equivalent of some $21,000 CAD in a year when the average yearly income was about $16,000 CAD. Quite a fee for a three-day job. When Father kept every penny and failed to shake the royal outstretched hand, I would call it an oversight, except I know the great detective made none, especially when it came to respect and money.

Did Holmes do the research I did years later?

Did he ever sit down with London newspapers and Scotland Yard dispatches to plot the travels of the King against the eleven unsolved deaths of women known as the Whitechapel Murders?

What significance did he glean from the dates of April 3, 1888 to 13 February, 13 1891? Did he see coincidence, or incrimination, in the timeline?

In March of 1888, the King arrives in London and hires Holmes. On March 23, the King is told Irene Adler has escaped. A mere eleven days later, on April 3, 1888, the first of eleven London prostitutes is brutally murdered.

Did Father suspect that Jack the Ripper was the King of Bohemia?

Centuries of men have murdered women for less.

It would explain why The Ripper was never caught. King Siggy left the county once the women he needed dispatched were murdered. It would also explain why they had to be murdered. Desperate to hide his syphilis long enough to make a royal marriage, the king made a veiled reference to this very thing, *"Then I must begin by binding you both to absolute secrecy for two years; at the end of that time, the matter will be of no importance."*

Why does the King say the photo will not matter in two years? Any accusation of an affair with an adventuress would matter to any crowned head at any time in his reign.

But the King knew two things Watson did not, things Mother knew from her European contacts. Firstly, in two years, the look-alike cousin the king had recruited to bed his grateful bride would have impregnated her, or another lusty Lothario would be hired to do so. Either way, the family von Ormstein was secured. Secondly, in two years' time the king believed both parties in the photo would be dead.

This, so sadly, proved true. When Watson published his version in *The Strand Magazine* in July 1891, he wrote: "*And yet there was but one woman to him and that woman was the late Irene Adler of dubious and questionable memory.*"

I'm sure it occurred to you, Astute Reader, to wonder if I am the progeny of the nasty bit of masked bravado Wilhelm Gottsreich Sigismond von Ormstein, Grand Duke of Cassel-Felstein and hereditary King of Bohemia?

I'd rather be sired by The Giant Rat of Southampton.

I can say with a relieved certainty – one no doubt matching the conjugal relief of his princess bride – I am not.

My mother was eighteen when she gave birth to me in New Jersey in 1876. When the King met her in 1879 at the Warsaw Opera, she was twenty-one and I was almost three years old.

This ancient Wiggins feels compelled to add that thanks to the sexual revolution of my day, I now see another vital moral in Watson's version of my mother's story. Today, I have zero respect for Holmes and Watson in their ever-so-manly attempt to rob an innocent woman of the one piece of evidence protecting mother and child from an abusive man. We've come a long way, baby, thanks to Victorian women like my mother who began a better game afoot.

Some men in detective stories kill women as quickly as the Ripper. But sometimes death gets dispensed at low doses, drop by drop, over time. Many smart, sophisticated men have this kind of toxicity, a distillation of their condescending view of women based on a deeply held Darwinian belief in their natural superiority as thinking creatures.

But my mother rewrote what could have been her death story with a much better plot. When she turned a story of abuse into her own woman-saves-herself escape story, all three toxic boys got beaten and bested by The Woman.

Had he ever read that line, I'm sure my father would have chided me, "tsk-tsk", and roundly protested at the great Sherlock Holmes being in any way equated to the chest-beating Neanderthal that was King Siggy.

That is exactly what I contend. As Victorian men, in one crucial way, the King, Watson, Holmes, were identical: they underestimated my mother because she was A Woman.

I know this condemnation of the great detective as being so ordinary, so very typically a man of his times, may bother many fans and scholars of the great detective.

But I'm a lame old woman in pain.

I have no more clucks to give.

Chapter Eight: A Deduction of Duncans at Diogenes

In the course of assisting my father, all the Irregulars met Mycroft. He avoided looking at me, but I caught his hooded eyes slitting over to Danny more than once. In all our days at the Diogenes, he stayed so sour as to be desiccated, so sedentary and corpulent next to Father's lean energy, I often wondered how they could possibly be brothers.

It pleased me to remember that Mother also had a secret spite for Mycroft, "My croft, is not and will not, ever be his!" As often as she muttered it, she would never explain it. My aunties just rolled their eyes.

Ask any teenager in history. You do not want to study when you hate the teacher and it is impossible to learn anything when you know the teacher hates you.

At the Diogenes, Mycroft's definition of teaching was to sit me in a hardback wooden chair and hand me lists of all things Mclean: births, weddings and deaths, the breeds in their barns and the crops in their fields. He would stare at the ceiling for exactly one hour, then take the lists away, testing me on how well I could regurgitate my forced-feeding.

No one will be lining up to buy his books on the education of women.

In my long first week as his pupil, Mycroft and I had but one conversation. We had graduated from lists to books when he handed me a most familiar one.

Mother loved all the books of the pioneering adventuresses Suzanna Moodie and Catharine Parr Traill. Together we had enjoyed Moodie's *Roughing it in the Bush*, and Parr Traill's *Rambles in the Canadian Forest* and *Canadian Wildflowers*. Without thinking, I flipped open to a page I knew well: *Hemerocallis Fulva*, known as the Orange Day Lily, the Tawny Day Lily, and given its ability to thrive anywhere, the Ditch Lily. Mother assured me they grew in wild abundance all over North America. Virtually indestructible, they were the first flowers she let me raise on my own in our Pictavian conservatory. My eyes filled with grieving tears.

Mycroft lurched forward. "Why are you staring at that lily?"

"I'm not. The book just fell open to it."

"That is a lie. Why are you weeping at the sight of that lily?"

That unnerved me. So I lied again, "I don't know. I've never seen it before."

"That is a lie. Why are you moved by that lily?"

"Because I didn't know they were wild. I thought they were a hot-house flower."

Here Mycroft snorted. "Where would you have seen a hot-house flower?"

"At Kew Gardens."

"Explain yourself. What would the likes of you be doing at Kew Gardens?"

"Fa-following one of Mr. Holmes' suspects. He was a botanist."

"I do not believe you."

"He had a particular interest in lilies. I reported it to Holmes."

"I repeat myself."

"That's all of it, guv. That's the truth."

"Obviously."

In case you have not ascertained it, Kindly Reader, I was not the best of liars and all my accents slipped when I was nervous. While I could improvise a flowing river of lies when it felt like a game, if I got anxious, if I got anywhere near Mycroft, I spouted nonsense. In deliberate punishment, Mycroft took the lovely lilies from my hands and handed me the same old family tree.

On January 6, 1891, after an interminable week wherein Mycroft crammed my insufficient skull with endless data Canadiana: trees both Red and Sugar Maple, cultures English and French, provinces Upper and Lower, livestock bovine and porcine, and a litany of lists Mclean, my father finally paid me his first visit.

The sixth of January is three things: The Feast of the Epiphany, Twelfth Night and Sherlock Holmes' birthday. Beyond the gift of twelve drummers drumming, Twelfth Night ends the frivolities of Christmas. *Twelfth Night,* in the first folio by Shakespeare, is equally fitting, being a play of conniving manipulations, deliberately mis-delivered letters, and a pair of cross-dressing twins, Viola and Sebastian. Separated in a shipwreck, the Countess Olivia falls in love with Viola who is dressed as a boy. Bodacious bedlam ensues when Olivia has no interest in the besotted Sebastian because she longs for the man who is his sister.

That kind of misdirected love is always comedic on the stage, isn't it?

That morning, reading mother's seventh letter, I found it far less humourous in real life.

July 1, 1875

My dear cousin Duncan,

I cannot bear this misunderstanding between us! Rumour and the wagging of tongues! Why, why, why are you listening to the jealous commentary of snide and sniveling minds! How can you possibly be unaware that it is only your own inaction that is giving them cause to gossip?

While it is beneath both of us to have to address the questions you so angrily asked me this evening, I will do so. But first, I might add that if you can grab my wrist and pull it meanly to your chest to interrogate me, then you can probably discover the ability to hold that hand from time to time, or possibly do what all the other boys did last night and ask a pretty girl to dance.

I am resolutely certain that if you used that dictionary that never leaves Home Boy's side to look up the words "Canada Day Dance", you will find the definition contains dancing on Canada Day. Even Home Boy himself, knows better. So, yes, I did dance with him, but that is all I did.

Your anger with me was baseless, based only on falsehoods, on gossip. Or perhaps you were really angry at yourself and turned it on me?

Because, no, I was not seen walking home from church hand in hand with Home Boy. I deny it. If you know me at all, you know I would never do such a wicked thing on the Sabbath. If once when I slipped, and you must allow the ground has been slippery given the rain, I admit that your erstwhile brother may have taken my arm for a moment to steady me, as would any gentleman in the assistance of a lady. Or should I perhaps amend that to any gentleman but you?

I indulge in this insult, knowing it beneath me, but I remain in such distress from the unkind and untrue things you said to me. I know they were said in anger. Perhaps, by tomorrow, I shall feel more charitable and attribute your fury to the depth of your feelings for me, but at this moment it simply feels hurtful and small-minded.

No, I am not "toying with you by indulging the affections of your gutter-born brother."

No, my actions are not "the calculated contrivance of a cold-hearted coquette", an appalling, approaching asinine turn of phrase, by the way, suggesting that your penchant for the music of alliteration has become an unhealthy and totally discordant obsession.

And, yes, the one thing you said that was true, I have admitted. For some time, Home Boy has taken your place, not in my heart – never in my heart – but at your violin lessons. You had clearly lost interest. You have no desire to make music with me at all. You wanted to be seen making music, but had not the stomach for the hard work it takes.

I sometimes doubt you enjoy any activity that cannot be done seated unmoving in a chair. So when Home Boy confessed that he had not just sat outside where you always left him, but that he had listened carefully to your lessons, I was flattered. He picked up Da's violin and with only a little assistance began to play. So, of course I helped him. Christian charity is something we all should have. Perhaps even Baptists.

To settle your suspicious mind, I shall tell you that Mutti knew and approved. Some weeks later, she came running into the study at the sound of a duet, expecting to see me and Father.

"How... When?" It left her quite speechless.

Home Boy answered both with a tip of his bow to me. "My apologies, Mrs. Mclean. I confess I prevailed upon Miss Catriona, who has proved herself a most excellent teacher. Should there be any blame or punishment for our music making, it must be entirely mine."

Knowing what would convince Mutti more than words, I quickly resumed the duet, to which she sat for a long time, her eyes tightly closed. And when she opened them, she smiled at us both, "What you have done together is extraordinary. I will not forbid it, nor share it with my husband who surely would do so. But if ever asked, mark me, I will tell the truth."

At that Home Boy's face spit into the first real grin I had ever seen from him.

"Exactly as life should be, Mrs. Mclean. I sincerely thank you for it."

As for rumours that we were seen "sharing favours" at the McLean family picnic, and again in the hayloft of our barn, do you really think it the best use of lips that have kissed me to use those same lips to call me a rutting animal?

If you still cannot admit to hearing the love in your heart, then I beg you to do what you otherwise do best – sit down, review the facts and listen to the reason of your intelligent head! What you are hearing instead may rob us both of our heart's true desire. What you are hearing instead is your own hesitation. I beg you to move past it.

Yours and trying so hard to be patient,

Reenie

I had no time to contemplate this new music making as Father arrived early. I meant my first words to wish him a happy birthday, but was shocked to see him in mourning, sporting the black crepe arm band demarking the death of a family member. I took breath to thank him, then realized I'd dishonour my mother by doing so. I had likewise forgotten that the first line was always his.

"Mycroft informs me you are doing an excellent job at most of your studies, Wiggins. To our specific surprise, you excel in learning to read and speak beyond your origins. But you have been entirely negligent, I am informed, in one appointed area. Why have you refused to memorize your new family tree? Have we reached the limits of your intelligence so quickly, within a short seven days? Or, for some unfathomable reason, are you opting to be an obdurate ingrate?"

Was Father was testing me? Taunting me? Pushing for exposure? What urchin would grasp the concept of "opting to be an obdurate ingrate"? But with his question, I realized that, yes, I was being exactly that.

It was a surprise to me, but once he said it aloud, I realized that I resented being handed a false family tree. I did not want to be an ersatz Mclean. If I had to be reborn, I wanted to be reborn as my parents' child. That desire was, of course, beyond ridiculous. I could not make any of it known.

I further resented that Mycroft would not answer my questions as to what branch of the family tree contained the new me. To this he would but shrug, "Irrelevant." If my father expected me to figure this out for myself, I could not.

The Mcleans of Mayfair weren't just a family tree. They were a bloody forest.

When the fifteen-year-old family founder, Duncan Alexander Mclean, crossed the pond in 1819, he had eight younger siblings in tow: Alex, John, Archie, Neil, Gilbert, Effie, Bella and Anne. What happened to his parents, why this boy was abandoned to care for this brood on a dangerous transatlantic journey, remains a mystery. Somehow, he got them all to Carradoc County, Ontario. He married in 1827 at age twenty-three. With his sixteen-year-old bride, Martha Mc Kinvin, he added another eleven children, founding the Mclean dynasty.

I was quite prepared to believe Mclean spawn had populated Ontario single-handedly.

To answer Father's question about my refusal to learn their family tree, desperate to save myself from more lists of livery and livestock, I answered in my new-found hybrid tongue.

"The family tree's too big. There's too many blokes what died afore I was born. If I say the first Mclean was Duncan, born in Kilcalmonell in 1803, came to Canada in 1819, that's enuff, ain't it? If I know more, I won't look like a long-lost cuz. I'll look suspicious."

Mycroft congratulated himself on the speed and efficacy of his teaching methods, then left the room. It did not escape his pupil that the argument of limiting what one puts in one's brain to what one needs to be there was the very stance Holmes always took for himself, but I had no chance to charge my father with hypocrisy when he proffered this patronizing rationalization.

"Perhaps because you have never been part of a family, Wiggins – particularly a large and closely knitted family that must pass the ennui and internment of interminable snow-bound winters – you understandably underestimate the importance of family stories. Stories are a family's true inheritance. They are the words that bind their provenance as a people."

I bit my tongue to blood to keep from yelling that of course I had a family.

And stories. Plenty of them. All true.

Some he could do with hearing.

Perhaps because this time he actually saw my distress, Sherlock responded in a softer tone. "It is only logical that you resent being cooped up here with Mycroft."

"He treats me like I was born in the gutter and should have stayed there."

"Really? I will speak to him. And I will say these two things to you. There is more to my brother than cruelty and a gutter is useful. Waste must be disposed of to keep us all healthy. And, as I understand it, some truly remarkable people have been reborn in gutters, not the least of which is the promising young person I see before me."

Here he grinned, the one he always used to urge himself on.

"For once, Mr. Twain put it eloquently: 'If it's your job to eat a frog, it's best to do it first thing in the morning. And if it's your job to eat two frogs, it's best to eat the biggest one first.' I suggest you catch your biggest frog, Wiggins, and fry it up forthwith. I am told it tastes like chicken, but do not believe it. It must, quite logically, taste like frog."

Here Sherlock reached for into the large case he had brought with him. Tucking his violin beneath his chin, he raised his bow then paused again. "I shall play some music while you scale the family tree, climb out of the gutter and swallow the webbed amphibian. I do not apologize for the multiple mixed metaphors." He grinned again. "When the frog fits, wear it."

When he finished practicing and reviewed my work, I deduced Holmes must have spent hours back in the fall of 1889, cross-examining Sir Henry Baskerville. His detailed knowledge of the Mclean provenance had a ring of personal experience that could not possibly be his own.

"The McLeans are very proud of their history. Mycroft has noted their participation in several wars, in politics, and their church. Their clan motto, *Virtue Mine Honour*, should be taken as gospel. Given that pride, they will accept you only to the extent you embrace it yourself."

"But surely no one will notice a few minor biographical discrepancies!" Hearing that dead giveaway exit my mouth, I quickly added, "And thems what do, they'll excuse me for a nipper."

If I thought I saw a fleeting wisp of smile, I must have been in error.

My father shook his head and his finger in my face.

"How quickly your vocabulary improves, Wiggins, but sadly not your powers of common sense. You need preparation if you do not want to let it slip that your name is actually Strand."

Here he enjoyed his own private levity for a moment, then frowned.

'If you are caught in the colonies by one of Moriarity's unleashed curs, Wiggins, it will not be a soft mouth that bites you. Appearances can save your life. That is why I trained as an actor – to be able to convincingly present myself as the man I intend others to see."

Holmes' history was a topic Mother had groomed me to encourage. Refusing to see inconsistencies in Watson's stories as his poor memory, or a detective's professional secrecy, she believed Holmes' backstory to be purposefully incomplete and contradictory. She scoffed at Watson's version, "Holmes' grandmother was no more sister to the painter Émile Jean-Horace Vernet than I am sister to Jumbo."

In advancing illness, she insisted we must prove Holmes a baseborn bastard, one who had crawled out of the gutter to which he reassigned me. With proof of vile illegitimacy, he could be ruined. If her low opinion of bastardy hurt me, I kept it from her, and largely from myself.

"So you're an actor then, sir, and you're advisin' me to see myself the same?"

"It is well known that I have said I had theatre training, or perhaps more accurately that Watson said I did," he grinned. "Or most accurately that I have let Watson say that I implied it."

Father held out his hands to an imaginary shelf from which he plucked a shape that evolved out of the ether and proved itself a skull.

"Alas, poor Yoric! I know deception well. In what other profession could I have learned the twists of the tongue from Brahmin to beggar, from Hebrides to Hereford, from Montreal to Michigan? Not to mention the transforming applications of putty and performance make-up? One does not learn any of those useful things entombed in Oxford," he paused with a deliberate moue, "Nor corralled at Cambridge."

He patted the unfortunate Yoric on the head, there being nowhere else to pat him, and returned him to his improvised shelf of oblivion.

"Beggin' your pardon, guv. Which college was it you went to, then?"

"Really, Wiggins, what need have I of either?" He dropped a sly wink. "Perhaps I am deliberately vague so as not to encourage either institution to claim my fame to credit their own?"

"Just tryin' to understand what you're wantin' me to learn about beginnings."

"Beginnings are plural by definition, aren't they? One invents oneself with plurals and parallel structures. But I don't have to tell you that do I, Wiggins?"

This alarmed me, but I did my best to let none of it show on my face.

"Watson, cow-towing to English gentry, would insist that in lives determined by bloodline like in-bred spaniels, our fates are set. But most of us begin like animals grunting in a barn, or splayed out in passion in a ripe spring field.

Many Londoners begin as a bubble in a gin pot. Does that mean we are doomed by our irregular creations? No! That is buckets of brazen balderdash."

Resolved eyes sought and held mine. His voice lost every scintilla of sarcasm or mockery.

"To contradict your restrictive Catholic religion again, Wiggins, whether or not we are born innocent is utterly irrelevant. It is a medieval, illogical, guilt-inducing sentimentalization of biological data. What matters is that we are born. What magic is it, that we are born! That we begin! I am Sherlock Holmes. I begin where and when I choose."

He sprang up to leave, then added, "And so, my dear child, do you."

I held my breath, fearing his next line would spoil the moment. Instead, he sat beside me, set his hand warm and ungloved on mine, and smiled.

"Our creation stories may indeed resemble tangled skeins of yarn, but no human being is born dirty. Our stories are made to appear dirty by small-minded others who are jealous of our originality. If, like all street urchins, you and I have irregular beginnings, if like frogs we are conceived in unloving squirts and thus viewed with public disgust, please also consider this: besides the two of us, Wiggins, what else on this planet is lucky enough to be spawned?'

I knew he did not expect me to answer. I was happy to wait for his.

"Science. Theories. Controversies. Social movements. Belief. Faith. Hope. And change itself. So, my dear Wiggins, I say it clearly: let spawn beget spawn! Let us defend our own spawned stories purposefully, passionately, profoundly, and proudly."

I need not tell you, Smiling Reader, how much we both enjoyed that sentence.

Chapter Nine: The Men with the Twisted Eyes

Whenever I could, I fled the Diogenes for tea at Pictavia. As much as I loved seeing my aunties, that escape increasingly became an opportunity to spend time with Danny without a dozen other Irregulars about. I missed his smile, his humour, his blunt intelligence and found myself increasingly missing his hands.

While this tale is not my love story, and our relationship is a part of my life I largely choose to keep private, I will tell you that our warmth for each other had kindled well before my mother's sad passing. Our glances held, then hands, then embraces. We shared our first awkward but glorious kiss standing hand in hand in the spot so important in both our lives: where Jumbo lived in the London Zoo. If my family knew or guessed, they said nothing. For once, we were all happy to keep it that way.

On one occasion when I arrived for tea, Danny proved thankfully elsewhere. Tante Gisela nodded at Tante Grizelda, who announced, "My sister finds herself disaccommodated on this subject, so I will speak for her. Gisela wants your permission, my dear, to begin the application of binding." She straightened her spine. "Chest binding. We can avoid it no longer. Our little Wiggins has breasts."

I gasped, providing familiar comic relief by inhaling my crumpet.

In a growing concern for my romantic teenage self, Protective Reader, you might well ask this: what did I know about the changes my body was experiencing?

Next to nothing. You need to see it as I lived it. The entire subject of sex might as well have been syphilis – it simply wasn't discussed. For all her progressive beliefs and bohemian reputation, at heart, my mother was still a good Catholic girl. She was also a woman who had been raped. In the silencing of the times, in the suffering of her own teenage trauma, she had told me little. And, as her eighth letter suggested, as a girl she had been even more confused about sexual attraction than I'd ever been.

August 7, 1875

My beloved cousin Duncan,

Now that my anger has abated and my redhaired temper no longer rules my words, I want to ask you something from my heart, as your cousin, your beloved and your life-long friend. Why are you afraid to touch me? Why do you never take my hand?

I do not understand you reluctance to embrace me and let the world know I am yours and you are mine? It cannot be a lack of confidence in my affections, as I have made my love clear since I was a girl of fourteen. Despite years of prayers, I still do not know how to give you the faith to face your fear. Of course you fear you have waited too long to declare yourself. Of course you worry that in my exuberant youth and the new-found wings of womanly pride

I might temporarily turn to another for flattery or comfort, or God help us all, simply for some harmless youthful fun.

Sometimes I despair of you. I despair and I agonize.

Do you even know what those words mean?

This much I know: I need my husband to be my partner in mind and body, spirit and soul. I want a love where I am valued as a peer. How can that be wrong?

I am seventeen years old. Of course I long for any word that I am bright and pretty as a wild lily, or laugh like a spring brook, or smile with the sweetness of the first touch of pixie snow to the tongue. For yes, these are all the pleasantries that Home Boy has offered me, and I have heard them all with a maiden's blush but also with a touch of sorrow, always wishing that even something half as sweet came even once from you. I cling to your only compliment: that I "sing better than Jenny Lind because in my contralto I embody the beauty of both women and men."

Those are the pretty words I need. That is the man I long for. It is clear that you are capable of speaking them and of being him. So why, or why won't you do so?

I beg you to stake a manly claim on my person before it is prospected by another.

Yours and longing to remain so, Reenie. But please remember, also a woman,

Catriona Magdalena Psalmonia Adler Mclean

While I fantasized that Danny might soon stake a manly claim on my person, I had no idea just exactly what that meant. I did not know what his stake might look like, or even exactly where he might put it. It occurred to me that my mother and my aunties may have devised the role of Wiggins at least partially to ensure that no such stake ever got taken in hand, let alone nailed in.

To keep me boyish, my aunties erased my breasts. Since my arms were strong from weekly rowing, they devised some clever padding to make it look like my torso was developing like a barrel-chested young man's. When they were done, Tante Grizelda, took the elephant newly arrived in the room by the tail.

"Someday soon, dear, you will get blood between your legs." Tante Gisela frowned, but Tante Grizelda failed to notice. "It is the monthly menarche. It is the cross of all women to bear, but not to fear. We pad ourselves up and go on with our lives. You will, too."

Tante Gisela looked unhappy, but when her sister left the room, she followed.

On the day I "became a woman," the day I "got my monthly friend", Tante Grizelda brought me an alarming array of belts, buckles, and linen pads, and showed me how to rig myself up in them. I felt as trussed as the Christmas turkey, and about as grateful.

But that was not the final problem.

It is easy to hide the swaddling crammed between your legs to absorb the dread horror menses when you are a

124

young lady in layers of small clothes, petticoats and skirts. It is quite another matter to stick a roll of bulky padding in a boy's crotch. The elephantine lump this created reduced my aunties to all kinds of tittering I did not quite understand. I knew it had something to do with what Tante Grizelda called "the indigent excitations of erections."

Tante Gisela pursed her seamstress lips and after much trial and error, fashioned a pair of underpants with a layer of oilskin between their padding and my breeches. But she made no promises. She said it might hold, for maybe twenty minutes. Both aunties then agreed – Wiggins must be "indisposed" on the days he got his period.

Please pause a moment, Tickled Reader, to enjoy that last sentence as I have.

We invented a backstory in the event that Father ever noted the periodicity of my absence. I told him that once a month I went to help my uncle the costermonger. Whether or not Holmes ever fell for those rotten apples, I honestly cannot say.

I can say that Victorian men perfected denial. As ubiquitous as street children, street sex for sale was everywhere, but no "respectable" Victorian Londoner was supposed to see it. As I told my twentieth-century students, estimates of prostitutes working streets and brothels range from 8,000 to 80,000. Progressive Reformers at our dinner table argued that if you added women occasionally driven by hunger to earn extra income, it would total 200,000. In a city of 5,000,000 this was 4% of the population, approximately one woman in every dozen. Young ladies like me, however, were never told one word about sex.

Victorian men assiduously protected all girls they had not yet deflowered.

I knew just enough about sex to know I needed to know more. I feared asking Tante Grizelda would elicit the swashbuckling tastes of Captain Hudson. Embarrassed, unsure of who or how to ask, I asked no one. In the end, Tante Gisela asked me. In the only time she scandalized me entirely, she hugged me as I left for the Diogenes, then protractedly cleared her throat.

"Dear, I assume you may have questions about the act of married love?"

I blushed redder than my hair. She set an enormous brand new book in my hands – *Ladies Guide in Health and Disease: Girlhood, Maidenhood, Wifehood, Motherhood*, a heavy tome by one John Harvey Kellogg, M.D., of Battle Creek Michigan. Of course, he was American.

"After you've read it, please feel free to ask me anything you want."

I imagine skepticism marred my gratitude. I'm sure she heard me thinking, "What could my sweet, unmarried auntie possibly know about the subject?"

She smiled from the doorway.

"You remember that my young man died at Gettysburg?"

I nodded.

"Well, sweetheart, every word in that sentence is true. My Henry did die. But he died a well-loved man."

One glance at the preface of the incendiary device she left behind, confirmed that Dr. John Harvey Kellogg had more in common with Sherlock Holmes than with Dr. John Hamish Watson:

The old adage, "A little knowledge is a dangerous thing", has done a vast deal of mischief, both in deterring those fitted to impart useful information on these topics from giving it, and discouraging those who needed such instruction from seeking it. We have never yet known a case in which a woman was injured by scientific information respecting her own body and its functions. We believe that enlightenment on this and kindred topics, and on all that relates to the physical, mental and moral well-being of woman is the surest means of correcting some of the greatest evils which curse the race at the present time, and which are sapping the very foundation of society.

Dr. Kellogg certainly believed in the primacy of data.

In six-hundred-and-seventy-six pages, he did not shirk and was no prude. He gave me pictures of my lady parts, diagrams showing how babies grew in my lady parts! Most liberating of all, he gave me words: ovaries, ovum, cervix, uterus, umbilical cord, and placenta. I learned that the correct term to describe menstrual flow was *catamenial,* a word that to this day seems more logically to mean the menial employment of felines. If, to understand human gestation, I first had to wade through the swampy spawning of frogs, so be it. When I saw how cells divided into a human baby, I saw Charles Darwin kissing the Virgin Mary. I saw the science of God.

As for the greatest evils which sapped the very foundation of society, Doctor Kellogg condemned red meat, prostitution and masturbation. The eating of red meat, which inflamed our constitutions, could be solved by the regular consumption of, rather obviously, Kellogg's flakes.

As for masturbation, to his credit, John Harvey admitted that "the sin of self-abuse" was practiced by both boys and girls. He then gravely warned girls it would make us ill, make us unfit mothers, and drive us mad. That gave me cause for pause, but it didn't keep my hands above the covers. Suffice it to say that if something called the *clitoris* was labeled on only one of Dr. Kellogg's plates, it was one of my lady parts I had already found quite nicely for myself.

It is also important to note that if upper-class Pictavia gave me some small measure of control over my life as a girl, in my Irregular life I had none. As Watson so aptly put it, the Irregulars had but one use: to put ourselves at constant risk as little servants, "to go everywhere, see everything and overhear everyone". Once I ran Father's errands, tailed and spied upon his suspects, I ceased to exist.

The Irregulars had less provenance for Holmes than an improvised object. We got pulled from a pocket at his bidding, to do his bidding, then disappeared. Some 30,000 beggared children swarmed the streets of London as ubiquitous as lumps of coal. Once we stopped being of passing use as bootblacks, chimney sweeps, and child prostitutes, we were entirely expendable. Our Irregular ends were regularly expected.

Father knew exactly what he asked when he ordered starving children to ferret out the most illicit and dangerous kinds of intelligences. We all knew that unless and until we did so, we would not eat. Like most of our class, we got paid in piece work, for errands, for pieces of information. For his princely fee of a shilling, little children risked their lives. And lost them. The bonus guinea – the Holy Grail in the Irregular Children's Crusade – was often awarded posthumously and sometimes not at all. Sometimes no grieving family member could be found to receive it.

Shrewd Reader, if you ask why none of these cases ever saw print, you must know that Watson would never publish a reputation-damaging tale. Maimed mudlarks and fatal failures? Such tales could not be told without besmirching both parties. Ergo, they were never told.

As a good friend and better publicist, Watson consistently sugar-coated my father for public consumption. He penned none of Holmes' anti-religiosity, nor his puerile penchant for punishing puns. Except for drafts that somehow went missing from Baker Street and found their way to my library safe, Watson destroyed all stories that did not play honourably or end well.

The world will never read them unless I someday decide to expose them.

For my lifetime entire, I have struggled with whether or not the world needs a straightened version of Watson's yarns. Would revelation correct the legend, or damage both legend and man? I do not want to stifle hope. I am loath to tell the world a shining example of decency could be indecent. I tell myself to let sleeping Watsons lie, that we should all be so lucky to be immortalized by our finest moments. But that does not honour my mother, the Irregulars, or me. And the one man who would never accept only half the data is Sherlock Holmes.

Please see his monograph, *Upon the Improvisation of Belief*:

The improviser must be the unsleeping detective of human behaviour. In all its vicissitudes, both its frailties and its foibles, its repulsiveness and its reason, no detail is too small. No data too insignificant. No stone not worth turning. In each moment of every day, the improviser's quest for patterns of truth must be unwavering. Human behavior is recursive. We repeat ourselves and find our humanity in seeing something new in each recursion. Accordingly, all improvisors must vow to look, look, and look again. Most critically, we must then make deductions from the data."

Consider the data I could expose! I own the only extant copy of *The Full Account of Ricoletti of the Club-foot and his Abominable Wife,* a woman who lured starving waifs to her home with the offer of a good meal, only to make *them* the meal. When she got her knives on Tansy's little sister, and Holmes didn't get there in time, without hesitation or regret, Danny and I pushed Mrs. Ricoletti down a flight of stairs. Watson alludes to these deadly cases in *The Musgrave Ritual*, via Father's veiled admission, *"They are not all successes, Watson."*

What Watson did not say of *The Tarleton Murders, The Case of Vamberry the Wine Merchant, The Adventure of the Old Russian Woman*, and the case Danny solved single handedly, *The Singular Affair of the Aluminium Crutch*, was that children died in the course of them. Instead, Watson cleverly exonerates himself by having Father falsely assert they occurred "before my biographer had come to glorify me."

I assure you that phrase was never uttered, except perhaps in the phantasmagorical spirit realm where Watson keeps his mythical Second Anglo-Afghan War wound, that self-aggrandizing "Jezail bullet" that magically circulates his body, from which he escapes death each time as adroitly as Houdini. Watson ensured no one knew about maimed children, lamed children, violated children, little ones he tended with his own hands and too-often failed to save.

Working for Holmes held the same devils and dangers as a workhouse with walls offered a century of Oliver Twists. But Watson was no Dickens. He had no crusading social spirit eager to expose the usury of beggars and orphans. Quite the opposite: the death of Watson's drunkard father which left him alone "without kith or kin in London" left him with little empathy for children who likewise had no one and nothing. Three decades of urchins risked life and limb defending the reputation and wealth of

London's upper crust, but Watson censored their injuries as too indelicate for the very persons who were beholden to them. In any choice between Irregular sacrifice and Victorian sensibilities, we counted less than a Highgate matron's blush.

The Irregulars were responsible for the success of some twenty cases, but Watson deigned to mention us in only three tales. On each occasion, he considers his world invaded by inferiors who had no right to be there. He calls us "the dirtiest and most ragged of Street Arabs that ever I clapped eyes upon." When Father waves his hand, Watson claims we "scampered away downstairs like so many rats." We were never anything more than an inconvenient infestation of vermin.

He looks even further down his uppity nose in his next tale, *The Sign of the Four,* set six years later in 1887. I degenerate to a "disreputable little scarecrow." Holmes repeats his request that he "cannot have the house invaded in this way," and that I alone must report to him.

I confess I ignored this request. But it was more than the chance to run the seventeen steps with Danny so we could wink at Tante Grizelda, more than enjoying her feigned protests and Watson's very real dismay. It went beyond the fact Father only protested in Watson's hearing and in truth enjoyed the horde descending as much as we did. We arrived in force because Father sometimes had what I shall euphemistically call "a forgetful Scottish side." If I did not appear with all dozen Irregulars, I might not leave with a full dozen shillings. If I wanted all my hands to be paid, then each child needed to storm the stairs of Baker Street to extend their Irregular little hand in person.

I note from personal experience, Understandably Outraged Reader, that the beggar boy named Wiggins was entirely erasable. I had fancied myself a beloved stitch in Watson's yarns, but unlike Father's death, which produced a public mourning befitting regicide, my death occurred without note. I simply disappeared. Watson knew a boy named Wiggins played first lieutenant from 1881 to 1891, but he either forgot my name or never bothered to learn it.

Instead, I am replaced in *The Adventure of the Crooked Men,* set in 1888, by some wholly fictional upstart named Simpson. To this day, I consider it a particularly nasty snipe to replace a starving boy with one named after the well-fed Watson's favorite supper club.

Now is the time to cue your best deductions, Skeptical Reader. Malnourishment notwithstanding, how did I stay young and small for a decade?

I can take no credit for this connivance; it belongs entirely to The Woman.

What Holmes and Watson never guessed, or at least never admitted, was that Mother's appearance in cross-dress in *A Scandal in Bohemia* was an encore, a repeat performance of an act she had debuted in 1879, when she premiered the role of Wiggins. Having joined the Imperial Opera of Warsaw after my birth in 1876, she took the job on the condition that she could make a permanent home in London and fulfil her contract touring. Suffice it to say that the first Wiggins joined my father to solve two years' worth of cases before he met John Watson in *A Study in Scarlet,* in 1881. She played the role of Wiggins for almost eight years until I took over 1887.

When I turned eleven, Mother decided that, unlike Watson, Father could count. Her Wiggins was getting a tad too long in the tooth. Since we looked much alike, especially with a face made filthy by soot, we considered, but rejected, the simple substitution of one Wiggins for another. Any resemblance that would fool Watson forever would not fool Holmes for long. He had to be told the truth, or more correctly, our version of it.

We approached him in Baker Street at twilight, one night when he was alone and already had one foot in a waiting hansom cab. As Wiggins, Mother stepped up and spoke her lines.

"I be goin' to work for me uncle, a costermonger, but me little bruvver can work for ya. The ovver Irregulars likes 'im. He's fast 'n smart. I learned'im everyfing what I do."

Father stepped up into the cab, pointed at me and then at the seat across from him.

"Let me tell you a tale about a giant rat," he said, as he closed the door on my mother.

Some ten minutes later he opened it to send me out into the street for the first time. He rapped on the roof, then shrugged out the window to fire his original apprentice.

"The child has the stomach for it," he told my brother-mother. Then he shrugged, "One Wiggins is as good as another."

For all his ballyhooed skills of observation, Father did not appear to notice that an adult female Wiggins had been replaced by an actual child, one eighteen years her junior. Watson took this short-sightedness further: he believed the Wiggins of 1881, who was Irene Adler, was the same even scrawnier and shorter boy six years later in 1887, who was me. But more is afoot here than Watson's well-documented density.

In his own class privilege, Father treated his limping Tiny Tim apprentice no better than Scrooge treated Bob Cratchit. At any hour of dark or light, expecting me to stand in, sleep in, or slug through the snow, he called for me whenever convenient to him, summoning me into existence like a master summoning his jinn to serve him. He never asked where or how I lived. Never asked if I received a nightly hearth or daily bread.

I must not de-sentimentalize the data. His missing sentiment is part of the data. He rescued me from a ditch so he could put me back in one whenever he pleased.

He kept me there by a circular, tautologous logic that made perfect sense to him: if I had none of the amenities of life, he had no responsibility to provide them to me, because he had no need of me having them. In truth, I was more use to him without them. He left me to survive by what Watson so pejoratively called "native cunning" – a phrase in which I heard the judgment that, like Watson's enemy Afghans, I was an inferior, subordinate, quasi-simian, creature.

Apparently, a Wiggins is as good as a Simpson is a good as a Billy.

In 1889, a page named Billy appears at Baker Street. Young Billy stays at his post from 1889 to 1903, when, in *The Mazarin Stone*, Watson famously tells him, "*It all seems very unchanged, Billy. You don't change either.*"

Unless Mr. H. G. Wells lent little Billy his Time Machine, during this fourteen-year time span, any discerning physician would have noted that Billy has grown both inches and a beard. As my ever-direct Danny put it, "Little Billy could have used his little willy to father several little Billys of his own."

I can only conclude that doctor, detective, and perhaps even you, Class-Bound Reader, all saw us Irregulars as little more than a two-legged servant species akin to Toby the Basset Hound. We could be patted on the head and replaced at any time by a new whelp from another readily available litter. We could be sent to fetch and deliver, and just as the king hunted my mother, as the ripper hunted women, we could be murdered as a step above game.

Over many a long and lonely Diogenes night, to bolster my confidence that I was worth anything at all, I read and re-read the late great Irene Adler's ninth letter, clinging to the hope that a Mother's loving advice is always a sweet scent worth following.

August 27, 1875

My dearest secret fiancé,

My chat with Mutti this evening has left me both blushing and bursting to tell you!

She came to my room with the smallest of candles, once Da was asleep. When she woke me up, I feared some disaster, such as the fire that took Lindstrom's barn, but she smiled to calm my fears. Then she lifted a corner of my quilt, snuggled in, and spoke to me like a sister.

"I was lucky my father was a doctor. He told me about the act of married love when I got my monthly friend, just as I did with you. But the most important thing, my sweet girl, he did not tell me. And in truth, I'm not sure I would have heard it. So please hear me now."

I confess I couldn't say a word. How I gripped her hand when she took mine!

"It is normal and natural to kiss a boy. It is God giving us a window on married life, and it is normal and natural to open a window. But do not settle for any window. When you kiss a boy, do not lose yourself in him. Do not just listen to your body, although it will have the loudest voice. Include your heart and your head. Be certain in all three ways that the boy you kiss kisses you back. That he truly wants you. Not just a girl to kiss. Not just because he enjoys kissing. Because it is you, and only you, he wants more than he wants to breathe. Find that kiss, then you will be happy. That is what I wish for you, my darling."

With that my lovely mother left the room.

I hereby resolve to kiss you like that tomorrow, Mr. Mclean.

No more pecks on the cheek. No more kisses in which you modestly pull away. I must know if yours can be the kiss my mother hopes for me and the kiss this daughter hopes for herself.

Your soon-to-be-more-than-kissing-cousin,

Reenie

Chapter Ten: The Adventure of the Bruised Departure Plans

For four long months, I jumped out of Diogenes' windows, wincing each time my feet hit the ground. In equal aggravation, under Mycroft's cold eye, I climbed every branch of the Mclean family tree and still wasn't told which one She-of-the-Execrable Name had budded from. Seeking comfort, I kept rationing Mother's letters. Even as they grew as concerning as this one, her tenth.

September 8, 1875

My darling Duncan,

I am in utter despair and must write quickly as I must not be caught with this letter!

But you must hear from me immediately that I apologize for the temper-driven oaf that is my father. He had no right, none, to go over to your house and yell at your father. He had no authority. He had no love in his heart for me, only his pride.

Mutti said he told Uncle John there would be no wedding, because he would always refuse to pay for it. He said he would forbid his uncle, Father Mc Kniven, to perform the ceremony. He said you weren't fit to wipe your shoes in our barn, and that if you ever set foot on our property again, he would burn down your barn with you in it.

He has returned in such a foul mood, spending the rest of the day in his chair nursing his bruised knuckles and refusing to speak to us after telling us what he said.

I am too afraid to provoke him. Just know that he does not, and will not rule me.

You rule my heart, but I rule my head.

Your still-willing wife to be,

Reenie

In contradictory irony, I was repeatedly assisted in following my heart out the window by the otherwise miserly Mycroft, who, in a manner typical to corpulent wealthy men, tended to indulge in rich, heavy teas. For mine, he let me eat nothing but crumpets. While vastly inferior to Tante Grizelda's, they kept my mouth busy and kept me from having to speak to him. My record was an even dozen in one sitting. Dr. Kellogg would have denounced us both.

After his third serving of mutton and sherry, Mycroft routinely drifted off.

I could exit the window without worry, as he always told Holmes that he never once closed an eye. If the Diogenes' staff knew of my covert comings and goings, they also knew their livelihoods depended on not seeing me in the first place. I had become increasingly aware that they were well-practiced at ignoring the comings and goings of Mycroft's special guests. The curious incidents of men moaning in the nighttime made it clear to me that members were forbidden to speak to each other, less for club reasons than for legal ones.

In February, when Holmes falsely put it about that he was off on a mission of "supreme importance" for the French government, he and Mycroft were actually engaged in hand-to-hand battle with a more powerful foe: my hair.

Used to being the arbiters of all things, they were loath to admit that a young lady's toilette defeated them. For reasons obvious, I wore my hair a poor boy's length, purposefully uncared for, frizzing over my collar. Unable to admit that they couldn't coax a chignon from a bob, combs and curling tongs got pitched into the fire, proving immolation the petulant pyrrhic victory for both boys named Holmes. While I knew how to dress both my person and my hair, Wiggins couldn't help. He knew even less than they did.

Father declared it a three-pipe problem.

Mycroft grunted and went to sleep.

On Valentine's Day, the great detective reluctantly concluded he would have to trust a woman. In a delicious irony, he opted to inform and swear to secrecy one of the two women who already knew I was not dead.

I thoroughly enjoyed Father's completely irrelevant and erroneous lecture cautioning me about what the frail Mrs. Hudson could, and could not, be told. He repeatedly pressed me to agree she should be told only that I needed her help to temporarily learn to hide as a girl for my safety. I was to impress upon her that her skill and her secrecy meant my very life. If she asked me anything I could not answer, Father advised pulling my cap down over my eyes. When I suggested Miss Euphemia would likely not be wearing said cap, he squinted.

"Fine. When in female garb, do something opportunistically female. Faint. Cry."

He really did not know my Tante Grizelda at all, if he thought those theatrics would work. But I applauded his every suggestion and promised to act the part.

Mycroft, however, was not so easily convinced to break the Diogenes ban on women.

"I would rather die than be the first to pollute its sacred rooms with uterine kind."

Father snorted so hard he nearly swallowed his pipe.

He asked me to leave the room, but I went no further than the armchair, behind which I could still hear him. He launched no counter argument, but simply began chanting a list – names he then suggested could be sent to various yellow journalists, enumerating all the women and – here he looked pointedly at Mycroft – some very lovely young men, who had already been willingly smuggled into the Diogenes' variously purposed rooms, including Mycroft's secret bedroom, which, as he heard tell, was awash floor to ceiling in the plush of red velvet and the snap of black leather.

Mrs. Hudson arrived that afternoon.

Father made it clear I must not to speak to my acting lady's maid beyond necessities or pleasantries. I had little opportunity to do otherwise; Holmes never stopped hovering.

It forced my auntie into a servile role, but she made Holmes pay for putting her there. Clamping her teeth on a mouthful of sewing pins, I heard words my liberal-minded auntie would never utter, "depraved," "unnatural," "Nancy boy" and "malicious mandrake." When I played my street urchin part and innocently asked what they meant, she needled Holmes further, throwing his words in his face.

"I don't need alienist tendencies to conjecture some unkind thoughts about the predatory intentions and proclivities of one Mr. Sherlock Holmes. They are as obvious as Jumbo."

It proved difficult to contain our giggles when he rapidly removed himself.

Under her breath, she called Holmes names learned drinking with sailors, but agreed to continue the charade. We pretended to take my measurements. We feigned a keen interest in the fashions of *Godey's Ladies Book*. She returned a day later with a smart lady's travelling case. I recognized it as clever indeed: Mother's valise had a false bottom, one which had once held the photo of her with King Siggy. It now awaited my precious stash of her letters.

Then, telling Holmes she could sew me into a lady much faster if she enlisted the help of her good friend Mrs. Turner – which I note again for the record was effectively true – Tante Grizelda went off and spent a few days at her leisure with Tante Gisela, only to reappear with several articles of a young lady's wardrobe which Holmes fully believed had just been constructed on a dressmaker's dummy.

I will avoid the much-too-easy line about who was the real dummy.

What my aunts had simply done, of course, was to open my well-appointed closet to select items from my existing wardrobe. Since they had sewn these garments under my mother's artistic eye, every item fit and flattered me perfectly. Then my stealthy pirating aunties took their own footsteps backwards. Mrs. Hudson stuffed her Baker Street mending bag with scraps of the same fabric. In the comfort of Pictavia, Tante Gisela would unpick the arm from one of my dresses. The next day, Tante Grizelda would sip tea with Holmes in the Baker Street kitchen and sew it back up, right under the great detective's nose.

They quickly realized that these shenanigans of subterfuge, while enjoyable, were entirely unnecessary: the world's greatest bachelor couldn't tell lining from laundry. Beyond complimenting Mrs. Hudson on the preternatural speed with which she and the diligent Mrs. Turner plied their needles, he never noticed a bloody thing. Thus was I quickly returned to being my mother's daughter; I became again the girl in the wardrobe my mother designed for me.

In March, Mrs. Hudson announced that the one thing she could not sew under any conditions was a corset. That required a visit to a corset maker. From the measuring look on Father's face, I feared he might try to whalebone me himself. Thankfully, he instead acquiesced to me going for a fitting, only after grilling me as to what I could and could not say at it.

Pictavia! I could spend a whole day at home. I could smell fresh crumpets and all but taste the honey.

Tante Grizelda and I hurried home to our family and my own corset ready and waiting in my closet. Wanting only to be with my loved ones, I made quick survey of said closet, hastily selecting further armor against the Canadian cold. I also pulled Mother's purple shawl out of my pillowcase.

"So that's where it went," Tante Grizelda smiled. "It was your mother's favorite. She always claimed it a gift from Jenny Lind."

Here we all smiled. While my mother often got many gifts from fans, it seemed unlikely that the Swedish Songbird was one of them. Tante Gisela's seamstress' eye took over.

"It's exquisite workmanship, wherever she got it from." She squinted at me, "She must have thought you were old enough to take care of it. You do know it must always be hanged and can never, ever, be washed. You'd lose all the beads. Promise me that, and I'll send it with you."

I'd have promised her anything that led to crumpets.

Tante Grizelda had perfected the art of crispy bubbles, ones that held honey while maintaining crisp edges. There is nothing more disappointing in this life than a soggy crumpet, but hers never disappointed. She said her secret was castor sugar, but like most things in life, I think it was timing. My exacting auntie counted off each second on drumming fingers.

Unbeknownst to all of us, the seconds ticking by us that afternoon were all the time we had left.

That last day with my Pictavians made it almost impossible to leave them. Under the table, I held tight to Danny's hand, and didn't care who may have noticed.

During sleepless Diogenes nights, I had often tried to talk myself out of going through with Holmes' plan, but always returned to the fact I had sworn my dying mother an oath with no escape clause. I told myself that at least now I would leave London wrapped in her shawl. But even that consolation proved bittersweet. When I looked in the mirror with it accessorizing my travel wardrobe, I saw someone my mother never got to see: a fully-turned-out young lady, a young woman from head to toe, wearing skirts that hid my feet. From somewhere – whence they would never say, although to this day I suspect grave robbers – my bootlegging aunties even found a waist-length wig of human hair, so exactly my shade of burnt auburn it looked all my own.

Tante Grizelda did, however, follow Holmes' final instructions to the letter. Pocket watch in hand, she ran me in drill after drill, until I could change from boy to girl, then boy to girl, in five minutes. I did so in daylight, candlelight and darkness, in closets, on, in, and under beds, and failed only at the ridiculous request to do it blindfolded with one hand. That took fifteen minutes.

Then, on April 24th, my wardrobe, my wig, and my understanding of quick change artistry complete, Mrs. Hudson informed me that Father had given her notice. As we gazed at the almost proper, almost pretty, young lady in the full length mirror, she laid a hand on my shoulder and asked me to forgive her. We had already said our private good-byes. This was a public performance. Having spotted the shadow of Holmes' boots under the door, Tante Grizelda could not restrain herself. Pent up words held back with pins pricked their way out.

Shedding tears to shame a crocodile, she wailed, "Forgive me, Wiggins! All I can tell you is what my mother told me: lie still and think of England!"

Trying not to laugh, regretting I could not say a true good-bye, I did my best to use my elocution lessons to give her what I could with Father listening.

"Mrs. Hudson, I promise you, this is my choice. There is nothing to forgive."

The genuine sobs that accompanied her exit from the Diogenes suggested otherwise.

I closed my ears to them. Unable to run, I had long contrived to discount my risk of sexual danger. Despite my repeated perusal of Dr. Kellogg's guide, I also did not want to admit that I remained truly confused about the play-by-play of the act itself. It seemed to occur spontaneously.

I could find neither plates, nor explanation of *penis* or *virgin*, two words I knew, but I needed to know what happened when one met the other. I still had no explanation of words all teenagers so desperately long to add to the plumbing equation, words like passion and pleasure.

No matter how often I re-read them, my mother's letters remained likewise tantalizingly incomplete on the subject. It was clear to me that Duncan had been a gentleman almost beyond bearing. I assumed Mother had been forced to take the situation in hand, so to speak, more than once. Her advice from her Mother made me long to have known my grandmother, Gerda Adler – a woman I perceived as having Tante Gisela's gentle manner and Tante Grizelda's pirate heart.

Wanting to say a proper good-bye to both my aunties, on the almost-spring April afternoon of Mrs. Hudson's departure, little knowing it for my last window exit from the Diogenes, I resolved to accept my Tante Gisela's offer. I visited downstairs with Danny, saying a long, private good-bye that we promised each other would not be one, then tiptoed into Tante Gisela's bedroom when everyone else was sleep. We wrapped ourselves in quilts and whispers.

"Let me tell you, dear, how I loved my Henry. And how it felt when he loved me back."

Knowing someone in our family had known true love, spiritually and physically, made it almost possible to quell the dread I felt every time I read my mother's eleventh letter.

September 30, 1875

My dearest Duncan and as of today, my husband-to-be:

Yes, yes, my answer is a life-time of yes! Your proposal was so sweet, so old-fashioned, so truly everything a girl could long for. I do not need to write it down, as it's written on my heart, but because it will give us pleasure in our old married days, I shall record it here for us both.

For once, we had evaded Home Boy. He had suffered, yet again one of his injuries. He is without a doubt the most accident prone farm hand I have ever known!

Since there was tension between you, no doubt because you so wanted to be alone with me, and he refused to take the hint, I ran ahead to the ravine. When you reached me, you took one glance to be sure he was far enough away and you got down on one knee right there beside the stream and collected your thoughts. Home Boy arrived just as you finally spoke in a clear, loud voice.

"Catriona, I have no choice but to claim you. My croft will always be yours."

How I love that you used that old-fashioned word, and how personal you made it!

How I love that you asked me at our ravine! Like our love, it flows eternally between our farms, or as Grandfather Mclean once put it in the Gaelic, telling my Da to make up with yours, "it's naught but water between your croft and mine." Now my croft will forever be yours! I knew it. I have always known it. Now we both do. And soon everyone will as I will be signing myself,

Mrs. Duncan Mclean.

On April 24, 1891, I told myself I knew everything I needed to know about sex. If DAMM was Mycroft and Mycroft was DAMM, I refused to even consider the possibility that either of them could possibly be my father. Even if it took a trip to Canada, I'd be damned glad to soon be rid of both of them.

That evening, my father returned in excellent spirits, nursing bleeding knuckles.

Chapter Eleven: The Finale Problem

Father's red knuckles needed no more than a sponge to remove the stage blood.

"For all his years of exposure to my methods," Holmes chuckled the next morning at breakfast, "Watson is not one whit smarter than when I met him. He believed me when I told him I evaded murder yesterday – not once, nor twice, but thrice – even though no attack was witnessed and no assailant can be found.

"On what possible evidence does he accept my flimsy assertion that these crimes can be attributed to anyone, let alone the dread Moriarty? For that matter, how can he know I have truthfully been attacked at all? While Watson is peerlessly devoted in heart, when it comes to the deployment of brains, he never fails to disappoint me."

Annoyed that he never once considered the endless ways that he had failed my mother and me, I answered in a less subservient role than I should have. Four months had restored me to myself and my station. I admit it: I enjoyed showing him exactly what kind of little Strand Wiggins Euphemia Hortensia McLean Frankenstein he had created.

"Begin' permission, sir, can I answer that question as Miss Euphemia might?"

Intrigued, my father nodded. He leaned in, poised to correct me.

"Watson takes your word as his friend. His faith in you is unassailable. On what possible evidence should anyone believe your flimsy assertion that Moriarty exists? It rests on the assertion of your word as a gentleman and a good man. Given that you lack both in the cruel way you continually mock Watson, you are correct: no one should believe, not in Moriarty, nor in you."

The great detective blinked, then busied himself in a long winding of his pocket watch.

"I stand corrected. Watson is a naturally happy man. My ridicule of him is petty, born of resentment and jealousy, as I will never know what my true nature might have been if life had not forced me from childhood to be suspicious and error-finding. You are entirely correct, Miss Euphemia, to see that as my loss. Not his."

After breakfast, I headed to Switzerland to rendezvous with a waterfall and a falling man.

I found myself dispatched to the Englischer Hof in Meiringen with Father's map in hand and worse – with Mycroft as chaperone. With instructions to speak to no one on the way, it took all my will not to scream all I knew at him. But that would untie all of Mother's plans, so I held back my hatred. Holmes explained he would follow us, but must first take Watson on a merry chase, in order to ensure we reached Switzerland first. Upon our arrival, we must locate a farm shed half a mile between Reichenbach Falls and the hotel wherein we must spend the night. Then, finally, Mycroft would depart and return to England.

I was further relieved to learn I would travel that leg of the journey as a boy with masculine clothes in my travelling case, and my female costumes secreted in my trunk. Father handed me a Swiss rucksack containing what he explained was the typical garb of a Swiss farm boy, one I should don in private only when we reached the shed.

I remained utterly flummoxed, however, by what he handed me next: a brand new pair of expensive men's hiking boots. When I began to protest how badly he had miscalculated the size of my feet, he snorted. It took him only a moment to approve them exactly the right size for me to pull on right over my own shoes.

When I asked what they were for, he prevaricated.

"Consider them water moccasins, Wiggins. Practice their bite and bring them to the falls."

Unable to sleep on the train, I worried Father was developing an unhealthy footwear fixation after saving Henry Baskerville, as he repeatedly reminded me, "based on nothing but a missing boot." As Mycroft snored, I checked my gigantic boots and was incommensurately relieved they did not read *Meyers, Toronto*, but instead the familiar brand of *P. Singer, London*.

What Father would have me make of this footwear became curiouser and curiouser when I spotted a lump under the sole of the label-bearing right foot. I pried it up and discovered a note addressed to Watson in a hand I did not recognize, signed by someone I did not know, named Peter Steiler.

I mulled over when, and where, and why, and even if I was expected to give said note to Watson. I jerked awake when a gnashing Rat from Southampton ran me down wearing gigantic boots on all four feet.

I have never admitted to another living soul that several consternated hours then passed before I made the obvious deduction and checked the other boot where I found a second missive, in Father's hand addressed to me. I told Mycroft nothing. At the shed, I told him I hoped never to see his face again. He grunted, shrugged and left me.

For once, I preferred to be alone. Father's note had left me colder than a Whitechapel gutter. It spelled out my role in the deaths that awaited us.

But, Comparing Reader, you must first hear Watson's version of Holmes' demise, as published in *The Strand* in December of 1893. Here, I have abridged *The Final Problem*, and again used only Watson's words to tell the tale. When the gullible and totally gulled good doctor gloats, "I alone know the absolute truth of the matter," I assure you, he is laughably mistaken.

In the winter and spring of 1891, I saw little of Holmes. It was with surprise that I saw him walk into my consulting room upon the evening of April 24th, his knuckles burst and bleeding. He requested that I come away with him to the continent to flee the criminal genius, Moriarty.

"He is a man of good birth and education. At the age of twenty-one he wrote a treatise upon the Binomial Theorem

and won the Mathematical Chair at one of our smaller universities. But the man had hereditary tendencies of the most diabolical kind. A criminal strain ran in his blood. He is the Napoleon of crime. He sits motionless, like a spider in the centre of its web, but that web has a thousand radiations and he knows well every quiver of them. His agents are splendidly organized. This was the organization I devoted my whole energy to exposing.

"But I must confess, Watson, to a start, when I saw the very man standing on my threshold. His appearance was quite familiar to me. He is extremely tall and thin, his forehead domes out in a white curve, and his two eyes are deeply sunken in his head. He is clean-shaven, pale. His face protrudes forward and is forever slowly oscillating from side to side in a curiously reptilian fashion. 'You must stand clear, Mr. Holmes or be trodden underfoot,' said he. 'If you are clever enough to bring destruction upon me, rest assured that I shall do as much to you.'

"I was out at mid-day when a two-horse van, furiously driven, whizzed around and was on me like a flash. I saved myself by a fraction of a second. On Vere Street, a brick fell from a rooftop and shattered at my feet. I called the police. They would have me believe the wind had toppled over some bricks preparatory to repairs. I knew better.

"Then I was attacked by a rough with a bludgeon. But no connection will ever be traced between the gentleman whose front teeth have met my knuckles and the retiring *mathematical coach. It would be best to get away for the few days which remain before the police are at liberty to act."*

Holmes then detailed his instructions, begging me to follow them exactly, by which I would take both hansom cab and brougham to Victoria Station to elude the cleverest rogue and the most powerful syndicate of criminals in Europe. He then disappeared over the back wall.

I obeyed Holmes injunctions to the letter and had no difficulty finding the train carriage. In vain I searched for my friend. I spent a few minutes assisting a venerable Italian priest then returned to my carriage to discover I had my decrepit Italian friend for a companion. A chill came over me as I thought Holmes' absence might mean some blow had fallen during the night.

"My dear Watson," said a voice, "you have not even condescended to say good-morning."

For an instant, the wrinkles were smoothed away and the dull eyes regained their fire. Then Holmes had gone as quickly as he had come. How he startled me!

"Every precaution is still necessary," he whispered. "I have reason to think that they are hot on our trail. Ah, there is Moriarty himself."

I saw a tall man pushing his way furiously through the crowd, waving his hand. An instant later we shot clear of the station. Holmes laughed, throwing off the black cassock and hat, packing them in a hand-bag. He gave me the news that Moriarty had set fire to our rooms on Baker Street.

"Good heavens, Holmes! This is intolerable."

"They must have lost my track completely. They have evidently been watching you, however, and that is what brought Moriarty here. You could not have made some slip in coming?"

"I did exactly what you advised."

"Did you recognize your Coachman?"

"No."

"It was Mycroft. It is an advantage to avoid taking a mercenary into your confidence."

When I asserted, we must have alluded Moriarty, Holmes replied that given Moriarty's intelligence equaled his own, the fiend would not give up but instead engage a special and catch us at Canterbury. When I suggested Moriarty be arrested on arrival, Holmes disagreed. Instead, we must get out at Canterbury without our bags. Moriarty would follow our bags and wait for us at the Paris depot while we treated ourselves to a couple of new carpet bags and made our way at our leisure into Switzerland.

I was still looking rather ruefully at the rapidly disappearing luggage van which contained my wardrobe when a special train appeared and sped past us.

"There he goes," said Homes. *"There are limits, you see, to our friend's intelligence. It would have been a coup-de-ma'tre had he deduced what I would deduce and acted accordingly. Had he overtaken us, Moriarty would have made a murderous attack upon me. It is, however, a game at*

which two may play. The question now is lunch. Here, or the buffet at Newhaven?"

Holmes had telegraphed the London police and, in Strasburg, we found a reply waiting for us at our hotel. Holmes tore it open, uttered a bitter curse, and hurled it into the fire.

"He has escaped! They have secured the whole gang with the exception of him. I think you had better return to England, Watson. I am a dangerous companion now. Moriarty will devote his whole energies to revenging himself on me. I recommend you return to your practice."

It was hardly an appeal to be successful with one who was an old campaigner and an old friend. It was a lovely trip to Geneva, but never for one instant did Holmes relax. I could tell by his quick glancing eyes and sharp scrutiny of every face that he was well convinced we could not walk ourselves clear of the danger dogging our footsteps.

When a large rock clattered down and roared into the lake behind us, Holmes raced to a lofty pinnacle, craning his head in every direction. When the guide said falling stones were common, Holmes said nothing, but smiled at me with the air of a man who sees the fulfillment of that which he had expected.

"I think that I may go so far as to say, Watson, I have not lived wholly in vain. The air of London is sweeter for my presence. In over a thousand cases, I am not aware that I have ever used my powers upon the wrong side. Your memoirs will draw to an end upon the day I crown my career by the capture or extinction of the most dangerous and capable criminal in Europe."

I shall be brief and yet exact in the little which remains for me to tell. It is not a subject on which I would willingly dwell, and yet I am conscious that a duty devolves upon me to admit no detail. It was on the 3rd of May that we reached the little village of Meiringen and the Englisher Hof, kept by Peter Steiler the elder. At his advice, on the afternoon of the 4th, we set off with the intention of seeing the hamlet of Rossenlaui, with strict injunctions, however, on no account to pass the falls of Reichenbach without making a small detour to see them.

It is, indeed, a fearful place. The torrent, swollen by melting snow, plunges into a tremendous abyss from which the spray rolls up like smoke from a burning house. The path has been cut halfway round the fall to afford a complete view, but ends abruptly, and the traveler has to return as he came.

We had turned to do so, when we saw a Swiss lad running with a letter in his hand. It bore the mark of our hotel and was addressed to me by the landlord. It appeared that an English lady in the last stage of consumption had been overtaken by a sudden hemorrhage. She could hardly live a few hours, but it would be a great consolation to her to see an English doctor.

It was impossible to refuse the request of a fellow-countrywoman dying in a strange land. It was finally agreed that Holmes should retain the young Swiss messenger as guide, visit the falls, then journey to Rosenlaui where I would join him that evening. As I turned away, I saw him gazing down at the rush of the waters. It was the last that I was ever destined to see of him in this world.

At the bottom, I looked back to see a man in black walking rapidly up the hill, but he passed from my mind. I hurried on, reaching Meiringen in about an hour, to see Steiler standing on the hotel porch. When a look of surprise passed his face, my heart turned to lead in my breast.

"You did not write this letter? There is no sick Englishwoman in the hotel?"

"Certainly not!" he cried. "It must have been written by the tall Englishman who came—"

In a tingle of fear, I ran for the path. But it was in vain that I shouted. My only answer was my own voice reverberating in a rolling echo from the cliffs around me.

It was the sight of Holmes' Alpine-stock which turned me cold and sick. He had not gone to Rosenlaui. He had remained on that three-foot path with sheer wall on one side and sheer drop on the other, until his enemy had overtaken him. The young Swiss boy had gone too. He had probably been in the pay of Moriarty, and had left the two men together. And then what happened?

I began to think of Holmes' own methods and tried to practice them in reading this tragedy. It was, alas, only too easy to do. The blackish soil is kept forever soft by the spray and two lines of footmarks were clearly marked along the farther end of the path, both leading away from me. There were none returning. At the end, the soil was ploughed into

160

mud, and the branches and ferns were torn and bedraggled. I lay on my face and peered over with the spray sprouting all around me. I shouted, but only the same half-human cry of the falls was borne back to my ears.

But it was destined that I should, after all, have a last word of greeting from my friend and comrade. The gleam of something bright caught my eye. As I reached for Holmes' silver cigarette-case, out fluttered three pages torn from his notebook and addressed to me.

"My dear Watson, I write these lines through the courtesy of Mr. Moriarty, who awaits my convenience for the final discussion of those questions which lie between us. I am pleased to free society from his presence, though I fear it is at a cost which will give pain to my friends, and especially, my dear Watson, to you. I have already explained, however, that no possible conclusion to my career could be more congenial to me than this. Indeed, I was quite convinced that the letter from Meiringen was a hoax, and I allowed you to depart under the persuasion that some development of this sort would follow. I made every disposition of my property before leaving England. Pray give my greetings to Mrs. Hudson, and believe me to be, my dear fellow,

Very sincerely yours,

Sherlock Holmes"

Expert examination confirmed that a personal contest between the two men ended, as it could hardly fail to end in such a situation – in their reeling over, locked in each other's arms. The Swiss youth was never found again, and *there can be no doubt that he was one of Moriarty's agents. As for the gang, the evidence which Holmes had accumulated exposed their organization. Of their terrible chief, I have now been compelled to make a clear statement of his career due to those injudicious champions who have endeavored to clear his memory by attacks upon him, whom I shall ever regard as the best and wisest man whom I have ever known.*

I apologize for such twaddle yet again, Long-Suffering Reader. Please let me approach the truth.

Of course, the "Napoleon of crime" was nothing but a Napoleonic red herring who was never caught or seen because the real Moriarty never once set foot in Switzerland. That was but another of my father's fictions.

Please note the arrogance it takes to say, *"This case is the most brilliant bit of thrust and parry work in the history of detection,"* when you are both the hero and the author of this fiction in the first place. In that hubris, in this creation of his nemesis, a modern alienist would also see transference. Holmes' description of the tall, gaunt Moriarty was so clearly a mirror image uglification of himself, a reflection of the way he saw himself in drug-induced nightmares.

Just as when Holmes used phony bleeding knuckles to boast about how easily he fooled his gullible friend, it is another of Father's ugly, manipulative moments when he makes Watson feel guilty. He tells Watson that Moriarty finding them is his fault – his "slip-up" in instructions.

As for Father's other ruses and manipulations throughout this story, I admit to a shameless part of me that admires them. Please consider how effortlessly he improvised and re-improvised.

Once Watson admitted he did not recognize his coachman, Father could have said it was Queen Vicky herself. I know it was not Mycroft; he was with me. As for costuming himself as yet another cleric, one doesn't have to be an alienist to see Holmes undisguised God Complex here. He liked being seen as more ethically evolved than other mere mortals. If he had truly wanted to travel incognito, why would he, in any disguise, sit next to his sidekick Watson?

It is a clever improviser indeed who identifies a random tall man in the crowd as Moriarty, only once the train is already moving and said tall man cannot possibly board it. But the train could easily have already been filled with Moriarty's henchmen. So why did Holmes take off his clerical costume as soon as the train left the station?

You only take it off if you know there is no danger. If there never was any danger. If you know the only fool you had to fool has been fooled.

Father had planned and set every brick of the edifice well. Of course, the Baker Street fire wasn't Moriarty. It was arson, set by an impatient departing chemist gleefully throwing old experiments into the fire. Mrs. Hudson extinguished it and told the fire brigade she'd burnt her cookies. Father should have burned with shame for leading Watson by the nose like a milch cow.

I note, for the record, that the first thing Holmes always does when he begins manipulating an unfortunate pawn is to deprive them of their clothes.

I will also admit that I enjoy the magical Moriarty who travels about like a Jezail bullet. First, the tall man Holmes identifies as Moriarty fails to board the train as it "shot out of the station." But Holmes needs to keep the threat alive in Watson's mind, so he plants the notion that Moriarty hired a second, special train. When a train appears behind them in Canterbury, Father's true improvisation skills shine.

Having told Watson that Moriarty will follow them in a special because he is Holmes' intellectual equal, Holmes makes Watson hide, because it must be Moriarty! But when this train fails to stop, it still is Moriarty, who is suddenly, almost, but not quite as intelligent as Holmes or his train would have stopped. In the unlikely event Watson spotted this illogic, Father quickly offered the best of all Watsonian distractions — lunch.

Any way you slice it, it's the baloney of bold-faced balderdash and improvising genius.

I'm sure you noted, Attentive Reader, that Watson never saw the telegram, allegedly from the London police, before Holmes threw it – where else – into the fire? It could have said anything and been from anyone. It might not have even been a telegram.

Of course, the tailor-made suggestion that the stalwart Watson turn tail and "return to his practice" equally achieved Holmes' intended opposite result. He knew when to push his hand and when to underplay it. He understood to his core that in improvisation, sometimes less is more. To jump at a falling rock, to accuse that rock of attempted murder by body language alone, that is a master improviser at the height of his craft.

Which is not to say that Watson was telling the whole truth, either. I do not for one second believe that even Holmes was ever vain enough to proclaim, *"The air of London is sweeter for my presence."* Perhaps Watson's inner Boswell got mugged by his inner Byron.

I would bet all my pink pages that Father also never said this, *"In over a thousand cases, I am not aware that I have ever used my powers upon the wrong side."* There are several reasons why that must be Watsonian hyperbole.

Father would have stated the exact number of cases, and chided Watson for numerical laxity. Secondly, Watson's estimate is mathematically impossible. Father had been detecting some twelve years – since 1879. That totals 4,380 days. Some cases were solved in days; some took weeks. As documented by Watson, Father also had languishing periods between cases. You do not have to be the Maths genius Moriarty to compute that Holmes could not possibly have solved a thousand cases. That would equal a case every four days, non-stop with no breaks, for the entire twelve years. Tante Grizelda estimated the truth as some three cases per month, which totals to four-hundred-thirty-two cases – a far more logical deduction.

For the record, I also note Father's continued manipulation of damsels in distress.

While the good doctor would have sprung to the assistance of anyone in medical need, Holmes skillfully blends paternalism and patriotism to fabricate Watsons's perfect patient – not just ill, but dying. Not just a lady, but an English lady in a foreign land. One who longs to die in the arms of a brave English doctor. Against such a perfectly presented prank, the poor man never stood a chance.

As for that Swiss youth who was never found?

Suffice it to say, that on May 4, 1891, when Watson and the man he trusted above all others began ascending Reichenbach Falls, and a boy came running with a note about a sick English tourist, Father's words from New Year's morning proved prophetic, "What is plainer than a child as plain as you hidden in plain sight? A dead child."

Watson looked right at me, thanked me for the note and patted my shoulder. But he never saw me. He never noticed that this boy limped. I grant that he believed Wiggins dead in a London grave. Ergo, the boy in a Swiss hat hiding until Watson exited could not possibly be me.

It took very little staging for Holmes to become "the man in black". He slipped unseen halfway down the path, turned his grey coat to its black lining, altered his gait, and became a tall man trudging back up the path. I saw him taking sideways glances to ensure Watson saw him.

What would Holmes have done if Watson believed he had spied Moriarty, and charged back up the hill waving his revolver? Conversely, what would either of them have done if Watson, in a flash of atypical brilliance as he headed down the path, had figured out when he glanced up behind him that since the nobody had passed him on their way up, the only man who could still be up there must be Holmes?

I do not know. I can only assume Father knew every bump of Watson's brain and had deduced that the lobe wherein Watson kept both his Hippocratic Oath and his masculine vow of chivalry would prove more dominant than any other part of his skull. For Holmes, Watson's departure was but a tactical diversion. It bought my father the time he needed to plant his pre-written letter.

Here, please permit me a moment's ire. It has long bothered me that of all the inane things Watson and his reading public swallowed, they believed a vicious criminal mastermind would call a truce in deadly hand-to-hand combat to permit his nemesis to calmly pen a romantic farewell to a friend.

The real Moriarty would have stabbed Homes through the eye with his own pen.

No one used Holmes' methods to expose the illogic. The note was written in ink. No one ever asked why Holmes, who always carried a pencil, suddenly went hiking through the Swiss Alps with a fragile crystal inkpot. When Watson notes *"the diction was firm and clear, as though it had been written in his study,"* it's one of his rare insights. That is exactly where it was written.

After pondering Holmes' usury of Watson for decades, this is the kindest I can be. In their last travels, Father gave Watson a great gift – the chance to do what he loved best for several days running. Next to saving damsels, Watson loved to share that tingle of danger, loved to feel himself the manly body-guard, the valued crime-fighting confederate of the great Sherlock Holmes.

But even if that letter was meant as parting consolation, it was also a nasty, final dig at Watson's lack of intelligence. Father flaunted the fact that he had instantly known what Watson did not – that the note and the sick English lady were fabrications. To this day, I find it vexingly vain to take credit for spotting a hoax you authored yourself.

But there is a further truth here. Perhaps the green-eyed monster is always barking mad, and I fully admit to being jealous of Watson. He survived unscathed. Holmes valued him enough to arrange a kind good-bye. I was the one who did not survive except with injury and trauma.

I was the one who let Sherlock Holmes murder me twice.

As Father's note detailed, upon Watson's departure, I was to come out of hiding and set the stage by fabricating signs of a death scuffle for two. Pulling the huge hiking boots from my rucksack, I laid down a second set of man-size tracks straight up the muddy hill to falls.

I did not hear or see the villain coming.

He attacked swiftly, from behind.

A man far stronger than I'd ever be, wrestled me through branches and ferns, dragged me to the rushing water. In that moment, I knew what it was to be my mother, to have an animal hold your life in his clawing hands. My heart yelled the word she made me fear all my life, "Rape!"

Then, at the crumbling edge, at the last possible instant, my father pulled his screaming child back from certain death.

He set me down, permitting me to recover.

Then he covered with a casual, improvised aplomb, as if nothing more serious had transpired than a scene partner had flubbed a line.

"The marks of scuffle must show a deadly desperation, Wiggins, thus I could not warn you. Your fear must be credible, and you could not credibly pretend it. You have my congratulations. That was a most convincingly terrified death yell you improvised for Moriarty. Now quickly, throw his large boots over the edge with the rest of him. We must not be caught with them."

I threw them, wishing they were him. Wishing I had a pink boot with guillotine kick.

Regretting, yet again, that I could never kick him. It would hurt only me and no one else.

Following his lead, we both walked backwards in his original footprints just as we had practiced innumerable times in London's mud and snow. It set the stage exactly as he planned, leaving his and a set of larger footprints approaching the falls, with no man's footprints leaving the scene. At a patch of hard ground, Holmes swiveled forward and ran us back to the shed. I opened the door on my travelling case, my trunk and a larger one, which I took to be Father's.

The reason for my training in quick change artistry quickly became apparent.

Five minutes later, our coachman, a white-whiskered Herr Froehlich, appeared exactly as instructed by Father's telegram. He drove in all haste, eager to earn the large tip the telegram promised if Miss Euphemia Mclean and her guardian met the evening train to Brussels.

When the real Herr Froehlich was later asked by Swiss authorities if he had conveyed any "unsavory characters" to the falls that day, he truthfully answered that no, he had not. After the previous night at his local tavern, where some American tourists had paid for many an appreciative toast to Swiss chocolate, Swiss misses, Swiss clockwork and Swiss cheese, he had slept all that day.

Unbeknownst to him, another Herr Froehlich met us, telegram in hand. He apologized for having to bring both his wife and a large cage of squawking chickens. Had anyone asked him, he would have said Miss Euphemia's namesake spinster aunt, Miss Hortensia Mclean, had been a bit of a flirt for her age, but given the generosity of her purse and her bosom, he had seen no reason to consider her "unsavory."

I have little memory of that carriage ride.

Until I both saw and observed.

Then, and only then, I began to cry.

Tears of relief joined tears of rage.

A voluminous polka-dot bonnet completely concealed Frau Froehlich's face. But beneath the Swiss hausfrau skirt that held held chickens sat a pair of pink boots.

Tante Grizelda's this time, but equally deadly.

In Herr Froehlich, I then recognized Godfrey Norton, aged three decades and clad in a truly transformative costume, including tiny ringing bells dangling from his hat and a luxuriant white moustache.

My real family had not abandoned me. They sat in silent symbolic solidarity as I wished I could have, with their backs turned on my murdering failure of a father, with their eyes on the horizon.

Chapter Twelve: The Escape of the Ersatz-Lady Euphemia McLean

We returned circuitously – of course we did – back from Brussels to Britain. At least I was not asked to walk the English Channel backwards in his footsteps.

After several attempts to draw me out, Holmes left me to myself. I retreated into the world of my mother's letters, noting that her father had likewise failed her in ways she did not deserve.

October 2, 1875

Dearest Duncan,

After days of ultimatums, outbursts and silences, Father sent Mother on a trip back to Egg Harbor City. He then came into my room last night to mount what I think will be his last objection to our union. I must say how sad he looked. I had not seen it before as he hid it under his anger.

I took his hand and told him how much I loved him. I said he wasn't losing his daughter. I'd be just across the ravine, safe on his brother's farm. I swore again I would stay a Catholic in a Baptist home.

I sought to comfort him, but for reasons I cannot explain, I gave him more pain. He lowered his head in his hands and groaned, "He does not love you. He cannot love you."

I pulled his hands from his face, smiled my best smile.

"Don't worry, Da. I love him enough for both of us."

With that, he left my room, sat down at his chair and reached for his whittling. About a half an hour I heard him, so soft it was all but a whisper.

"Fine, daughter. I have done my best, but cannot stop you. Enough is enough."

It is the only blessing we will ever get from him. But he is right. It is enough.

Yours, and finally soon to be so, in wedded mind, body and soul,

Reenie

I must not gloss over the parallels that hurt me afresh with each re-reading of this sad letter. My own father had likewise issued unexplained orders, but not ever shared the true concerns so clearly on his mind. He not only failed to save me from heartache; he caused the heartache. Then he expected me to keep following his plans and orders without explanation or apology, as if he had done nothing wrong.

Father held Watson equally in thrall. He correctly assumed Watson would run back to the hotel to raise a loud hue and cry with the Swiss authorities. But, waiting for him on the front steps, Watson found a pretty Swiss Miss with a second note from Holmes stating that in the event that anything happened to him, Watson must promise to elude the dread Moriarty by immediately taking the next train back to

London. He must equally promise to say absolutely not one word to anyone about Holmes' death until he first broke the news to the good Mrs. Hudson.

Accordingly, the "examination by experts" Watson mentions is a lie. It never occurred. While Father felt it likely that the Swiss Police were even less expert than Scotland Yard, he could not take the risk of their examination for fear of exposure. Ergo, he ensured that no one but the inexpert Watson ever examined the scene of his murderous hoax.

The improvising theatrics Holmes pulled next can be seen as solicitous and selfish, as kind and unconscionable. I think it a contradictory both, and leave its judgment to you.

As Miss Euphemia and her elderly great-aunt guardian, Miss Hortensia, we not only took the same train as Watson, we also sat beside him. Father had, of course, failed to warn me of this impromptu test of my improvising abilities. A despondent Watson said little. For once, Father had the good taste not to provoke the poor man for sport.

When Watson apologized for being a poor travelling companion as he was struggling with sudden death of a dear friend, Father clutched Watson's hand to Miss Hortensia's ample bosom, and offered condolences. Yes, Disgusted Reader, you do recognize Father's spoon-fed words as later dutifully regurgitated by Watson, "He is the best and wisest man you have ever known."

I have always said the last line was always his. My hat is off to him, in my deepest bow. Only a master improviser could write the last line of his own eulogy.

At least the Wonderful World of Duping Watson kept Holmes from any close examination of other passengers. Safe from scrutiny in another car were a clean-shaven Barnardo official, a.k.a. Godfrey Norton, travelling with two plain-bonneted Quaker ladies, escorting homeless children bound for American ports unknown.

What a caravan of deception and deceit we made!

As Godfrey followed Watson to ensure he made it safely to Baker Street, and the Irregulars fanned out from the train station to slow Watson's passage, another cabby sped ahead. Behind the closed curtains of that carriage, a pirate demonstrated her own quick change artistry, by doffing a pair of pink boots and donning Mrs. Hudson's apron.

Secreted as great-aunt and niece in a hotel near the train station, Father and I awaited our departure. Holmes wanted a fast trip to North America via the best that modern science could supply, and so had chosen a steamship in the White Star Line – *The Majestic*. It had made its maiden voyage from Liverpool to New York a year earlier, in 1890, in an amazing six days and ten hours. A serious improvement over sailing ships like Captain Hudson's good ship *Grizelda*, which took weeks. On our voyage, Historically-Savvy Reader, you might be interested in this: the *Majestic's* captain was E.J. Smith, soon and better known as the ill-fated captain of the *Titanic*.

I thought it good omen that we boarded the ship on my fifteenth birthday – June 23, 1891. Of course, this little bastard could not tell my father and there was no celebration.

On our voyage, we had no icy collisions except that of wills. I could fathom no reason why Father had reserved us such a small set of second-class rooms in the aft of the ship. He certainly had means for a more comfortable passage.

Our tiny bedrooms held but a bed and a trunk. I kept my travelling case, with its secret compartment of Mother's letters, under my bed. We shared a water closet the size of the confessional at St. Ambrose, and a sitting room containing two chairs and a tiny dining table. It did double duty as my school desk and displayer of Father's maps.

To the best of his knowledge, we both retired early and slept all night in our own rooms.

Always at home on the water, I loved the rolling of the ship. But being cooped up with a green-faced gumshoe was enough to make me say I'd gladly have boarded the *Grizelda* for a month-long crossing in steerage, complete with uncooped chickens, dung-dropping cattle and any number of odiferous families. Anything would be better than being locked up in a hot cabin and grilled like a porterhouse about my delimited deportment at our dubious destination. I am particularly partial to the sizzling excesses of this last paragraph and do hope you enjoyed it.

But I mustn't overstate my plight. I was no prisoner.

I had redressed as a boy for the voyage, Father deducing it would better serve to hide me as a girl in Canada. As a boy, I was able to join him for hearty constitutionals on deck, walks that often devolved into a spirited Hide-and-Seek-Tag. He also created several treasure hunts for me, leaving clues around the ship that led me back to him. But our recreation took place under strict schedule, always and only for ninety minutes precisely at 10:00 and again at 2:00 every day. We walked each time along the port side to amidships, crossed over, and then jaunted down the starboard side. I was forbidden to make a full lap of the ship, or to leave our cabin without him.

This aroused my suspicion, not to mention my teenage pride. This little Wiggins had a map of London in her own head; I would not get lost on a boat. What could possibly be in the fore that was not in the aft? While I knew an Irregular nothing about ships, beyond what I'd gleaned from *Mutiny on the Bounty*, I could neither stop worrying, nor ask the question that soured my mind – was Father so ashamed of limping me that kept me from meeting the first-class passengers?

But I never protested.

I only asked why I could not go out alone.

Father's Captain Bligh rightly saw no danger from my fledgling Fletcher Christian. He waved my inquiries away with a breezy hand.

"There are dangers on a ship with which a city lad like you is entirely unfamiliar. I must be with you in the event that you encounter Moriarty, or anything, or anyone, you should not."

While I wanted to retort that after abandoning me to fend for myself in a Whitechapel ditch, his new concern felt more than a tad too little, and fifteen years too late, to matter.

"Tread softly, Wiggins," he said noting my scowl. "There are things I cannot explain. Please accept that as your custodial adult, I have your best interests at heart."

For the first night, I obeyed him and stayed put. I hummed the song of Skye boatmen as the ship rocked me to sleep. To my surprise, I heard Holmes take up its refrain on his violin. On the second night, not even Bonnie Prince Charlie, himself, could have comforted me. I would suffocate without the stars. If I grieved my mother when I opened my eyes each morning, if her loss hit me again at any moment throughout the day, it was only at night, alone with the sharp tiny points of light we both so loved, that I could open my heart to missing starlit London, and all that had been my Danny, my Irregular family, and the warrior home I had been forced to abandon.

Little germane to our story occurred at sea, with two important exceptions: *The Mendacious Matter of Manufacturing Myths for Watson,* and *The Calamitous Incident of the Kiss in the Nighttime.*

Let me, for once, put Watson first. I believe Father missed him terribly. I imagine he also missed Mycroft, no matter how glad I was to be free of him. Indisputably, Holmes missed London. He read and re-read his last copy of the *Times*, then sat, eyes closed and morose. No doubt some of his green around the gills was home-sickness. To keep some part of home and hearth with him, he spent a great deal of time gleefully planning what to tell Watson about our absence from London.

The question of Holmes' whereabouts from 1891-1893, romantically referred to as "The Great Hiatus", began as a game – a simple pastime. To entertain each other, we tried to come up with the most outrageous places on the planet Watson would eventually be told Father had been, lies all fabricated to mask the years he would spend in Canada with me.

To be clear, there never was a Norwegian explorer named Sigerson. Like the boy in my grave, he was but a decoy replacement for a not-so-dead Holmes. I've often thought Father borrowed his name from King Sigismund. It would be a fitting jibe at the vile king to steal his name for an indigent commoner, to rub it in his class-proud face that a vagabond named Sigerson had sons he would never have.

Father also used our hiatus banter to continue my teachings in world geography. He would unfurl a map, I would close my eyes and point, and he would tell a tale of that location and culture so real and in such dazzling detail that I could not tell if it was imagination or experience. He made it all so tantalizing, we could not settle on which spots to offer Watson.

We considered Pitcairn Island, Prussia, Patagonia and Poughkeepsie. I pointed out the impossibility of anyone's destinations all commencing with "P."

Father laughed, then spouted an improvised lecture on *impossible* vs. *improbable*.

I tuned him out to think about Pitcairn Island, made famous by a mutiny on the good ship *Bounty*. It was maddening not to be able to regale Holmes with my enthusiasm for it via Lord Byron, Jules Verne and Mark Twain. I'd already made the grievous error of letting him see I was not a literary blank slate. Hoping he'd be tempted by its early-manuscript library, rivaled only the Vatican, I pointed to Mount Sinai and suggested St. Catherine's Monastery. When he asked how I knew about it, I covered poorly. In truth, it was Tante Gisela's dream to pilgrimage there. Unable to say so, I said I'd seen a picture in a Bible as the spot where Moses saw the burning bush.

"Should we ever encounter a burning bush in Mayfair, Wiggins, whether it is the Messiah masquerading as a maple leaf, whether it ever utters so much as 'pass the crumpets,' we must sell it to make our fortunes. What do Canadians call eternal warmth in winter? A miracle indeed."

In mutual entertainment, egging each other on, we became geographical hucksters; a pair of P.T. Barnums, manufacturing hokum explanations for the hiatus as fantastical as the Feejee Mermaid. We sent Holmes to the head lama in Lhassa, to the Khalifa in Khartoum, to Montpellier in pursuit of the pleasures of coal tar. I feared our self-indulgence guaranteed exposure, but Father assured me Watson and his almost-as-gullible fans would gobble up every sticky-pudding word.

At his second mention of food, noting my travelling companion keen of eye and no longer any shade of green, I asked him something verboten before I thought better of it.

"Your medicine? Did you take it today?"

Father's eyes darkened.

"I had hoped not to need it in our travels together, Wiggins. I had hoped for a fresh start. I'm sorry to say it was necessary today. I assure you, however, it is a clear mind that selects our dissembling destinations. I promise you, they will all be believed."

In this, as you know full well, Loyal Reader, he proved entirely correct. Every lie we told, Watson duly inscribed, *The Strand* duly published, and like a plate of honeyed crumpets, the public hungrily, gratefully swallowed. Father's explanation haunts me still.

"It is firstly true that the public is eager to believe the good-hearted Watson. His is a voice they know and trust. They believe he speaks directly to them as confidant and friend. It is likewise true that he has already established me as larger than life. But sadly, Wiggins, please also mark this: human beings tend to believe whatever they are told. They especially believe the story they hear first."

Here he must have seen me smiling as he paused to let me share it.

"Like the street gossip all Irregulars hear. Folks start defendin' whatever story they heard first. As if it belonged to 'em. As if anybody else was making things up. People got right vexed. Stuck to their story even if it got proved wrong. Like it was their own face they were saving."

Father nodded. "Them, Wiggins, with a t-h. But otherwise well spoken, even astute."

Unable to take a compliment, I bowed, then halfway through turned it into a curtsey.

Father laughed. "Storytellers like Watson – exuding good humour, authoritative confidence and a soupçon of humility – can sound truthful even when they have only shared but Watson's Half of the Story. In other words, only that portion of the data that leaves teller, story, and reader, all in the most flattering and comfortable of lights."

His comments returned to my mind later that evening. They offered an eerily accurate explanation of how my young mother in love couldn't see in her unlucky thirteenth letter that the deceptive voice telling her only Watson's Half of the Story was her own.

October 10, 1875

My Dearest Fiancé Duncan, how I love to write that word!

How proud I was when Father Mc Kniven read the bans in church today! The greetings of all in the parish were so warm and flattering. I was only sorry that you, Uncle John and Aunt Ida could not be there. But I have promised Mutti that you shall be changing faith soon and that she has no reason to fear for my immortal soul. Please tell me that is true?

I have finished sewing my new dress, trimmed with some perfect French lace sent by Grandmother Adler all the way from Egg Harbor City. I am sorry they will not attend, but it is a long journey. I will also wear the lovely purple shawl I won from Jenny Lind on the night we first sang together. I am ready, so very ready. I count each day and each long, lonely night.

In the one sour note, I saw Home Boy today when he came for his violin lesson. I hoped he would congratulate me, but instead he stood in the doorway, struggled with an emotion neither he nor I could name, then ran from me as if I might spread some kind of foul contagion.

Oh, well. He is gone and of no import. Soon, and then always, to be yours,

Reenie

Chapter Thirteen: The Adventure of the Missing Barnum

No doubt you have been wondering, Engaged Reader, why I have so far omitted from my tale one vital scene: my tearful good-bye with my own beloved Danny. Perhaps you have been wondering where it occurred. Was it a final stolen moment on the dock, in our kitchen, or at our own private bolthole? Those are good guesses, but all would be wrong.

Do you yet have so little sense of my character? Have I so inadequately warned you of my stubborn pride? I was a teenager in love. I would no more say good-bye to Danny than I would abandon my beloved cap.

In happy coincidence, thanks to the truthful and tactful penmanship of Tante Gisela, Danny had his own good reason for coming to America.

The Honorable Phineas Taylor Barnum
Marina Estate, Bridgeport, Connecticut,
The United States of America
March 8, 1891

Dear Sir,

In recognition of the unorthodox nature of this letter, and in full appreciation of the likelihood that any man might rightly look askance at such an intrusive correspondence from a total stranger, please permit me to first assure you of both my character and my sincerity.

My name is Miss Gisela Adler, and while I am now a resident of London, I hail from your part of the world: Egg Harbor City, New Jersey. Before moving to England in 1879, I was a schoolteacher, and eventually headmistress, in my hometown's Transcendence School for Girls, based upon the visionary teachings of Bronson Alcott, a man I believe you know well through your joint work in abolitionist causes. For five years, I was a nurse in the Civil War and opposed slavery with my heart and soul. As did my father, Doctor Laurenz Adler, who is now Chief of Staff at the Egg Harbor City Hospital. Please feel free to write him as to my credibility and authenticity.

I must also state, Mr. Barnum, when I gathered evidence to determine whether or not to send this letter, I was most impressed by all I learned as to your own character. Here in London, newspapers emphasize the sensational aspects of your life: Tom Thumb, the Feejee Mermaid, the sad death of Jumbo, the burning of the American Museum, the fabulous wealth generated by the tour of the Swedish Nightingale, Jenny Lind. These stories cast you as larger-than-life and, forgive me, as a grandstanding impresario.

I was delighted to learn you are also mayor of Bridgeport, humanitarian, teetotaler and temperance lecturer, founding Board Member and largest donor to Tufts University, President and principal benefactor of Bridgeport Hospital, a man who served his country in the Connecticut legislature for several terms. I am willing to look beyond the circus of rumor and reputation. This second man is the one to whom I am appealing today.

The nature of my request is personal to the extreme. I shall endeavor to handle it with all possible sensitivity. For the past three years, since 1887, my family and I have had the good fortune to know a local boy, a young man we hired to run errands and do odd jobs for our somewhat irregular household of women, being my twin sister, my niece and her daughter. This young man has proven himself a most intelligent, trust-worthy, good-humored, amiable, and quick-witted lad. Not only has he become indispensable to our household and the trusted best friend of my niece, we all value him as a member of our family. His sad years as an impoverished street urchin left no permanent stain on his character. He has become a fine young man.

To be direct, Mr. Barnum, his name is Daniel Phineas Barnum. His birthdate is March 8, 1875. Today is our Danny's sixteenth birthday. And today and every day, he proudly believes he is your son.

As the young Mr. Barnum has been told his story, after your first wife died in 1873, you sailed for London. On this trip, you first met Jumbo, the elephant you eventually purchased for your circus, when you attended the London Zoo with Sir William Henry Flowers, his children and his children's governess, one Amelia Worthington. She was Danny's mother.

This much I can corroborate – your first wife of forty years, Charity Hallet Barnum, died November 17, 1873. Sir William Flowers is a surgeon and anatomist of indisputable repute. Besides being decorated by the Queen for his service in the Crimea, he has also, since 1879, been the President of the London Zoological Society which runs the zoo. One Amelia Worthington did work for the Flowers family as their governess until 1875. Members of the household affirm that Sir William did indeed meet you through the zoo in 1873. You stayed some weeks at Sir William's home at 26 Stanhope Gardens. He still counts you as one of his closest friends.

I assure you, Sir, these inquiries were detected through a professional third party with the utmost of discretion, by a man who did not, in any way, or at any time, suggest or imply, that you might be linked to Miss Worthington in any manner, let alone a romantic or scandalous one.

Amelia was greatly valued by the Flowers family, who were most saddened to hear of her death in childbirth. Danny lived the first eleven years of his life knowing nothing about his father. Whenever he asked his grandmother, she refused to discuss it. There was no one else to ask.

On her deathbed in 1886, his grandmother finally confessed. Grief-stricken by her daughter's death, desperate to keep something of her daughter with her, she had written you falsely claiming that both your wife and child had died. When she begged Danny's forgiveness, it is so telling of this kind young man's generosity of spirit, that he immediately and unstintingly forgave her.

For the last four years, three of them with us, Danny has lived in a limbo of uncertainty, longing to contact you, but unsure how to do so, both excited by and dreading your response.

I have taken the liberty, Sir, of having two copies made of the one photo Danny has of his mother, revealed to him from its hiding place by his grandmother right before her passing. I enclose said copy with this letter. It depicts a young woman in a simple lace wedding dress, and an older man who looks quite like Danny, with the same snapping eyes and curly black hair. As also confirmed by the Flowers household, the woman is definitely Amelia, and the gentleman is exactly as they remember their famous American houseguest, one Phineas Taylor Barnum.

Let me now be blunt. Someone with your wealth and notoriety, my dear Mr. Barnum, has no doubt already encountered would-be blackmailers. Unscrupulous sorts who would take a perverted pride in attempting to hoodwink "The Prince of Humbugs." My entreaty has nothing whatsoever to do with money. I assure you that such a vile thing as blackmail never once crossed my mind.

It is with all delicacy that I further admit that I am aware that certain newspapers and persons various already claim you have another illegitimate son, one who is training at your expense to be a doctor, and who I understand you have treated well. That is all I wish for Danny.

Likewise, Daniel has no agenda. He does not know I have contacted you. Having discussed the matter at length with my sister and my niece, we agreed that, as his custodial adults, we must send this letter in secret. We uniformly decided to share only the result with our Daniel to spare him weeks of tangled hope and worry the knowledge of this correspondence would bring. Our only desire is for you to be fully apprised of the facts, to make your own informed decision.

Our family happily has both the means and the love to continue caring for him for life, but in the most fundamental of human ways, Danny is still alone. I trust you agree with us, an innocent child has suffered enough. Please know my family sees you as similarly blameless – you were never told you have a child. In light of your advancing years, we do not want either of you robbed of your last chance to know each other.

Conversely, Mr. Barnum, if you do not claim this boy, it is better to break his heart now, while he still young and resilient enough to mend. He deserves to know your answer so he can either look his upon his father's face, or turn his eyes to a future of his own making.

I close with your own words from your most-uplifting autobiography, "The Life of P.T. Barnum: Written By Himself," a speech made as a member of Connecticut Legislature in support of the ratification of the Thirteenth Amendment which ended slavery, "A human soul that God has created and Christ died for, is not to be trifled with." You hold a child's fate, their very hope, health and happiness in your hands. I beg you not to trifle with Danny's immortal soul, nor with your own. I leave this matter to your most capable and, I hope, compassionate conscience.

I stand ready to answer any questions you might ever have of me. Your obedient and hopeful servant in the loving mercy of our Heavenly Father,

Gisela Adler

Marina Estate

Bridgeport, Connecticut

March 28, 1891

To the Dear, Kind-hearted, Conscientious Christian, Miss Gisela Adler,

Yes, yes, a lifetime of yes! I must tell you forthwith, Dear Lady, that I am over-joyed, delighted, and frankly shedding an old man's grateful tears to receive your remarkable correspondence. Eternally yes, I knew, and loved, and married, the precious woman in the photograph you sent me. To see her smile again raises my spirits to stratospheric heights! For it is indeed the smile of my bride, and we truly were the most ecstatic of newlyweds. I trust that you and young Daniel will give me permission to keep this copy you sent me? I once had my own.

It traveled with me always, in a special cabinet designed to hold my dearest photographs, including those of my first wife and four darling daughters. I have long been *despondent at being unable to save it in the fire that broke out in my hotel rooms on that dark night of September 15, 1884, when Jumbo died. In my advancing age, to be able to gaze again on my departed darling's beloved face again – that is a gift I never expected. Please tell Daniel, what I soon hope to be able to tell the dear boy myself – I loved his mother and grieved her loss as the loss of my own life.*

For I did indeed receive the devastating letter from Amelia's mother, Mrs. Lucinda Worthington, announcing the childbed death of Amelia and our newborn child. And, again yes, if God had blessed us with a boy, we had decided to name him Daniel. What a fine name it is! It pays homage to Amelia's father, to the victor in the Lion's Den, and I confess, to one of my equally brave childhood heroes – he of the Bowie knife and the Alamo, one Daniel Boone. If for no other reason than this, the self-same perfectly chosen name, I am certain he is my son.

In further deceit for which I have no explanation, Mrs. Worthington's false letter, also falsely claimed the stillborn child had been a girl. Had I any reason to doubt my new mother-in-law's veracity, I would certainly have investigated. But who would lie about such a horrific thing?

I cannot conceive of any reason to justify lying to her daughter's husband and then for the rest of her life to lie to the very face of her own flesh-and-blood grand-child! Perhaps she did not want the boy raised here in America? Perhaps she felt my circus was immoral? Or perhaps in her grief of losing her daughter, she simply could not also lose her daughter's child? I can only speculate as to her motivations, but I can assure you this, Miss Adler, had she ever written me truthfully, had I known my darling son lived, I would never have abandoned my own dear child.

Oh, the years she has cost us both! It beyond bearing, but her sins are with God. Blaming life for being life is always a fool's mission. When life hurts us, however cruel and arbitrary, we must simply go on living. For years, I have mourned the loss of my wife. Now I mourn the loss of my child's childhood. Yesterday must be accepted as a loss that can never be recovered. But today is still ours. Some good can come of yesterday's loss.

Please be advised that my third wife, Nancy Fish Barnum, is both a good woman and one of my oldest friends. She has known her own sorrows. We married, shortly after Amelia's death, to provide each other home and comfort. I have shared your letter with her and she, too, wept tears of joy. Both Nancy and I would be delighted to make the young man's acquaintance.

When you feel the time is right, my dear Miss Adler, please give my dear son this letter. I have today also seen to the deposit of £100 in his name at Barclay's Bank of London, and I shall happily send him any further funds he might need for his present comfort, and hopefully, to soon make the journey to my home in America. Should you, and any of your family be willing to chaperone him, I would gladly pay your expenses as well, and would welcome the opportunity to thank you for the years you have devoted to his care. I know he has been in excellent hands.

Not wishing to cast a pall on this happy day, I must in all conscience and pointed truth add that Daniel should know I have not been well. Time is a hovering thief, looking to snatch up what little happiness we might have left. Should he be willing, I would love to claim him as my own and offer him, if belatedly, the chance to shake my hand as his father, and meet me as my son.

Thank you again, Miss Adler, for your heaven-sent intervention in this matter. I remain, your most grateful servant and a very proud new father,

Phineas Taylor Barnum

Only a short few days later, an already ecstatic young man received from Tante Gisela yet a second letter from his father. One that my aunties understood in all its implications, but I did not.

March 30, 1891

My dear, delivering Miss Adler,

While it is unusual to send a second letter before your reply to my first, I confess that I find myself giddy in anticipation of it, and made even more so by another letter which I have only this morning received from your father, Dr. Laurenz Adler, in Egg Harbor City.

I must, in all fairness, confess that I did contact him, dear lady, but only after I accepted your letter in and of itself as genuine, and had replied to you on faith alone. Dr. Adler, as I knew he would, confirmed your authenticity and sincerity, and also shared with me the most extraordinary piece of news – that your niece was one of the most respected names in opera, the late, great, Irene Adler. My condolences to you and yours for your inestimable loss.

This brings me to one of my life's greatest inexplicabilities, and I cannot adequately explain just how excited I am to share it with you. I like to think it is kindness come full circle.

Many years ago, a lifetime ago, as Dr. Adler reminded me in his letter, I had occasion not only to meet him in person, but also to bring a young couple together when they were but little older than my son is today. If I may blow my own horn for one moment, I was one small link in the chain of events that led to Irene Adler's operatic destiny. How is this possible, you ask?

On tour with the Swedish Songbird, Miss Jenny Lind, in the autumn of 1851, we were in the lovely town London, Ontario. Ms. Lind's carriage was detained, and I was desperate to keep the over-flowing crowd happy. In every audience, there is always a girl with some singing ability, and so I asked, as I had often done before, for my assistants to seek one out and put her on stage. It usually produced a sweet, if amateurish, version of a modern ditty. It also gave some brave young woman a lovely, once-in-a-lifetime memory and held the crowd until my star arrived.

I was totally unprepared, however, when my assistants found both a strapping local Canadian farmer and a pretty American tourist, visiting London with her parents, who were speaking at a local Anti-Slavery gathering, the very one that I would be attending myself the next day. Both these young people were stubbornly adamant that they wanted to be my opening act.

I threw up my hands saying I could not decide between them and they must sing together or not at all. Knowing there can be no admission of coincidence or accident in the theater, knowing you must always bow and take credit for both, I went out on stage and sold it as a magical moment – two star-crossed strangers, a boy and a girl chosen by fate, performing here on our stage together for the very first time. The crowd went wild.

She was such a tiny thing in a green velvet dress, her sweet face so serious, framed by long red curls. He looked an unlikely musician, a lumbering Scottish farm boy. I confess I feared she would faint and he would sound like a milch cow, but they produced some truly lovely harmonies singing "The Sky Boat Song." When the sweet girl took the shy boy's hand, they sang as if they were the only two hearts in the room.

To this day, I believe we witnessed two people falling in love in front of our very eyes. When Miss Lind arrived, she waited in the wings, refusing to interrupt until their last note.

195

As the crowd rose to their feet, Miss Lind ran on stage and hugged them, bestowing on the now shivering Miss Adler, her own purple shawl, in a most gracious thank you.

This young couple were, of course, fated to become Miss Irene Adler's parents. The young woman was your older sister, Gerda Adler, who as I remember was all of sixteen at the time. The next morning, there was quite the commotion in the lobby when the young Mr. Mclean bravely returned the young lady to her parents. He insisted there was no reputation ruined, that Miss Adler had sought him out entirely of her own doing, and they had sat up chatting in his hotel lobby until dawn made it safe to return. Despite his white knight defense, Dr. and Mrs. Adler acquiesced to their daughter's firm insistence that the two lovebirds must be married immediately.

I understand that your newly-wed sister continued to corresponded with Miss Lind for years after this event, and they grew to become friends. I understand she entrusted some of her marital concerns with the kind Miss Lind and, I am certain, she provided sage advice.

It also later came to my ear that sometime in 1875, after a fire in which Mr. Mclean was presumed to have perished, that Gerda's seventeen-year-old daughter had both abundant talent and good reason to leave home. Miss Lind happily sent her letter of introduction. I understand this is how the young Miss Mclean, now calling herself Miss Adler, met Wladyslaw Prysybylinski, the director of the Warsaw Opera. And, as they say, the rest is history.

I do not know, my dear Miss Adler, if you were aware of this connection between us, but I hold it as divinely serendipitous. Time and time again life proves it true: human history is so often akin to hokum; borderline believable, full of the strangest coincidences imaginable. At the end of my history, I hope to spend my last days as a whole man, as an imperfect father to all my children.

Anxiously awaiting your reply, and hopefully one from my son, Daniel Phineas Barnum,

Your most grateful servant,

Phineas Taylor Barnum

Understandably delighted by both letters, Danny carried them about on his person at all times. If I only read the second letter once and handed it quickly back to him, if I soured to read how easily, instantly and lovingly, his father claimed him, I assure you, Concerned Reader, that green moment quickly passed. I also noted that, privately, my aunties seemed less than celebratory. They huddled together, frowning, more than once.

"We are just surprised, dear," Tante Gisela explained. "We don't cast aspersions on Mr. Barnum's version of the story, as we were young when our sister Gerda married, but we were always told your grandparents met at an Abolitionist meeting and that a love-struck Alexander proposed on the spot." She shrugged and glanced at her sister. "But it is true that Gerda was a decidedly modern girl."

Tante Grizelda grunted. "Merciful Mother, wherever can she have gotten that from?"

"But still, your mother appeared late on the scene and remained an only child," Tante Gisela added, still looking troubled. When she asked, "Do you have any quest—?" one pink boot kicked another quiet.

I deduced their discomfort had something to do with the contradiction between their sister's quick marriage, but much-delayed birth of her only child. A delay, I confess, I longed to know how to repeat.

In his "information on the limitation of offspring," John Harvey Kellogg went so far as to claim this was actually desirable for reasons of health or poverty. He suggested that certain times of the month may be less likely to result in conception. He even made passing mention of the use of "shields, veils and sponges," none of which I understood, except as a mortal sin.

I had no explanation how a young couple desperately in love when they married in 1851, held off having a child, my mother, until 1858. I did find pictures of babies with clubbed feet that looked so much like my feet I had to close the book. But no matter how much that hurt me, I could not even contemplate the other method of "limitation" Dr. Kellogg mentioned: THE HEINOUS CRIME OF ABORTION. For him it was an abomination and, as priests had drilled into me for all my life, it meant eternal hellfire. I didn't dare ask my devout Tante Gisela about it.

Believing my own story because I heard it first, I repeated the error most people made with the seventeen steps: I saw the facts of Danny's letter, but failed to observe them. I didn't note that my grandmother met her farm boy husband in London, Ontario. Or that Alexander, and thus his Mclean family, were the ones "local" to Ontario.

Since I was born in New Jersey, and my Adler grandparents lived in New Jersey, it had never occurred to me that that my parents could have grown up anywhere other than New Jersey. All the addresses on my mother's letters had been erased. As I read them, I assumed, despite the repetition of the name Mclean, that the farm she described was in New Jersey. Today, I can only assume my aunties stifled my curiosity in the hope that what you don't read correctly can't hurt you.

But off, course, Dr. Kellogg, Sherlock Holmes and I, we all knew differently.

Given how I missed my mother and had to suffer my ill father in close quarters, Daniel P. Barnum had a much better time on the good ship *Majestic* than I did. With his own money for the first time, he could easily have paid for first class passage. We considered dressing him up befitting his new station, hoping that the clothes would make the man and fool the detective, but concluded we could not risk discovery. The cramped quarters of a boat offer a finite number of places to hide. If all Irregulars looked alike to Watson, Father was not so short-sighted.

In fitting irony, Danny solved the problem by hiding a boy in plain sight.

He joined a family in steerage, whose last name – I swear it – was Witty. Costermongers from Whitechapel, they already had eight dark-haired children. When Danny paid them the price of a first class ticket to annex him for the voyage, they welcomed him into the Witty fold. The Witty father played fiddle; Mother Witty and the little Wittys sang. Every night, I snuck down to steerage to join them. Danny's voice was changing and we all enjoyed those discordances.

My elbow found his ribs, as my memory found his words and repeated them. "You sound like a burping bullfrog. It's bloody god awful. Please stop."

To which he whisked me away to our private spot in the aft lifeboat, and whispered, "This bullfrog shall continue singing, unless you can think of a better use for his lips?"

I won't romanticize steerage; it was dark, cold and cramped, but we were happy there. In further truth, its relative discomforts can only be measured in comparison to previous lodgings. All the little Wittys agreed – compared to a Whitechapel ditch, or a freezing bolthole, our third-class accommodations included a warm fire, a roof and daily bread, and plenty of adventures.

Danny and I often snuck away, scouring every deck trying to deduce why a full half of the ship was forbidden. We failed. In first class, we did discover a set of rooms that the crew sternly informed us were out of bounds as the captain's quarters. They seemed large for one man, but we found nothing to prove that Holmes was hiding me from someone, or hiding someone from me.

No, Hopeful Reader, it was not a pair of twins in pink boots. It was not my aunties. Although that is indeed an excellent guess. Both sisters were outraged at the temerity of Holmes' departure plans, and never for one second intended to hand me over to the inconsistent care of a pyromaniacal bachelor. Instead, we made our own operatic plans. Together, we overcame several seemingly insurmountable problems.

Tante Grizelda first worried that the sudden disappearance of Mrs. Hudson from Baker Street, so soon after the death of its famous tenant, would get publicized by all the newspapers in the world. It would not do to raise Holmes' suspicions. Tante Gisela worried about abandoning Pictavia, period. I wondered if Tante Gisela was generously suggesting she wouldn't go, because Tante Grizelda shouldn't. One did not have to be a detective to deduce it less than advisable for her to show her wanted pirate face on any boat, particularly not one taking her back to America.

I admit being likewise filled with guilty panic at the thought of no one left behind to visit Mother's grave. I awakened screaming and choking, as a tangle of maple leaves pierced her coffin, thrust up from the ground, forced their way down my throat and between my unwilling legs. Yes, Dear Readers with Fertile Imaginations, you don't have to be a modern alienist to see rape in that.

This time, Tante Grizelda saved the day. Having so often quoted her own dear husband, whose life depended on his gift of the gab, and knew that, thankfully, most people believe whatever story they hear first, Mrs. Hudson decided to ensure what John H. Watson heard first.

I imagine, Wise Reader, you already know the vital moral of her story?

Never wrong a pirate.

Chapter Fourteen: The Calamitous Incident of the Kiss in the Nighttime

Having long ago perfected a fine forger's hand for the falsification of shipping bills and government writs for sailing ships, the pirate of Baker Street took her revenge. She fashioned a note in Holmes' hand, one she planned to give Watson when he arrived from the continent bearing sad news. Before he could open his mouth to share it, she handed him the missive she had skillfully styled as Holmes' final instructions, "To My Most Bosom Boswell."

If Tante Grizelda indulged herself on the envelope, she got positively unguent inside it. I'd call her manipulation of her borders' friendship unwarranted had I not seen how often Holmes hurled things into fires that risked burning her to death, and how Watson ordered her about as if she was not his home-owning landlady, but a dirty and dismissible Afghani camp lackey. Their smug superiority proved ever hurtful to a woman raised to fight servitude heart and soul. In Yankee ingenuity, in an inspired burst of her own Barnum, she bilked them both in one fell swoop.

My Dearest Old Chap,

If you get this note, it means you are grieving my loss. My deepest condolences. I alone appreciate the depth of this loss: for if you have lost me, old friend, then I have lost you.

But I call on you, Watson, to do what you have always done, to rise to the occasion. I ask you to accomplish what I reluctantly admit the great Sherlock Holmes could not. I beg you to thwart the evil Moriarty one last time. Despite the best efforts of Scotland Yard, you and I both know Moriarty's henchmen will not all be caught. But those that skip the snare must be humbled.

In short, no one must be told Moriarty has bested us. No one must learn he has finished me off. It would embolden any number of felonious fiends to reach next for your throat, or perhaps for Mrs. Hudson's. I fear the recent Baker Street fire was arson, set by just such a callous fiend.

Please do not mention this frightening possibility to the frail good lady before you.

Please simply advise her of my last, unalterable wishes. She must board up 221b, untouched forthwith. For the next two years, should anyone inquire, you and she are to say exactly and only this, "Sherlock Holmes is dispatched on an extended matter of import in the personal service of our Queen." No embellishments, Watson. That, and that alone, is all either of you must ever say. Mrs. Hudson must go post haste to live with her friend, Mrs. Turner. Be insistent, dear Watson. A good woman's very life is in your hands.

And perhaps more than one. I equally fear that Moriarty's minions might also seek their perverted revenge on you own dear wife, she with the most unforgettable name. The thought of that fiend harming even one hair on any woman's charming English head—intolerable!

I shall be direct old friend: you must take the mantle from me and transfer it to your own broad shoulders. As you have no doubt already deduced, given your own unique grasp of my methods, you must make it appear to the Empire entire that the great detective Sherlock Holmes is inescapable, all-seeing, omnipresent, if not omnipotent, and yes, most importantly, still alive.

How are you to accomplish this, Old Friend? Firstly, by doing what you do best – recording our exploits together. This is the subterfuge that keeps everyone safe. (It is also the subterfuge that, if I may momentarily argue the pecuniary, will earn you far more than your medical practice, sufficient to provide you, your wife, and the future pattering feet of some little Watsons, all the comfort and leisure you deserve.) Your persistent publication, My Dear Boswell, will save lives and ensure the Empire. If there is one thing I know, it is this: the man named John Hamish Watson can be counted on to do what he truly believes is in the best interest of his country and his best friend.

Secondly, and I recognize most difficultly, Watson, you must tell no one that I am dead. Not Mrs. Hudson. Not Mrs. Watson. Women's tongues can never be trusted. I know your doctoring heart would seek to comfort their aching ones, but I implore your most manly courage here, Watson. You are a soldier in your last campaign. You must not fail your last comrade in arms. You must fight the good fight as I often did, wearing a disguise. As the secret voice of Sherlock Holmes, your tour of duty must last two years. Then, it will no longer matter.

In two years' time, you may tell your wife, our landlady, and the Empire of my sad demise. Then, and only then, you may share your grief. Until then, whenever you miss me beyond bearing, whenever your resolve begins to flag, then simply look for our flag. As it stands proud in the wind, we stand as two proudly British brothers together. Onward, ever onward, my beloved Boswell!

I remain ever in your debt, and always and forever, your most grateful friend,

Sherlock Holmes

Apparently, my auntie missed her true calling as a ghostwriter for Winston Churchill.

I can only imagine, Chuckling Reader, the pathos of the scene! When a weeping Watson recovered himself – a process requiring more than a few medicinal shots of brandy – he dutifully conveyed the letter's instructions to a tearful Mrs. Hudson. After asking him many questions to be certain she understood, which was, of course, actually Tante Grizelda grilling Watson to be sure he understood, she suffered a paroxysm of pure grief. Watson was sure the poor dear lady had no idea what she was doing when she threw Holmes' letter into the fire.

After a liberal application of "Buck up, old girl!" and smelling saults, Mrs. Hudson recovered. She kindly handed Watson a piece of pink stationary so he could copy for posterity all he remembered in his own hand. She reports having several cups of tea and three crumpets, as Watson's memory turned a two-page letter into four. But this new version in his own words ensured no one would ever be able to trace any words back to her.

She sent him home to his wife with a peck on the cheek. A traitor's kiss? You decide.

As you and history know, Faithful Reader, Watson followed his instructions to the letter. Of course he did. He always did. How he felt doing so puzzled us all. But none of us could ask him. I was dead. Danny and the Irregulars had disbanded. Mrs. Hudson had followed her own instructions and gone to live with her sister. Although she did not provide Watson an exact address, she did get the last word and the last laugh – she told him it was on Sticky Pudding Lane.

I'm amazed poor Watson had any trouser legs left to pull. But now, having had sufficient fun at his expense, I must give him full credit.

In an homage that did his friendship proud, Watson would keep his grief close to the chest. He did not reveal Holmes' death until he published *The Final Problem*, in December of 1893. In this, I see only the best of him. I see the genuine attempt to obey a loved one's dying wish, and I respect it, knowing the toll that promise takes. I must in all fairness, however, also report that I sometimes also see it skewed at a less flattering angle. Watson spent a full two years after Father's death doing exactly what anyone would do when someone they love is murdered on their watch – getting rich, exploiting his legacy, enriching themselves by fictionalizing a dead friend's deeds.

Without Holmes to logically advise or correct him, without Holmes there to stop him, Watson's fictions became entirely his own. When Holmes "died", Watson had published only two tales – *A Study in Scarlet* in 1887 and *A Sign of Four* in 1890. In a prolific outpouring over the next two years, Watson then published a full twenty-four stories in *The Strand*. This equates to an astounding average of one story per month, every month, for two long years.

When he finally admitted Holmes' death, twenty-nine months after it occurred, one could cynically conclude Watson got the last laugh on all of us. To paraphrase Holmes, "although his grief was credible, Watson quite credibly spent two years pretending it did not exist." Whether or not this practiced duplicity ever calmed his eyebrows, or improved his game of Whist, I cannot say, but it does make the smaller fiction of a Jezail bullet appear far more in character.

I also confess that Watson's good fortune made me more than a little green.

If *The Strand* paid him the astronomical price of one hundred dollars per word, what would they pay me for the whole truth? My two families would never want for anything ever again. But therein lay another trap and tangle – I could provide for them only by exposing them and myself.

Instead, I did nothing. I waited. I hesitated and grew old, then ancient. But again, I digress in my own mashed carrot ramblings, and must not.

Of course, my auntie got more than a pirate's revenge; her letter punched our ticket out of London. In one blow, she dispatched both Watson and all her duties at Baker Street. Next, to care for Pictavia, Tante Gisela hired a new housekeeping couple, freeing herself and Godfrey to make the journey. Grateful for all of Mother's kindnesses to them, some older Irregulars volunteered to visit her grave.

I found our copy of Catherine Parr Traill's *Canadian Wildflowers* and marked the *Hemerocallis Fulva* as Mother's particular favourite. Since her regular Irregular mourners would not take payment, I insisted they always be paid with full stomachs and full pockets of food.

Having no clan of their own, John and Eliza Barrymore were delighted to open Pictavia to some lively children. These kind pair you will know, Faithful Reader, as the sister and brother-in-law of the convict named Selden from *The Hound of the Baskervilles*. In 1889, they had done no wrong but kindness – Mrs. Barrymore had left food out on Grimpen Mire for her starving brother. But they had felt duty bound to resign their positions at Baskerville Hall. Holmes had mentioned their subsequent hardship, asking Mrs. Hudson if she might know of a position. Tante Gisela swore them to secrecy as to the irregularities of our warrior household, and hired them forthwith.

So how do I know my aunties weren't the secret stowaways in the captain's quarters?

Well, the dark-haired Witty father looked nothing like Herr Froehlich and even less like our groom, but he did have Godfrey's light touch on the fiddle. The Witty mother had cut her hair very short and used a whole bin of walnuts to look as raven-haired and Witty as possible. In worn calico homespun, in sturdy brown boots in which she could have mucked a barn, she looked as unlike a rich, redheaded pirate on the run, as any rozzer could imagine.

It is an excellent day, Impressed Reader, when my poor pen produces that smile. More to the point, two pairs of pink boots stood ready, secreted in a steerage steamer trunk.

Tante Gisela proved harder to costume. She refused to dye or cut her long auburn hair, but neither bonnets, nor wigs would survive the gale of a ship at sea. Danny solved her problem by "borrowing" items from Tansy who, thanks to Mother, had secured a post at the St. Ambrose parish as their laundress. My aunts clucked at his sinful ways, inspected, measured, and copied his pilfered items, then reached for their rosaries to ask forgiveness. I'm sure Danny knew exactly what he was doing when he gave my quiet, devout auntie the role of her childhood dreams.

Deep in steerage, the good Sister Magdalena politely looked up from her Bible from time to time to smile and clap at the Witty music. From a little Polish town only she could pronounce, Pictavbartitsushynski, she could not socialize with other passengers as she spoke only the oddest of dialects, a hybrid of Polish, German and Gaelic designed to be incurably incomprehensible to all but her chosen clan. This ensured that, for once in her life, she got exactly what she had always wanted – to be left blessedly alone. In full habit and a pair of thick spectacles, no one noticed the slightest similarity to the vivacious raven-tressed Witty mother. Not even the great detective could have imagined that a shy nun had waist-length curls swirling like scarlet serpents beneath her wimple.

As for the Witty children, surely, Perspicacious Reader, you guessed all along. Tansy and several of the others already had dark hair. Walnuts are cheap. After we lined them all up for their Witty beautification at the Salon de Pictavia, the Irregulars all became quite beautifully regular. Say it with me – one Witty urchin is as good as another.

And, yes, I have successfully avoided that calamitous kiss in the nighttime for a growing pile of pink pages and must not continue to do so. That moment, the end of life as I knew it, began when this little obdurate ingrate nearly lost her mother's shawl. An heirloom made even more precious by the recent confirmation of its provenance by way of Jenny Lind to my grandmother, from Gerda to her only daughter, Reenie, and then finally, from my mother to her only child.

On the fateful evening of July 1, 1891, we were preparing to disembark the good ship *Majestic* for all the splendors of New York City. Father had announced I would exit the ship as a boy, but to confound all followers, in our first carriage we would both change into our female aliases. He instructed me to pack a set of Miss Euphemia's clothes in my travel bag.

Wanting to see again how fine I looked in Mother's shawl, I opened my cabin window, hoping the angled glass would create a mirror. Instead, in fitting punishment for my vanity, it created a vacuum. In a gulp of wind, the shawl flew from my shoulders and my cap sprang from my head.

I could only save one. I thrust my cap back on my head and ran outside to look for my shawl. Fearing it lost, I discovered it had landed, thankfully, not in the Atlantic, but in a tangle around a deck chair. Sadly, it was sodden, so heavy with salt water I feared it ruined. Back in my room, smoothing it out with my hands, wondering how to save it given Tante Gisela's injunction it must never be washed, I felt a strange lump: a thin oilskin pouch hidden in the hem.

October 14, 1875

If I were to say it cannot be true, if I were to say that nowhere in the most secret part of my soul, did I believe it possible, I would be lying to you, to Home Boy, to my mother, and to myself.

I can do so no longer. I must believe what I saw, what I observed with my own eyes. Perhaps I should have seen it all along. There are so many things it explains.

How often was Home Boy covered in bruises? Too often. I made excuses for it. I told myself that life on the farm is a dangerous place. When he struggled to write his lessons with a broken arm, when he limped into school on crutches, I believed your stories about how he had been kicked by your family's ill-tempered plow horse, how he had lost his balance trying to catch a heavy bale, or fallen from the moving hay wagon onto a large field rock and broken his leg.

These are all common farm accidents.

Why should I not believe you?

If I noted over the years how Home Boy increasingly disliked you, I was too much bedazzled by you to pay it any mind. If I sometimes noted that your scrapped knuckles, were oddly coincident with his injuries, I thought little of it except for what I assumed the rough-housing of brothers. Having none, I could only assume it a normal, friendly rivalry.

Oh, I was such a fool! Such a stupid, vain and careless fool! When Home Boy summoned his courage, when he warned I must not marry you, I laughed at him. I thought it simple, green-eyed jealousy and sent him away.

When he told me you beat him, beat him for years because of what he refused to do as soon as he got big enough to refuse it, I put my hands over my ears and refused to hear him.

But the third time, this very evening, when he arrived out of breath, having driven himself, his horse and his haycart far too fast to be good for any of them, there was such a look in his eye, an urgency that could not be denied.

"For the sake of your own life, Reenie, for the sake of any children you might ever hope to have, for the sake of truth in the sight of God, please, please, come with me now."

God and Our Lady help me, I grabbed Mother's shawl and jumped into his cart.

In the irony of the devil himself, it was a beautiful starlit night. There you were, hidden in the ravine. There you were, in the very spot where we all so often sat in childhood, next to the stream. There you were in the place where you proposed me marriage.

There you both were, blaspheming under God's holy sky. I saw it with my own two eyes. You, who never held my hand. You, who kissed me only when I cajoled or begged. You were naked, moaning, kissing, and caressing!

The vile hands that touched your naked body – I have seen those fingers whittle delicate little boys. I have heard those hands play Mozart. I have seen those lips kissing my mother, and I have felt those lips every night of my life, kissing me good night. The man in your embrace, the man commanding your embrace, was my father.

I felt my heart break into a thousand falling stars.

Thankfully, before I screamed, Home Boy pulled me away. He took my hand and we ran. Then he whipped the horse to make it run even faster. We only stopped when we got to the school. Desperate to hide, we drove the cart straight into the barn behind it.

I know I was crying. I know he was trying to console me through his own tears.

I remember the next horror, the moment we realized Mother's shawl wasn't in the cart. I must have dropped it.

I remember clinging to him, and sobbing, and then moving because the bottom of the cart had splinters, moving into the soft sweetness of freshly-cut hay. I remember that he held me. When he kissed me, I kissed him back. Words came spilling out of me. I told him that I loved him and had always loved him. I admitted I had hidden it from him and even from myself. I remember more kissing, then deeper kissing, then writhing, and panting, then screaming, screaming too late, that no, he must stop, stop, stop!

Then there were voices, and we were exposed.

Two men. One with my shawl. One lifting a lantern. My father threw that lantern at us. The flames caught.

Da grabbed me by the hair and tried to pull me into them. Home Boy lunged forward. Both of you hit Da repeatedly and he went down. I grabbed my mother's shawl as it fell. I ran as the hay, the barn, and the school burned.

I did not stop to see which one of the three of you entered hell first. No longer yours, no longer anyone's, no longer myself. No longer certain of anything on earth.

I can never be Reenie, or Catriona, or anything Mclean again. Alone in her shawl, I will be only my mother's daughter,

Irene Psalmonia Adler.

Chapter Fifteen: The Valley of Fear and Fairy Dust

Please permit me, Indulgent Reader, to jump ahead some months in our story.

Before I kiss Daniel, before I share my most impulsive mistake and a moment of deadly malice, I would like to share a harmless story. A delightful one. A memory that reminds me that, yes, I somehow lived beyond the sorrow I must share with you next.

In the chilly autumn of 1891, as Aunt Hortensia and Euphemia, Holmes and I boarded a train in New York City to cross the border into Canada at Niagara Falls. The next morning, after signing out of the hotel, my father emerged from the alley behind it dressed as himself. When I asked why, he said only, "Today, Wiggins, as myself, I shall revisit a true wonder of the world."

We stared at Niagara Falls for all of ten seconds.

Then agreed we never wanted to see another bloody waterfall ever again.

After purchasing a horse and carriage, I saw good reason for his garb as Holmes drove up top. I sat alone inside. Having slept poorly in nights riddled with nightmares, I fell asleep on the day Father drove down Longwoods Road into the tiny hamlet of Mayfair. When I awoke, I did not realize we had arrived, only that we had stopped. Noting that Holmes had come down from his perch and fallen asleep on the seat across from me, I unlatched the door and stepped outside.

Nothing in my dirty London life prepared me for it. No painting I had ever seen did it justice. As I slept, the most pristine of blankets had enveloped the land, covering every bit of brown and green, laying the world to sleep only to greet it the next morning with the clearest of all blue skies. For the first time in my life, snow was white, gloriously white. Not grey. Not black. Not yellow with piss pots thrown from windows. Not brown with horse dung.

White.

I saw Mother's fairy dust. Pixie icicles winked good morning. I gloried in the depth of my footprints.

Just because I could, just because no one was expecting it of me, I walked expertly backwards in them. When I met my first snow drift, I jumped, and rolled in it like Toby the Basset Hound. For the first time I put out my tongue to taste a snowflake and did not taste cinders. I even made my first attempt at sliding on a frozen creek. It hurt my feet far too much to attempt it a second time, but I am still very proud to say I have done it once.

I hid at the ridge of the creek, made an arsenal of snowballs and called for my father.

"Quickly, Holmes! It's extraordinary! It must be all of six inches!"

Whenever the great detective retold that story, one of the few funny stories in our travels as father and daughter, it made him laugh to hysterical tears every time.

But pixie dust materializes out of the ether and returns to it. It never lasts.

When the good ship *Majestic* pulled into port, I would never have believed that a winter day months away would be my next happy moment. I had no apprehension of disaster. Danny and my aunties were with me. Our plans were set. Since Holmes wanted to spend weeks in New York City – doing exactly what he would not say – it gave Tante Gisela time to take Danny to meet his father in Connecticut. I regretted not going with him, but we could concoct no believable tale to pry me from Holmes for that long.

I promised Danny I'd meet the man who loved Jumbo the next time.

I didn't like leaving him any more than my aunties liked their separation, the first in their lives. But we all told ourselves and each other the same reassuring thing: it was temporary. The Wittys would follow Holmes and Wiggins around New York City in whatever costumed incarnation we presented ourselves. We knew Holmes had booked the Dakota Hotel. We planned to leave each other messages there from "Mr. Daniels."

It was, of course, Tante Grizelda who insisted we must also have a contingency plan.

She suggested the one she had with Captain Hudson. Before each port, after poring over maps, they chose a local landmark. If they got separated, they knew to appear there each day at noon until reunited. Because our maps put it near the Dakota, and for romantic reasons obvious, I chose the statue of Daniel Webster in Central Park. When Danny pointed out I could only get there by giving Holmes the slip, Tante Grizelda added a failsafe. If we lost contact, we would place a personal ad for Mr. Daniels in *The New York Times*. If all else failed, Tante Gisela assured me, they had plenty of maps and weren't afraid of beavers. They would find me in Mayfair.

It now seems like such a conceit – after tailing the great detective through a sprawling New York City that none of us had ever visited, four adults and an Irregular handful of children were blithely proposing to follow him some five hundred miles into the wilderness of Canada.

And we all convinced ourselves no one would notice. Of course people notice.

When the passengers of the good ship *Majestic* saw a calamitous kiss in the nighttime, we were so close to a safe landing together we could touch it. But, thanks to me, we lost everything.

After reading the devastating letter hidden in my shawl, I flew from my room to tell Danny, but couldn't find him. A setting sun illuminating New York City, and the fact that the captain had opened the top deck to all, ensured that I found it far more crowded than it had ever been.

As Holmes had taught me, I surveilled the scene without appearing to do so. At stage right, I saw Sister

Magdalena thanking God in prayer. I closed my eyes and further down, stage left, heard the excited voices of several Witty children. I found Danny leaning over the railing, searching for the evening's first stars. Bursting with news, I could say nothing given the crowd.

Suddenly, it was all so urgent. I had so many things to say. Things we had put off saying.

It became pressingly clear that this would be the last I'd see him for some time. Perhaps the same thought occurred to him. He fell uncharacteristically shy, shifting his gaze to the horizon.

That enabled me to take a good last look at him without embarrassing him. Years of good nutrition, daily bartitsu, and a warm, safe bed, had all done wonders. He still had that boyish upturned nose, but in every other way he had grown from a scrawny urchin into a handsome young man, now easily five inches taller than yours truly. To all appearances, to all the other travelers and sailors milling about, we were just an older and a younger boy; friends, standing side by side.

After moments of silence, Danny grinned and reached into his pocket.

"Seeing as we're finally out of reach of the London rozzers, I thought I'd give you this."

When I pulled the scarlet ribbon off the bit of pink paper that wrapped his gift, I recognized it immediately – a tortoise shell comb, one with mother-of-pearl insets along the edge. A truly lovely design, one I had liked from the moment I first saw it some five years ago when I took it from Mr. Sally's Pawnshop and Emporium. That night, when Danny had gone back for my cap, he must have also helped himself to the comb. He had kept it with him all these years.

I immediately understood what he was actually giving me – the past and a future.

It meant he remembered. It meant he wanted me to know that he remembered. He was telling me my old life wasn't lost as long as we were together to remember it. He wanted me to know that London mattered, that Mother mattered. That I mattered.

He was looking forward to my being a full-time girl. His girl.

Without giving one instant of thought to where we were or how it would look, I threw my arms around his neck and kissed him. It was not a peck on the cheek, not a kiss you give a kissing cousin, and most demonstrably not our first kiss. It was young love's kiss. The kiss you and your first beloved share when you are a hungry and hopeful fifteen and sixteen years old.

It ended everything.

A pair of hairy, tattooed hands grabbed Danny. More hands pulled us apart. I lost my balance and went down hard, hitting my head on the deck. While I was merely held down, Danny got much worse. Men began to punch him. Both sailors and passengers. A snarl of angry men were yelling, outraged, pointing at me, screaming words that the ringing in my ears wouldn't let me understand. In a truly alarming, damn near impossible coincidence given the letter I had just read, slowly, their malice grew clear.

"He's buggered the boy!"

"He's a bloody sodomite."

"A fiend. Kill him now!"

When more hands pulled me up, I observed what they saw. As irregular as ever, I had been visited days early by my monthly friend. I was not wearing my oilskin underwear. In a boy's thin breeches, dark red blood had seeped straight through my crotch and up between my buttocks. I tried to pull away, to explain, but instead fell forward, smacking my face into the railing.

Now, before this next coincidence seems beyond impossible, Rational Reader, please imagine your typical nineteenth-century ship's deck. In the rolling of wake and the gusting of squalls, passengers lost all manner of things. So it was not surprising to me to find my face stuck into a newspaper that had wrapped itself around an upright of the railing. What was surprising was the headline at the end of my nose: "P.T. BARNUM DEAD OF A STROKE IN BRIDGEPORT, CONNECTICUT."

I lifted my head and I screamed, "He's dead, Danny. Your father's dead.'

That sad news was the last thing I said to my beloved boy. Thankfully, when his assailants paused, and glanced over at me fearing I'd gone mad, Danny seized their moment of hesitation to pull from their grasp. In one smooth, graceful movement, he vaulted straight over the side of the ship.

It will always be the longest moment of my life.

Eyes closed and breath held, praying to hear the sound of a splash, not the deadly thud of a dock. In a fast-flitting kaleidoscope behind my closed eyes, I saw Danny's first smile, the burnished black of his curls, the sooty London cobblestones with our first joint footprints, and the diamond of honey on his chin as he enjoyed his first crumpet in our kitchen. When I heard a mighty splash, relief evaporated into fresh dread.

If Danny had grown up in Bridgeport, next to the ocean, he would have had a chance. But Daniel P. Barnum grew up in the streets of London. He couldn't swim. As I clutched his present, held but moments ago in his own warm hands, the mottled tortoiseshell and the glowing mother-of-pearl insets danced and buzzed.

As you will remember, Solicitous Reader, I had hit my head. It reset the world in a slow motion of living colours.

Did Father really call murder "a scarlet thread running through the colourless skein of life"? I find the tangled metaphor too apt and astute to be Watson on his own. But I can say this – the moment I murdered my beloved is not scarlet. His murder will always be blue.

The flash of Danny's p-coat flying over the side. The aquamarine waves that darkened into indigo with the setting sun. The rich, royal blue of the sky that, second-by-Danny's-absent- second, turned the blackest navy. The ice blue stars that poked the sky, then fell with my tears.

Then I did see red. The colour of blood. Of sacrifice.

The Witty mother, her red roots showing, uttered obscenities that frightened the sailors. Being both the strongest swimmer of the clan, and the one with a pirate curriculum vitae that included frequent jumping from ships, she leapt overboard yelling Danny's name.

Sister Magdalena shed both her habit, and any pretense of being anything but a girl from the Jersey shore, as she leapt after her sister.

The Witty father would have done likewise, but for Witty children clinging to his pant legs.

When I tried to do likewise, the crowd held me back.

At the last possible split of a second, just before Mr. Witty attempted to wrap his coat around my shoulders but accidentally threw it over my head, covering my eyes, I saw a flash of turquoise.

A familiar blade cut the ropes of the aft lifeboat in one vicious bartitsu swipe. As the rowboat dropped, I saw the back of an emerald gown with two strong arms reaching confidently for the oars. Against a velvet collar trimmed in pink rosettes, bounced a long auburn braid.

I did what any self-respecting Victorian young lady would do.

I fainted.

Chapter Sixteen: Far Worse than Rippers or Rats

The children were right – it was a crime against nature to watch The Wonderful World of The Starship Enterprise on that old black and white TV. It helps to know that tonight is *Star Trek* night and more than one good crew in living colour awaits me. I need only do a little writing after breakfast and then, after a long afternoon nap, can reward myself with several rapt great-grandchildren joining me in intergalactic adventuring. I need to know that before I can write this next difficult chapter. I shall need to glance up repeatedly at all my thumbtacked photos. I need to both see and observe the safe passage of time until I know this for certain: I lived through the deadly despair that followed that calamitous kiss.

How do you live after watching your entire family die before your eyes?

How do you live knowing their deaths are your fault?

I first awoke in our cabin to a cold cloth on my head and the sound of someone weeping.

In my father's lean hand I thought I saw the hidden letter, but I know I saw a syringe.

Holmes said only this, "Close your eyes, Wiggins. It is not yet safe to open them."

When I awoke the second time, I recognized nothing. No longer in Wiggin's clothes, I wore a woman's long nightdress, one I'd never seen. Unlike my tiny stateroom, my enormous bed had multiple brocade pillows and a lovely gold eiderdown. The room held a soft turkey carpet and a tall picture window. My letter and the syringe were gone. Only my father remained the same.

I said the first thing that entered my woozy head.

"I saw her. I saw my mother."

"How are you, Wiggins? You have been insensible, having badly hit your head."

I sat up and wished I hadn't. But I stayed sitting up to face him.

"What did you give me? I saw the syringe."

"Only something to help you sleep, Wiggins. Nothing more, I promise."

"You mean, you drugged me to ensure I could not go after them."

Looking like a crumpet would not melt in his mouth, improvising perfect innocence with a soupçon of incredulity, my father smiled. "Pardon me, Wiggins? Go after whom?"

"Treating my brain as addled, does not make it so."

"That is a logical deduction, Wiggins. Good. I trust your memory will soon right itself."

"My memory is just fine, thank you. I saw my mother. She is alive."

"Think carefully, Wiggins. Your mother from Whitechapel? On board our ship? That is supremely illogical. You distinctly told me she had died. Of the drink, I believe?"

"Yes, I thought she had died. But I was wrong. She lied to me. They all lied."

Then, of course, I began to cry.

Father patted my shoulder. "It is understandable, Wiggins, that in times of duress—"

"Piss and poppycock," I spat at him. "I saw my mother in the lifeboat. I saw you. I saw your knife cut the ropes of the boat so that it dropped into the water. I saw her, I know I did."

Father held his role as if it were not one. He leaned in and smiled.

"Let us examine this logically, Wiggins. Please tell me precisely what you saw."

"A long red braid down a green back. Two strong hands reaching for the oars."

"I see. So you saw a sailor with a queue, such as many of them have to keep their hair from their eyes. A strong sailor in a green shirt."

"Certainly. A shirt that flounced to the floor over white petticoats. I believe they call it a dress. With black silk piping and pink rosettes. I know it well. I buried my mother in it.

"Hmmm... I see. Not your typical seafaring garb. Perhaps—"

"Damn you, Holmes, tell me the truth for once in your sorry life!"

I had never screamed at him. Never so much as raised my voice. Desperate to press him further about Danny and my aunties, I could not. He must not know they were on the ship.

He dropped to my bedside chair and closed his eyes for the longest time.

"I cannot supply what you seek, Wiggins. I truly cannot. Suffice it for now to say that all will be revealed in the fullness of time." He opened his eyes and smiled. "Please trust me now."

I threw the only thing I could get my hands on at his head. He caught my shawl, looked at it a moment with a muddle of emotions, and hung it gently on the back of the armchair.

Then my father did what he always did best.

He bowed and made his exit.

I remember little of the next few days. Some of it was my head injury and the hellfire headache that burned behind my eyes. Dizziness worsened my already poor balance. It took a week before I could leave my bed to walk across the room. But I flatly refused to speak even one word to the lying cur who called himself a consulting detective who had never once consulted me.

I could see how this worried him, but did not care.

I hoped to hurt him, intended to give him his due share of my pain.

When I realized he must have been the one to remove Wiggins' bloody clothing and put me into my nightdress, when I realized he now knew for certain I was no boy, my nightmares shifted. Now, before raising his turquoise knife to my throat, Holmes first slashed off my clothing. When I was exposed as a runty, deformed girl, my father laughed, then ended my life.

Each night in my nightmare soaked bed, I told myself the same thing, "Tomorrow. I will hear from them tomorrow." As grief grew and hope waned, as one day became three, as one week became three, I kept looking for a sign. Perhaps a note smuggled in with a food tray? Perhaps the tallest Witty would pose as a maid with a letter stuffed up her sleeve? I checked the soles of my boots repeatedly. I strained to spot a beloved face from my hotel window.

The Dakota overlooked Central Park. In true serendipity, from a room that towered over the trees, I could see the raised clearing that held the stature of Daniel Webster. I watched every day at noon, and hours afterwards. Every glint of red hair, every young man with dark hair lifted my spirits, then dashed them dead again.

Had Holmes lied to my family and sent them away?

Perhaps they now believed I had abandoned them?

Perhaps, like Danny's grandmother, he had told them their child was dead?

On hotel stationary, I placed an ad in the *New York Times*, smuggling it out by tipping the housekeeping staff. I got no reply. The explanations I deduced for that silence vacillated back and forth between hopeful consolation and hopeless dread. I decided that when my family did come for me, I had better be ready. Each day at dawn, I got fully dressed, and waited.

And waited. And waited. And still heard nothing.

Catapulting between rage and remorse, incredulity and invective, no matter how I tried to tell the story, it made no logical sense. Even in the worst of scenarios, even if my mother and both my aunts had died in an unsuccessful attempt to save Danny, why weren't their heroic deaths in the newspapers? Godfrey Norton and the Irregulars were still breathing. Why didn't they seek me out? Had Holmes tracked Godfrey down and killed him? And all the little Wittys, too?

In the total absence of data, I hypothesized without logic and beyond reason.

And I made Holmes pay for it. I refused to answer the liar who spent all morning hoping I would to speak to him. When he invited me, then ordered me, then begged me to eat breakfast with him, I did not. When he implored me to eat at least the orange, to eat anything at all, I ignored him. After his second cup of tea, promptly at 11:45am each day, he gave up and made his exit.

Once he left, I cried non-stop.

Little things enraged me.

The hotel didn't serve crumpets. They put milk, not cream, in my tea. I had to let my breakfast get cold, which doubly infuriated me, even if it was my own choice. It made me increasingly angry each morning to watch my father eat, as if he deserved nourishment, as if the world had not ended.

Once he left and I reached for the gelatinous eggs and cold toast, it tasted like cardboard. Forcing myself not to vomit, I told myself I had to keep up my strength to escape when my family arrived. When I realized I could order a second breakfast from room service, I kept forgetting that if you wanted a cup of tea, as if it wasn't bloody obvious, you had to say "hot tea" or the Yankee fools brought you some hideous brown bilge water with ice.

When my father returned each evening, yet again, he proved worse than no help at all.

When he sat with me, I wanted him to leave; when he left, I resented being left behind. He got to go off adventuring. He got to explore New York City, and I got entombed in yet another lonely Diogenes. I wanted to hear what he had done all day and, simultaneously, didn't want to ever hear his voice again. My window offered my only comfort, and even it came with a price. As lovely as my own Hyde Park, Central Park made me miss my Pictavian life yet again.

Unequipped to deal with teenage obstinacy, Holmes made a bachelor's logical choice – bribery. He brought unspeaking me Broadway theatre programs and music playbills, tempted me with the brand new Carnegie Hall, opened that spring by the great Pyotr Ilyich Tchaikovsky.

I ignored him.

He brought me menus from Delmonico's and Katz's Delicatessen which I ignored until he left the room. He brought brochures for museums and art galleries, the Botanical Gardens, and The Empire State Building. When he brought me the program of the Metropolitan Opera House, I collapsed in fresh tears and threw it into his stricken face.

That night, I opened my window wide and stood on the ledge.

I could keep my loved ones with me by jumping, as they had, into oblivion. The idea felt safe and comforting. It offered me a way to end the pain. It felt like what I deserved.

I pulled my beloved cap tight to my head and made ready to make my last exit.

As luck would have it, in the last good-bye sweep of my room, my eye fell on a handbill for Madison Square Gardens and, thank goodness, I took it as a sign.

I didn't want to die just yet.

I wanted go on a pilgrimage.

For it was in that very arena that P.T. Barnum had triumphantly exhibited Jumbo. For my dear departed Danny's sake, I could visit all the sites we had hoped to see together. I could walk the Brooklyn Bridge. After a rumour of its imminent collapse caused a stampede that killed twelve people, Barnum had saved the day by parading Jumbo across it to prove it stood strong. I could visit the site of Barnum's American Museum, home to Tom Thumb and the Feejee

Mermaid, open fifteen hours a day before it mysteriously burned to the ground. If I felt up to it, I could even go to the American Museum of Natural History to witness the clean, bare bones of Jumbo's skeleton.

The next morning, when a particularly lovely autumn breeze blew through the window, I decided I'd had about enough of my Jumbo-sized self-entombment.

"So, Holmes, you said we can go anywhere I like. Is that correct?

Hope lit his face at the return of my voice. "Yes, anywhere!"

"Fine." I picked up the *New York Times*, chock full of coverage of the upcoming November election. "There," I pointed. "I want to go there."

I enjoyed watching his face fade from victory to that of a sputtering man with a hedgehog caught in his throat. I fully expected he would veto my request to hear the slate of candidates from the Socialist Labour Party, including their leader Daniel De Leon who was running for governor.

To his credit, Holmes swallowed the hedgehog and nodded.

"It is tonight. I will happily escort you."

After the speeches, after a spirited discussion and a fine dinner at Delmonico's, after agreeing to take me on my Jumbo pilgrimage, when we returned to our rooms that night, true to form, my father spoiled the moment yet again.

"I shall eagerly escort you to anything you might like to see in this truly remarkable city, Wiggins, but I must confess I also have ulterior motives for being here."

"There it is," I thought. "The bloody man always has his own selfish second agenda."

Holmes turned the desk chair backwards, rested lean arms on its back, and leaned forward.

"I am a man of science and will be direct. First, I want you to know I am here to seek treatment for the addiction that has plagued me most of my life. I have been going back and forth each afternoon for treatment and am cautiously optimistic that I see improvement."

I could manage only this, "I am glad of that. Thank you for telling me."

"But that is not my only motive for coming here." He avoided my eyes then straightened his spine. "I apologize in advance if I speak indelicately. While we are in New York City, should you wish to take advantage of it, I have asked both Mycroft and Watson to use their contacts. Appointments have been booked with multiple American doctors, the top specialists in their field."

"See any doctors you like. You don't need my permission."

"Not for me, Wiggins, for you. I thought you might wish to consult these experts about your feet. From my reading, I understand advancements have been made that might benefit you."

I said nothing. I wanted to keep hating him. I absolutely did not want to be in his debt.

"I would be honoured to accompany you on these consultations, but should you prefer to go alone, or not at all, I will respect your wishes." From his coat pocket he pulled several sheets of paper. "I have written a monograph in comparative elucidation of their education, experience, expertise, and empathic bedside manners, or lack thereof. Please let me know what you decide."

That time, when he fled the room, a tiny glowing bit of my heart went with him.

A week later, great-aunt Hortensia and Miss Euphemia attended my first appointment.

We visited seventeen physicians – a number I absolutely assert Holmes had chosen for each step of Baker Street. In every consultation, my usually garrulous aunt stayed silent. She let me lead the discussions, asked questions only once I was done, and only with my permission.

I cannot adequately explain the relief it gave me to hear doctor after doctor say that since there was no history of deformity in my family, my feet were likely not caused by heredity, but either by nature's accident or by corseting. Several said they had seen similar injuries done to babies by corseting. They all advised women to stop the practice upon first learning they were with child.

By the fifth doctor, I asked the vital moral question. One I had never spoken aloud.

"In your opinion, will I pass my deformity on to my children?"

The clearest answer came from the eleventh doctor. "No woman has a guarantee of a heathy child. But I see no reason to fear any extra risk. In every other respect, my dear, you are an entirely normal, remarkably healthy young woman. I believe all your babies will be fine."

He said *babies. All my babies.* Plural. As if he knew my greatest secret.

One I had not dared hope for, but longed for all my life.

My great-aunt beamed. "Such wonderful news, my darling Euphemia! We must celebrate!"

After each appointment, we went to a restaurant to discuss the new advice and compare it to other opinions garnered. Discovering a joint appreciation for ice cream and spaghetti, my disability grew easier to discuss each time. After due consideration, we rejected the surgical option that the rather zealous doctor, unlucky number thirteen, had proposed, deducing it too risky.

The last doctor, the seventeenth, surprised us again. He was a she.

I had never met a woman doctor. It hurt my heart to realize I could not rush home to tell my aunties and my mother. Dr. Garland, a fellow of The New York Infirmary for Indigent Women and Children, had studied with its founder – the great Elizabeth Blackwell herself. I knew her to be the first woman doctor in the United States and a strong progressive reformer that my aunties had met when they worked as nurses in the Civil War.

In second surprise, explaining that she believed in a treatment called "passive movement," Dr. Garland took my feet in her hands and slowly, carefully, began to rub and manipulate them. When she asked if my Aunt Hortensia could sit closer to observe, I hesitated but agreed. When she asked if we would return tomorrow so she could train Aunt Hortensia to do this for me, I wanted to say no, but could not. It helped so much, relived the spasticity and the pain so effectively, I agreed.

The next day, I closed my eyes and opened my trust. I let my father touch my feet.

By the time the leaves of Central Park had fallen in scarlet ribbons, thanks to the collective medical wisdom of New York City, for the first time in my life, I had a full and medically current course of treatment for both my mobility and my pain – passive movement, personal exercises, hot baths of Epsom salts and oils, new drugs in tablets and powders, and best of all – several pairs of custom-made shoes and boots. I walked longer, with more certainty, with new calm and pride.

As time flew by, as medical science advanced, my choices improved again.

Horrific lessons from the carnage of World War I produced more effective treatments and pain medication. Thanks to organizations like The War Amps, people who limped became a little more welcome in the public eye. The first time doctors saw my feet in x-ray, saw proof of missing and malformed bones like the tiny bones of birds, they expressed surprise that I could walk at all. They shook their heads, saying I could not possibly walk all my life and would soon have to stop.

My feet disagreed. Their frail little bastard bones are stubborn. We kept walking.

After World War II, surgeons and physiotherapists developed all kinds of new treatments for all kinds of irregular bodies. I used a cane in my forties and leaned heavily on crutches in my fifties. Eventually, I did have surgery. But the true credit for walking for most of my life belongs to the warm hands of my family. Thanks to a lifetime of nightly foot rubs, my feet have stayed supple and strong, and I walked longer than anyone ever expected.

Their love still fuels an old lady in her wheelchair eagerly anticipating *Star Trek*.

But first, I must again give credit where it is due. Holmes and I really did go somewhere neither of us had gone before. At every appointment, I had a parent who spoke to each doctor, and then to me, without a scintilla of embarrassment or shame. A parent thrilled to take me out for more than covert rowing on the Thames. My great-aunt toured The Big Apple with her disabled niece proudly on her arm. She sat patiently and divertingly wherever and whenever I needed to do so, and cared not one whit if people stared. More than once she stared back until they stopped.

In Macy's tearoom when a richly dressed man gapped at tired me limping to my seat, utilizing an aim perfected tossing things into fires, she threw a cube of sugar straight into his open mouth.

"You, Mr. Nosy Parker," she advised him, "are in serious need of sweetening."

On the morning of our last breakfast at the Dakota, which included an American, almost reasonable facsimile of crumpets called waffles, on impulse, I asked my father directly.

"Are you now convinced my feet are not a shameful punishment? I always assumed, given your interest in Darwin and phrenology, that you would see them as proof of my inferiority."

It was the one time I truly shocked the great detective.

"Shameful? Inferior? How could you possibly be…" Then he stopped himself. "No, Wiggins, I do not believe for one second that your feet are either shameful, or any kind of punishment. They are simply your feet. Flesh and bone, not magical metaphor." Here he smiled, "They are irregular feet, because they belong to the very best of the Irregulars."

When we left Niagara Falls, we made one stop before reaching Mayfair. A destination I had requested, but one I dreaded. Having already made inquiries and consulted maps, Holmes drove straight to the railway yard of St. Thomas, Ontario.

When I asked to grieve alone, he drove off a respectful distance.

As that sad night of September 15, 1885 played out before me, I saw Jumbo hit by a train. I saw him fall. Saw him quiver and die. At the end of my pilgrimage, I cried for all the lost loves of my life. Until I had no more tears. Until I felt cleansed. For once, Holmes stayed silent. When I returned to the carriage, he handed me his real handkerchief, nodded, and drove us onward.

This was the new separate peace my father and I had constructed, the limited truce we had co-authored, as we approached Mayfair. He still called me Wiggins, although he knew I had never been one. I wanted to tell him the truth, but could not. He owed me an explanation first.

Once I share that with you, Patient Reader, this ancient Wiggins will be done.

When I tie up all my pink papers, in your mind's eye, please see my lean arthritic hands using the last of the scarlet ribbon that has secured my family stories for over a century. The first length held Reenie's letters. The second and third bits lifted the earflaps of two adventuring caps. The fourth strand once wrapped a tortoise shell comb and now holds every note, card and letter my Danny ever sent me. I want you to know now that my brave beloved boy, survived years as a heroic World War I fighter pilot, only to die of the Spanish Flu in 1919.

Somehow, I have lived half a century without him.

But there has never been a day I have not felt him with me, his hand and heart in mine.

As I do, please carry the happy image of our wedding photo with you. Please enjoy his snapping eyes, dark curly hair and incandescent smile. Please see me, equally glowing, pregnant, yet again. Both of us resplendent in our Royal Flying Corps uniforms.

When I use the very last bit of ribbon to bind this literary love letter to you, Dearest Reader, please know I do so with my best wishes for your own scarlet adventures.

Chapter Seventeen: The Mayfair Improvisers Take Their Final Bow

In the valley of fairies and pixie dust, once we returned to our carriage and stopped laughing at the popping sound a snowball makes when you pelt it at a person's pate, Father settled tartan blankets about our knees then reached into his breast pocket.

"When it was time, your mother asked me to please begin with this."

I hesitated. After longing for the truth for weeks, after damning him to hell and back for refusing to give me any kind of explanation, after planning and failing to run away, or to hold a turquoise knife to his throat until he talked, I was no longer sure I wanted to hear the story. For the first time in my life, I had been free of pretending, free to simply be a child, to let adults deal with adult matters. I found I rather liked it. I slept better. I could throw some snowballs.

But nothing can hold back change, or a changing adventuress.

I expected the letter to be an apology from my family. Again, I was wrong.

October 14, 1875,
My dearest Reenie,

Regretfully, I have very little time before I leave, but I must tell you two things.

The first is this – you are my first happy memory. Before you, I had only a blur of sadness, snatches of unhappy colours and sounds. I remember a horse's scream. The smear of blood on cobblestones. A gravestone. A woman's tears. I remember a cold train and a freezing boat. The sound of a small body, my brother, I think, dropped into the sea. Then I remember nothing, until I see myself – a lad of perhaps six, sitting alone on the steps of the Mayfair General Store. I'd been dumped off like a worthless package by a harried driver. A boy with a misspelled sign on his chest.

Then I saw you. And you did something no one else had done. You saw me.

You were such a precocious little thing with your mint green dress and your new pink boots. You marched right up to me. Your green eyes locked into mine.

"H-O-M-E-S B-O-Y. Why do you wear a sign on your chest that says Homes Boy?"

"Because that is what I am. That is my new name."

You pulled off your tiny glove and held out your hand.

"Welcome to Mayfair, Homes Boy."

Here is the second thing. I must beg your double forgiveness, but do not expect you to grant it. For the unconscionable wrong I have done you, for the loss of your Da. Whatever else he was, he loved you. For that and only that, I mourn him. For it is something we share.

Today, I am running from Mayfair, running from a man who will kill me if he is alive, and from being accused of his murder if he is dead. But please know this – wherever I go, I will always have two homes. My physical abode, wherever it may be, and the permanent home in my heart that I hope one day to share with you. For now and forever, you and only you are The Woman for me.

Should you ever want to find me, I will have a new name. Improvising from the one you gave me, tonight your Homes Boy has made himself Holmes.

It names me a whole man, one who can make more than one home. It acknowledges the double strands in my life story and the double beating of your heart in mine. For the rest of my life, whenever anyone speaks my name, I will hear this truth – you and you alone, Reenie Mclean, have the one sure lock to my heart.

I am now, and will forever and always be yours,

Sherlock Holmes

When I lifted my head, if my eyes were misty, Weeping Reader, I'm sure it was the snow.

True to form, Father spoke before I could.

"Please let me first set all fears to rest. Your good friend Danny and your Tante Gisela are safely in Bridgeport, Connecticut. He will sadly not get to meet his departed father, but has been embraced by his new family. Grizelda and

Godfrey are safely with the Irregulars in Egg Harbor City, visiting your Adler great-grandparents. ”

"How do you — you knew! You knew all along!"

I saw him puff up and expected to hear, "Of course, I have known all along! I am Sherlock Holmes."

Instead, he closed his eyes.

"I think this will proceed faster, my dear, out here in the frozen wilderness, where we lack the warmth of a burning bush, if you let me tell this story whole and ask your questions later. We will perhaps then see the vital moral of the story secured."

Unable to seize his pants for the whipping he so clearly deserved, I nodded.

"I asked your mother to the altar many times, Wiggins, both before and after you were born. When I left Canada, I wrote to her in Mayfair. I used my new name, my old name, my best entreaties, and never received a reply. When you were born in 1876, I was perhaps twenty and your mother eighteen. I knew nothing of your birth until 1879 when I had a letter from your grandmother, Gerda Adler. She confessed to having read and burned my letters to her daughter. Informing me I was a father, she told me her daughter was in Warsaw and, she feared, in trouble.

"It was in Warsaw that I saw you for the first time, a moment I shall never forget.

"But a more stubborn creature has never been born than Reenie Mclean. She would have none of me. I brought too much risk. We did not know if Alexander Mclean had perished in the fire. His body was never found, but neither were mine, nor Mycroft's. She did not feel safe from her father, or the authorities. And, she proudly announced, she was being courted by a king.

"You must understand, dear child, how I prevailed to change her mind. I read her poetry. I conjured whimsy. I dressed as Romeo and wooed my Juliet. I dressed as Juliet and cajoled my Romeo. I sent her baubles and books. I stood under her window and played Paganini. I appealed to her beauty and her brains, her profession and her reputation, her heart and her head. Whatever might have won her, I never had it, nor found it. She was too young, too wounded, too frightened, so very badly betrayed, and incandescently angry. She flaunted the king in my face.

"Reenie told me you knew I was your father. She had told you just enough of our story to make it easy to keep us apart. It is my greatest regret, that the harm I caused your mother and my inability to make amends made you what I was – another lonely, fatherless child. For that, I am most unreservedly sorry."

"You need not apologize. My mother loved me. I never once felt your absence."

I knew that shot wounded him and did not care. He continued in visible pain.

"When Reenie fled Warsaw, I gave her what she wanted – a life on her own terms. The idea anyone could hide from me anywhere in London is ridiculous, but I let her believe she had eluded me. My second Irregulars, the Kings of Kensington, reported on Pictavia for years. I appointed their leader, Billy Simpson, in your place when you met your unfortunate demise."

"Your starving street servants play short roles. Did you kidnap this Billy, kill him, or both?"

Again my father blinked, and drew a deep breath to continue.

"I did not attempt to kidnap you in Hyde Park. That bit of botched unpleasantness in April of 1882 was engineered by the King of Bohemia. He had sent Reenie threatening letters. I confess to intercepting them. In growing madness, when she would not return to him, in an attempt to force her hand, he sent her a list of women he had defiled in revenge."

He dropped his eyes. "I will return to that list anon," he added, taking a breath to continue.

"When you mother still refused him, knowing it mathematically impossible, but fearing he would never have children, the king then insisted you were his heir and attempted to kidnap you. Thankfully, your family remained on high alert and kept you close at all times. I regret how that precaution made you a home-bound child, but Reenie acted out of love in order to protect you."

If he saw my shame at misjudging by mother, he had the decency to say nothing.

"When the king sent an unlucky underling to your carriage window, Gisela saw a man with clean jet black hair, with muscles and mustache too well-tended for a street thug, and correctly assumed him a Bohemian threat. Quibble him kidnapper or assassin, she dispatched him justly."

"How could you possibly know all of that?"

Father smiled. "I was there. Disguised as an elderly cleric. Had Gisela not dispatched the villain, I would have done so. Then returned you instantly and anonymously to her arms."

That rankled.

"We didn't need you. We all lived better without you."

Here he grimaced, fought for control, and eventually found it.

"For years, I longed to know you. I had no way of knowing my dear Reenie already had a plan in place. To hide you from the king, to give you freedom from the house, she trained you to be a beggar boy. Then she launched the second act of her plan and introduced that boy to me. Her own appearances as Wiggins were some of her finest work. Of course, I recognized her immediately, but said nothing, happy to keep her with me in any way she chose."

Here he smiled. "As always, since childhood, we make a very fine team."

"When she later sent you to me as little Wiggins, understand that she did not know that I already knew her to be the first Wiggins. She did not know I recognized you immediately. It was all too easy to oblige her and make you my new apprentice. But, my dear, it is not the role you were born to play. You are no more a spy or a street tough than a little lost kitten."

When I protested, he extended the all-too-familiar stopping hand.

"To ensure your protection, I sought out the first Wiggins. Your ersatz brother agreed it would be wise to provide you with an irregular entourage. Please note this: I spoke to Reenie as if I had no idea who she was, or who you were, as if the concept of using street urchins as informants had only just occurred to me. Only one of your merry Irregular band ever knew the double nature of his employment. I offered him a guinea a week to tail you. He soon quit, to stay by your side by choice. After pulling you from the peril of that perfidious pawnbroker, he pledged your life as dear to him as his own."

Danny. Of course, he meant Danny.

My beloved had been lying too. Right from the start.

"You and I had many fine London adventures, all designed, from your mother's point of view, to give you the chance to know me in secret, and to give you the incognito skills you needed to escape the king. But in the spring of 1888, when he returned to England, Reenie recognized the sad names of Polly Nichols and Mary Kelly from his list. In one last effort to secure an heir, in utter depravity, the king committed the Whitechapel Murders. Snuffing out all the women he had ruined in your mother's place, he said her your death would follow if she did not give you to him.

"Horrified at unleashing The Ripper King of Bohemia, Reenie decided to take me into her confidence. Dressed as her lovely herself, she arrived at Baker Street with a packet of her old letters and a full explanation. Mrs. Hudson brought us tea and crumpets and her own confession.

"I freely admit it – I was bested by your aunties. When Grizelda, Gisela and Reenie stood side by side, the resemblance was clear, but I had not seen it. I knew Reenie had twin aunts in Egg Harbour City, but had never met them. I equally never suspected Mrs. Hudson had a twin. She fooled me entirely. Reenie is The Woman, but the formidable Mrs. Hudson is truly The Pirate."

"Right. You respect her so much you burnt down her house."

"Not exactly. Grizelda and I needed a pretext for closing up Baker Street. We set off a few smoke bombs just like the one she had kindly made for me to use at Briony Lodge. It fooled the fire brigade. It kept both you and Watson from returning. We believed the king would have my premises under surveillance and could not risk either of you being apprehended."

When I again tried to interrupt with a blast of questions, he simply waited.

"That first night reunited with your mother, when I read her old letters to Mycroft, I realized Reenie had never guessed the true nature of my many injuries. Who could blame her? No one saw that the boy she loved for years had spent those years abusing another boy, one who lived in his home, one who never gave in to his advances without a fight."

When I shrugged and looked out the window, he continued.

"Reenie further confessed that she had guessed that I had guessed the truth about two boys named Wiggins all along. I apologize for that sentence, Wiggins, and hope its meaning is clear?"

I did not say I had not known that she had known that he had known. I simply nodded.

"When I asked how she knew I knew, she said that from childhood, she had watched for my rare unguarded moments. That in them, I looked at her, and at you, with love I could not hide."

What could I say? That I had seen those moments?

That Mother trusted them, but I did not? I said nothing. But I knew he knew.

"That first night after so long, as I gazed into her face, one Watson quite rightly called 'the daintiest thing under a bonnet,' I saw what I have always known. I loved her as child, I loved her as a young man, and I loved her still. I pledged my every breath to help you both.

"Using Mycroft's connections when the king returned to England in March of 1888, he was advised to hire me. This led to the events I gave Watson to record as *A*

Scandal in Bohemia. His tale was the public piece in the permanent escape Mycroft helped plot for us all."

"You mean DAMM, Duncan Alexander Mycroft Mclean? I'd have killed him long ago."

After the longest pause, he asked only this, "When did you realize I was Home Boy?"

"I deduced it quite early on, but did not want to admit it, not even to myself."

"As Mycroft still lives, you might wish to know why? And why I still call him brother?"

I shrugged. "I'd prefer the pair of you dung beetles simply crawled off and died."

If there was a smile, Holmes did his best to hide it.

"His parents were good to me. John and Ada Mclean gave us all their savings to help us escape Mayfair. Assuming the authorities would be looking for impoverished lone Canadians on the run, Mycroft and I settled in London posing as wealthy British brothers. When we took the same last name, it created a bond I cannot logically explain. We have been brothers ever since."

"But he, he was a... He hurt you, repeatedly. That isn't brotherly. It's a crime."

"That is true and always will be. I shall never forget it, nor minimize it. When you are brutalized as a child, it rewrites your story. You lose a piece of your heart you can never regain."

Father reached for his pipe and spent some faltering time attempting to light it.

"Boys fight. Boys are encouraged to do so. At first, I thought it no more than that. When it became more, Mycroft was older and stronger. I was ever conscious I lived as a servant in his home. If his parents were ever forced to choose between us, I knew they would not choose me."

"But you said they were good people?"

"John and Ada Mclean were the best of people. But they were also ignorant, isolated, hell-fearing Baptist farmers who lived in a community they could never leave. Please note this, I do not accuse them of doing nothing. They separated us. They sent Mycroft away to school. I was allowed to continue my studies far longer than any other Home Boy I have ever met. Whenever I got injured, at least whenever they could see the injury, they sought medical attention."

Here, Father needed several long drags on his pipe before he could continue.

"When Mycroft hit me with a hammer and broke my left foot in three places, they took me to a doctor. If he saw a Home Boy as Mclean property, as but another beast of burden, and so repeatedly shot a child full of painkillers of excessive dosages, that was the practice of the day."

Father's medicine. That explained it. Given to him after beatings. As a child. Making him an addict long before he was old enough to understand or refuse.

I pushed my sympathy away.

I did not want to see or observe it.

"After one injury too many, Uncle John took me out behind the barn himself."

My face must have showed my alarm. Father intervened quickly.

"To teach me how to box. Queensbury rules. Uncle John had been quite the bare-knuckled boxer in his day. As I am certain he realized, my long reach and quick footwork soon gave me an advantage over the slower, heavier Mycroft. After I broke his nose twice, Mycroft left me alone."

"That explains his ugly face. I'm glad to know he has to see it each day in his mirror."

Rather than smiling, the man before me looked defeated.

"Unfortunately, to exact his revenge, Mycroft then proposed to your mother."

"Why didn't you snap his damn neck?"

"It is only later in life, after professional combat training, that I would have been able to do so."

"That's how you learned bartitsu. From my mother."

"Not exactly. The Pirate and I sparred daily at Baker Street. Unlike her, I have not had the pleasure of visiting Japan, and am unlikely to do so, given it does not begin with the letter "P.""

He may have thought his feeble comedic relief well-timed. I did not.

"Then kill him now. Mycroft is no better than men you've sent to the gallows."

Here, Father looked protractedly out the carriage window before responding.

"What do you see here, Wiggins? What can you both see and observe?"

I had no patience for guessing games, but knew he would not continue except for my answer. So I gave it, listing the few buildings, a farm in near view, a long curving road, and endless acres of snow.

Patiently, my Home Boy father waited.

"I see our prints in the snow, over the ridge and down to the ravine below."

Still, he said nothing.

"This is the ravine? The very ravine where — You brought me here?"

Father nodded.

"Again, at your mother's insistence. Your nightmares have long troubled us both. She hoped that if you faced the full truth from the moment of your arrival here, the rest of Mayfair could not hurt you with its ghosts." He smiled. "I believe she wants that for all of us."

"I have been lied to and hurt by real people. I do not need to fear ghosts.'

"Please look again. This was our whole world – two family farms, a ravine between, a road to school and church, and trips to the Mayfair General Store. It was stultifying.

"Consider this – Mycroft suffered at the hands of your grandfather from the time he was far younger than you are now. His rage and confusion, his fear and loneliness, were unspeakable. I believe in his violence against me, he wanted to be exposed. He hoped to force his parents to demand the truth.

"Sadly, they did not. But since reaching adulthood and London, Mycroft has learned the meaning of the word *consensual*. He has repeatedly apologized to me and to Reenie in both word and deed. Each year on my birthday, he gives me a priceless gift. The first was the day itself.

"I do not know my birthdate, never had a birthday until Mycroft chose The Feast of the Epiphany. Each year, he gives me the name of a homeless London child, one he has sponsored for life. He does not ship them off to a foreign land. He gives them a new life in their London home. Of the fifteen children to date, some have gone on to Oxford and Cambridge," he smiled, "And one to Pictavia."

Danny. That explained his timeline, his educated speech, and why he could read and write.

The vile DAMM, the horrid Mycroft, I had him to thank for giving me Danny.

"If I sometimes accuse Mycroft of trying to out-redeem Ebenezer Scrooge by saving his own small army of Tiny Tims, I see saving fifteen children from London gutters as commendable redemption for a man who once beat a Home Boy bloody in a backwoods ravine. In that, Mycroft has earned my forgiveness. In his work, he has earned the thanks of the Empire. Without an unfaltering trust in his redemption, Reenie and I would never have left you alone with him."

"You do know he left me unchaperoned every afternoon, falling asleep after tea?"

"As instructed. So you could visit your family in the safety of daytime, rather than at night."

If I looked more patronized than impressed, at least he noticed.

"Your mother thinks my early life with Mycroft explains why, for my second chosen brother, I selected someone like Watson. Someone affable, chatty and charming. Happy to follow my lead. Unfailingly kind and loyal. A man whose unshakable creed is this – first do no harm.

"Your mother's alienist theories aside, here is my truth. I am not a religious man. A childhood like mine makes a cynic of any thinking creature. But I must believe in something. So I believe in the intrinsic worth of John H. Watson, and I believe in the redeemed goodness of my brother Mycroft. He is transformational proof that change is possible. His example reminds me to continue to seek redemption and forgiveness here on earth, each and every day, for myself."

I speared my eyes to his, spitting all the venom of broken feet and bastardy.

"But you're no better than Mycroft. You did what he did. You did it to my mother."

To his credit, Holmes met my gaze and accusation without flinching.

"Yes. I hurt her in the worst way a man can hurt a woman. But know this – I have thanked the universe each and every day for your birth." He leaned across the carriage to grasp both my ungloved hands in his. "Please hear me. You are my rare wild lily, and I treasure you."

Here it was my turn to busy myself with my blanket, to brush at my eyes. But, as always, Sherlock Holmes pushed his audience for more.

"It is no excuse, but it is factual and pertinent. I had no experience with love or passion that was not accompanied by brute force. I misunderstood and failed Reenie that night, with repercussions for which I can never atone. Note, dear child, I do not mean you. I mean that in running from what I had done to her, she ran straight into a royal fiend's arms."

Leaning forward, he continued with greater urgency.

"We had hoped that the staged marriage to Godfrey would be enough to deter the king, but in 1890, as his own marriage grew ever-more unhappy and true illness set in, he began threatening your mother yet again. That left us no choice. You and your mother both had to die. Once believed dead, you could disappear into safety. Unfortunately, removing and relocating you proved to be the most difficult – nearly insurmountable – part of our plan."

"I am sorry to have been such a burden. Perhaps you should just have left me where you left my unfortunate doppelganger, frozen in a Whitechapel gutter."

I gloated. And should not have done so.

"There was, of course, no dead boy on the Baker Street woodpile. Shame on you, Wiggins, for believing that of me for even one second. One of Mycroft's resurrected red-headed children happily agreed to lie dead as a proverbial doornail until I scooped him up and drove him tearfully away. The impossibly named Strand Ambrose Wiggins does have a grave, but it is blessedly empty. I admit to saving some money on your headstone by using only your initials."

"Because you didn't care enough to use my name?"

"No, because *The Strand* did not begin publication until 1891. In fact, the magazine you spotted at Baker Street was the very first issue. A child claiming to be born on May Day in 1878, could not be named after a magazine that did not exist."

When I started to protest that I could have been told the truth, that I could have been trusted, could have been treated less like a baby in diapers, Holmes shook his head.

"It was not a matter of trust. We could not change your nature. We all tried to train you in the arts of defense and deceit. We failed. Your inability to run and fight is not your fault. Neither is the fact that deceit is likewise not in your repertoire. Every word, every syllable of feeling, shows on your face. You are, my dear girl, quite simply the worst liar I have ever met."

"But Watson, his eyebrows—"

"Next to you, Watson is a veritable Sarah Bernhardt."

"But surely, there were times when I fooled you?"

Father shook his head. "Compared to you, Watson's eyebrows are Sarah Bernhardt."

"You lied to me because 'my grief must be credible and I could not credibly pretend it.'"

There it was.

That rare crinkle of softness that warmed his eyes.

"Recalled exactly!" He tucked the blanket back around my ankles, casually, carefully, touching my feet. "You have the best memory for spoken language of any human being I have ever met. I am quite in awe of it. Weeks later, months later, I dare say, years later, you can replay whole conversations verbatim. It comes so easily to you that you do not recognize it any more than a leopard values its spots. But I see it plain. I gave you that phrase about Watson knowing you would remember it. I wanted to help you see that everything we did was done to save your life."

"Just exactly how did all of you take it upon yourselves to do that?"

He blinked. "Let's see. Your mother's people are free-thinking abolitionists. Your Amazon aunties exited the womb shouting, "Votes for Women." Pictavia welcomes friends named Marx and Pankhurst, and you are actually asking me how we decided something?"

Tickled and outraged, I tried to show only the later.

"You voted?"

"Indubitably. We extended the franchise to all. Your parents, your aunties, your Daniel, Mycroft, Godfrey, and every Irregular old enough to say yay or nay. It was all but unanimous."

"Surely Danny voted against deceiving me?"

"No. I have no doubt of his affections, but the naysaying vote was not his."

"My mother?"

"No. It was her idea."

"Tante Gisela?

"No. Her kind heart hesitated, but was convinced by a pirate."

"Who was it?" He waited until I deduced it. "You!"

"Correct. I especially did not want to continue lying once you feared your family dead. But, on that first night in New York, while you slept, the rest of us consulted. With reluctance, we voted to maintain the plan. If the king had a spy on our ship, or watching from the docks, he would have seen Irene Adler alive. If the king attained you, it remained vital you did not confirm it."

I quoted him from that long ago morning, "By conspiring to expire, we save other lives."

He nodded. "Everyone's safety hinged on your grief. If you knew the truth and then fell into Bohemian hands –

disaster! You would have spilled every one of the proverbial beans. None of us wanted to put you at that risk."

"Instead, you lied. You all risked pushing me into a real grave. How commendable."

"I agreed only on the condition I could tell you the truth the instant we reached Mayfair. Here we are all doubly safe. King Sigismund believes Reenie is from New Jersey. I planted that lie in his head by pretending to read it from my index on the night he hired me. We likewise removed all the addresses on your mother's letters in case they ever came into his possession. Secondly, if your grandfather is alive, this is the last place he will show his face. Accordingly, my dear, I hope you will please accept my unreserved apology for every omission, half-truth and outright lie I ever told you."

I closed my eyes.

"I was not given all the data I deserved. I may have misjudged you, Holmes, but for your part in withholding the truth from me, I cannot forgive you so quickly."

"Expected and understood. I shall continue to seek forgiveness in word and deed. Here, in your parents' home, as you meet your grandmother Gerda Adler Mclean, who longs to meet her only grandchild, I hope you will give me the honour to introduce you as my daughter?"

There was not a trace of arrogance in his voice.

Only humility. Tinged with paternal pride.

"Before you answer, you must know this. For reasons obvious, I cannot be introduced as Sherlock Holmes.

Likewise, under suspicion of murder, I cannot use any name I was known by as a child. But – and we hope this pleases you – I can travel legitimately as your mother's husband."

He reached again into his breast pocket and handed me two papers, the first being the Marriage Certificate between Godfrey Norton and Irene Adler.

"It was a sham wedding. It certainly does not make you my mother's husband."

"Well observed, my dear. The first document is indeed false. To permit your mother and I to hide as Mr. and Mrs. Norton here in Canada, Godfrey graciously permitted us the use of his name. He has no use for it, being far too busy enjoying himself as Jasper Witty, husband of the raven-tressed Corona Witty. But please note the second document. There was a true wedding that day. Your mother was the bride, but I was no witness. I was the groom."

"That is not possible. It is preposterous, utterly outrageous!"

"Heavens, Wiggins, you sound just like Watson! Consider this – in his version of *A Scandal in Bohemia*, Watson wrote exactly as I instructed. What he did not know was that when Reenie went on her drive, I met her carriage at the registry office. We married with your aunties in attendance. We used Watson to make it public that she had married Godfrey Norton, barrister, and had left the country.

To see the truth, please read again Watson's version of Irene's letter. What did she tell me to tell the king? I cherish the words, "*I love and am loved by a better man than he.*" When she signed herself, "*I remain, dear Mr. Sherlock Holmes, very truly yours.*" I am delighted to say that, as of that afternoon, my beloved wife meant every word of it."

I shook my head, but it did not clear.

This was Sherlock Holmes. There was always more.

"Today, in my barrister's suit, my London upper-class accent perfected, being inches taller and several stone healthier, with my limp visible only when I am very tired, no one in Mayfair will see a Home Boy. As you have often rightly noted, Wiggins, no one ever really looks at us."

My whole face burned. My poverty lasted only as long as my costume; his ruined his childhood and ruled every day since. But I had seen little beyond my own reflection.

He gestured at the farm before us, one with a curving lane to the door.

"As Mrs. Norton, Reenie has been safe here, but she misses you beyond words. We can visit here, the three of us, then reunite with the rest of your family. But the decision is entirely yours. If you prefer to see only the back of me, I will leave you here and depart alone."

I said nothing. Having finally attained the spotlight, I did not intend to squander it.

"Please permit me a few last words." He closed his eyes. "The Science of Deduction is a gift and a curse. It is a profession I did not choose, but chose me as a child. When you fear attack at any moment, you must learn to observe trivialities, to deduce from minute observation, or be again a victim. That diligence left me distant and alone. I do not recommend it. I am today a cold curmudgeon because I was forced to be bitter, wary boy. I am the secondary victim of a predator too clever to be caught, the truly evil genius known as Alexander Moriarty Mclean."

I gasped, visibly injured by this last brick flung at my head and my heart. Not only was Moriarity real, he was my grandfather. Holmes waited until I nodded for him to continue.

"But thanks to you, my dear, I found a new game afoot. My days with you have returned a measure of my lost childhood to me. I am beyond grateful for this hiatus with my daughter. I thank your family for allowing it, and you for sharing it. Together, we now have a chance to undo past harm and write our own family future together. Or," here he did his best to try on a smile, but it fit poorly, "in my departure for places beginning with P, I shall perchance begin with Poughkeepsie."

In his eyes I saw something I had never seen. Longing. And a fragile hope.

In that moment, I saw him. Not as "The Great Detective", but as an ordinary man. One I might like to get to know. But not right away. First, I had to make him suffer.

"I give you your own words, Holmes, re-improvised for the occasion." I cleared my throat and intoned them as he would. "*Upon the Deduction of Lies: Like their human creators, lies have provenance. They neither materialize in the ether, nor return to it. To do the most damage in a credulous world, lies must have, and must be seen by all to have, a trusted genesis, a familial first appearance, an identifiable on-going use, and a clear result of pain and harm.* I do not care if you regret your lies now. It is too little too late. I spit on your apology."

I puffed up my cheeks, leaned forward, and mimed my best shot straight into his face.

Pulling the same improvised hanky from his breast pocket, he wiped his cheek, crumpled the hanky, then returned it from whence it had come.

"I deserved that, Wiggins." He bowed. "Please give my best to your mother."

I waited until he had unloaded his luggage, finished the slow finger-by-finger of his gloves, and raised a black hand to wave good-bye. I especially waited until he had taken exactly seventeen steps away in the snow.

Then, and only then, I protractedly cleared my throat.

"Had you chosen Pitcairn Island, I would have let you go, if only to have received your letters from it. But Poughkeepsie is neither probable, nor possible. You would not face a sufficiently painful or protracted punishment. For that, Father, you must stay here. With us."

He flashed a transformative grin – one that caught my heart in its similarity to Danny's, my darling who was not dead, but would be when I got my hands on his sorry neck. My mother likewise deserved a frosty reception, but one I knew I could not give her. I knew that the second I saw her.

As I glanced at the farmhouse, I saw a woman running through the snow. I saw the face of my lovely mother, upturned to her beloveds and the winter sun. If only for her, I would improvise a truce with my father.

Once I was certain she was well, once reunited with my truth-pirating aunties and thieving Danny, I would make them all walk the truth plank and unleash the tongue lashing of the century.

My father laid down footprints in the snow for mine, and held out his hand.

"Welcome to the next chapter of your irregular story, Miss Lily Psalmonia Adler Holmes."

With a purple shawl around my shoulders and a beloved cap on my head, I took his hand and limped confidently forward into the warmest, best-dressed morning of my young life.

-END-

Afterword and Acknowledgements

How can I explain what it means to me to have had a life-long relationship with Sherlock Holmes? Thanks to his methods and his companionship, I deduced my own worth.

In 1964, the hottest summer of my life, I could not swim at my cottage because my foot was entombed in a cast after the first of many operations to correct what were then called "birth defects" in my feet. Having read all of Trixie Belden and Nancy Drew, I feared I'd never read anything good again. My grandmother smiled and handed me *The Hound of the Baskervilles.*

For all that long hot summer, I chain-smoked Sherlock Holmes.

I can pinpoint the exact moment when I became a Sherlock fan for life. In *A Scandal in Bohemia*, when Holmes asks Watson how many steps there are at 221b Baker Street, like most able-bodied folks, the good doctor hasn't a clue. Sherlock responds, "Now, I know that there are seventeen steps, because I have both seen and observed."

When I gasped, Sherlock casually jumped from the page to my bedroom chair.

"How are you? You have been counting all the steps in your own life, I assume?"

Yes! This was my game afoot. I counted steps nonstop. In his seventeen steps, Sherlock saw and observed each limping, painful step of my life. He saw me. In Sherlock's methods, I saw not just counted steps, but something I'd never seen and truly needed – an adult who validated and praised counting them. Quite simply, Sherlock changed my life. He gave my life purpose.

I decided that it didn't matter if I limped; it mattered that I could think. Sherlock encouraged me through high school and fueled my degree in 19th Century History. Over twenty-three years as a Drama teacher and improv coach, I learned to see The Great Improvisor in The Great Detective and brought Sherlock Improv into tours and festivals, including 221B Con in Atlanta.

Once I retired from teaching, I began the book to honour my life-long companion.

I wanted a book that did not sentimentalize the data. I longed to bring a new, disabled lens to Sherlockiana and to include my other identity as an adoptee who found her birthfamily. For seven generations, the very real McLean farm in Mayfair, Ontario, housed my hardscrabble Scottish ancestors. In 1819, my great-great-great grandfather, Duncan Mclean, left Kilcolmonell, Argylshire. Age fifteen, he sailed for Canada with eight little siblings and no parents in sight.

His son, Alexander, was my great-great-grandfather. Real life brothers Alexander and John Mclean lived in side-by-side farms on Longwoods Road. When Alexander raised his family, there is no data to say if his brother and neighbor, John Mclean, also raised a Home Boy, but it is possible.

There is no record to prove John's son and the Home Boy both courted a Mclean cousin, but cousins married often in my family tree. The real Alexander did not meet a headstrong American girl at a concert, but Ms. Lind and Mr. Barnum did appear in London, Ontario on their tour.

The equally real St. Thomas, Ontario, boasts a larger-than-life monument to Jumbo who, sadly, did meet death in its train yard. The Mayfair school, Caradoc Academy, is also real. It matriculated boys and girls to university until 1857 when it mysteriously burned to the ground.

Please permit me, Dear Reader, to celebrate my own operatic feat. After half a century related to no one, this ancient writer built herself a new family where I am simultaneously related to Irene Adler, Mrs. Hudson, Mrs. Turner, Mycroft, Moriarty, Wiggins, P.T. Barnum, and to Sherlock Holmes himself.

I created this irregular family, because I truly believe Sherlock didn't tell the exact truth in "*The Greek Interpreter*" when he said, "my ancestors were country squires." His skill set clearly demonstrates farm origins.

In *A Scandal in Bohemia*, why was he able to pass himself off as a groom, to spend a day chatting up "horsy men?" Why was he able to perform so many different tasks of menial labour, such as plumbing? Why did he know about soils, geology, hoofprints and beekeeping? Because the "county squires" were a biographical improvisation to throw clients and the class-conscious *Strand* public off the scent.

As for his birth, the only true provenance Sherlock Holmes could ever logically have is this: he was spawned by the streets of London. There, he gave birth to himself.

Of course Duncan Alexander Mycroft Mclean and Alexander Moriarty Mclean are not my real relatives, but hybrid inventions. Did I shirk at making my relatives, and Lily's father, abusers? No. Through Lily, I exposed the vital moral question of my life: is it possible to forgive your father for raping your mother? In Lily's case, I am glad the answer is yes. In my case, it remains no, and thanks to Sherlock and Lily I have reconciled myself to it.

Does this story reduce the great detective in any way?

Quite the contrary. Sherlock Holmes has always been a father figure to me. Permitting me to tell his dark backstory, one which he faced, and strove with heart and head to overcome, makes him even more of a hero.

In helping me birth this book of my heart, I would like to thank my early readers: Peggy Perdue, Lahring Tribe, Janet Berkman, Marianne Froehlich, Pam Singer, and Angela Misri. Before I left The Bootmakers of Toronto, I was honoured to receive the rank of Master Bootmaker and thank all at my former scion society for their Sherlockian expertise.   At Orange Pip Books, I'm grateful to publisher Steve Emecz, my eagle-eyed editor Des, and especially Nicko Vaughan De Wheel for her kind consultations. Thank you also to my agent, Emmy Nordstrom-Higdon and Westwood Creative Artists for encouraging me to follow my heart.

Last, but never least, to my family and friends: thank you all so very much for putting up with me for all the time I spent away from you fulfilling my childhood dream to go off adventuring with Sherlock Holmes.

Also from Orange Pip Books

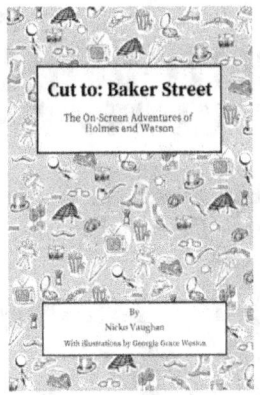

It is well documented that Sherlock Holmes is the most depicted literary character on screen; he even has an entry in the Guinness Book of Records to prove it. This reference guide covers depictions of the world's most famous detective, and his faithful companion, from the first silent film Sherlock Holmes is Baffled (1900) to the Will Ferrell, John C. Reilly comedy Holmes and Watson (2018). As well as cinema and television portrayals, this book by Nicko Vaughan (Author of The Wordy Companion: An A-Z Guide to Sherlockian Phraseology) also covers documentaries, animations and web series adaptations alongside début feature artwork by graphic artist Georgia Grace Weston.

Combining encyclopedia, biography and reference structure, this book comprehensively explores the many celluloid faces, cathode-ray shapes and digital sizes of Sherlock Holmes and Doctor John Watson, so far.

Also from Orange Pip Books

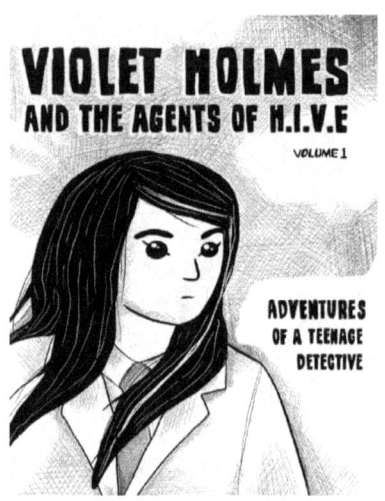

Violet Holmes is not an ordinary teenager because, well, nothing is ordinary when you're the adopted daughter of the great Sherlock Holmes. Having been home schooled for her entire life she has decided to take the plunge, at 14, and attend Bardle Secondary School to study for her exams. But after a week, she notices that the school hides a deep secret, and she's determined to crack it wide open. Are the current spate of school thefts the work of criminal masterminds? Is there really a secret society behind closed doors? Can a girl like Violet make friends and fit in?

Also from Orange Pip Books

Just the place for a Nark!" the Detective cried,
As he eagerly surveyed the scene;
With the stout-hearted Doctor alert at his side,
And the Dog standing guard in between.

Imagine a world where the logic of Sherlock Holmes meets the nonsense of Wonderland! *The Hunting of the Nark* combines the best of Lewis Carroll and Arthur Conan Doyle's adventures into a madcap collection of verse, including the novella-length case, *The Adventure of the Twinkling Hat.* Holmes and Watson will discover that anything can happen at 221B when you're the White Knight...

Also from Orange Pip Books

Dr. John H. Watson is a man of medical science, a man of action and a man of letters. His life has been one of adventure and romance. In 1894 he finds himself alone following the death of his great friend Sherlock Holmes three years earlier and now the passing of his beloved wife, Mary. His loneliness is all encompassing and only a true friend can help him to see there is still reason to continue living. But when that friend, Inspector G. Lestrade of Scotland Yard suddenly and mysteriously disappears, Dr. Watson takes it upon himself to discover the reason for the abduction.

Also from Orange Pip Books

It wasn't that John couldn't tell the story. It wasn't that we didn't know the truth. It was that nobody would believe us. But we cannot keep Sherlock alive with silence. The reader smiles when Moriarty appears on the page. So does Moriarty. And Sherlock Holmes follows him. We smile because we recognise them. Scarlett Vendalle is recognised by nobody, except for John Watson. With no recollection of her own identity and a suspected criminal past, Scarlett is the perfect case for Sherlock. As they follow her tracks, red threads appear in their lives that make it more than clear - Scarlett meeting John and Sherlock was no coincidence. Someone has drawn her shadow on the wall before she appeared. Was it Anne Boleyn who haunts Scarlett with visions of her past? Was it Moriarty who attracts Sherlock like a magnet? Or was it another shadow from the past? With Moriarty's men on the one hand and the secret service on the other, the stage is set for a game with deadly rules, as Sherlock, John and Scarlett slowly become aware that something larger is guiding their steps... Is there another story being written?

Also from Orange Pip Books

Lestrade realized abruptly that he was not alone. He turned to face his assailants. Outnumbered, he braced himself for an unfair fight with no delusions of winning. Light glinted off metal as one of the men drew a blade, and Lestrade realized that he was in for more than just a beating – these men fully intended to kill him.

London. 1867. Against the advice of his senior partner and mentor, newly promoted Inspector Lestrade agrees to look into a case no one else wants, only to find that there is more to investigate than a simple disappearance, and that his fellow Inspectors may not be as trustworthy as they seem. Determined to carry on, uncertain who to trust, Lestrade faces danger and corruption both in the city-and within Scotland Yard itself.

www.ingramcontent.com/pod-product-compliance
Lightning Source LLC
Chambersburg PA
CBHW070844250626
47159CB00003B/930

* 9 7 8 1 7 8 7 0 5 7 2 3 4 *